I0562356

BULLETS HAVE NO EYES

Cavon D. Mills

CAGED BIRD
Publishing

ISBN: 978-1-7368788-5-9 paperback

Photographer: Jo'sef Haynes
Djnowphotography@gmail.com
Cover Model: Christopher Hankins
Cover Concept and Graphic Design: Danielle Ferreira

Published by: Caged Bird Publishing
www.cagedbirdpublishing.com

CAGED BIRD
Publishing

CONTENTS

Prologue...1

Chapter 1...5

Chapter 2...25

Chapter 3...41

Chapter 4...61

Chapter 5...73

Chapter 6...97

Chapter 7...125

Chapter 8...149

Chapter 9...173

Chapter 10...195

Chapter 11...215

PROLOGUE

A rain of bullets swept our street, making me drop the birthday cake I just took from the fridge. Everyone in the kitchen ducked for cover as the smell of buttercream frosting invaded my nose. I scrutinized the smushed pieces of cake that made it out of the box while bullets broke through the front room window and into our cinderblock walls. *This must be personal*, I thought to myself, witnessing the walls of the kitchen quickly becoming infiltrated with panic.

We began squirming around the floor looking for safe places to take cover. My homeboy Rico made it to the pantry while Gigi managed to crawl under the kitchen table. Gigi's fair-skinned face blushed with an expression I've never seen on her. Fear. I wedged myself between the lower cabinets under the sink, leaving me the most exposed out of the three of us. Our bodies remained pressed on the concrete tiles, helplessly waiting for the shooting to end. The sound of guns exploding outside wasn't a strange occurrence in our neighborhood, but a midday shoot out on our street was a bit peculiar, even for Harrow Park.

Screams began to grow outside, making me uneasy, drawing all types of awful conclusions.

"Da-ddy!" Love screamed clearly over the sound of the bullets, snapping me back into the realization that she was still outside. I stood up and ran to the front, disregarding the shots still being fired, knowing I had to get to her.

"Wisdom, get back here!" I heard faintly from the kitchen, as I continued. I felt the presence of someone trotting close behind me, but I ignored it, staying in full pursuit for Love. Arms stretched around me, and I found myself being tackled to the living room floor, pinned down just inches away from the screen door.

"Get off me!" I demanded, looking up to see that it was Rico. I attempted to fight out of his hold. But his arms only tightened.

"Wiz, are you crazy?" Rico asked, trying to keep me in his grip. Shots continued firing over our heads.

I pondered his question while wrestling my way out of his tight hold. People always say, "Love will make you do crazy things," and here I was demonstrating how right they were. I bent Rico's fingers back. He screamed in agony and released me out of his grip. I made it to my feet and went charging towards the screen door.

"Wiz!" Rico shouted. "Wiz!"

I burst through the screen door, barely catching a glimpse of a dark SUV drifting down the street. The sound of their tires screeched across the pavement, fleeing the scene, weirdly adding a sense of calm to the chaos they created.

Everyone was dispersed, putting a huge dampener on the birthday party we were throwing outside. I looked out around the front of our clustered brick houses. All the food and decorations we had in our yard were now scattered across the entire length of the street. A small crowd began to draw in towards a lifeless body in the middle of the road. The only thing I was able to make out from my skewed view on the porch were some black jeans, a pair of Jordans, and the pool of blood. All of that was ignored when I saw my daughter's empty motorized power wheels SUV turned on its side. It was right next to Ms. Corrine, my daughter's babysitter, who was crying on the ground tightly holding her arm. I took off towards her direction, silently praying for the best.

I dropped to my knees sitting Ms. Corrine up just slightly, examining the wound on her arm; her blood-covered hands swatted me away.

"I'm fine, I'm fine!" she snapped. "It's just a graze," Ms. Corrine said. I shook my head at her stubbornness, turning my daughter's motorized SUV back on its wheels.

"Where is Love?" I asked, that now becoming the only important question after finding out Ms. Corrine was alright.

"I'm not sure," she replied with a slight tremble in her voice.

We both aimlessly looked out across the yard, and my stomach began to turn with worry. Ms. Corrine's eyes started to swell with tears. She pointed her bloody finger a few feet from our very spot. I turned around hesitantly to see my daughter lying face down among the tall grass.

"Love!" I cried.

CHAPTER 1

Tick-tock, the clock goes around slowly teasing everyone with its control. Tick-tock, the one thing man can't take charge of, yet grows frustrated when it doesn't work out in their favor. It's too fast, it's too slow, and depending on the situation, no one is left completely satisfied. Tick-tock, tick-tock, the one thing that will never compromise. Time.

Come on, 2:05. Ain't it funny how time works? When you don't want time to end, it speeds up. And when you're ready to go, time procrastinates. It's like being stuck behind an old big boned lady at the supermarket. She drags her feet with her whole body perfectly centered in the middle of the aisle. She leaves no room to get around, keeping one stuck with only the anticipation for more desired endeavors. I dread moments like this.

2:01. *Dang, it's still not 2:05,* I thought to myself, glancing at my phone to ensure the clock on the wall was correct. I watched the clock intensely, as Mr. Joyner, my creative writing teacher, blabbed on and on about our final writing projects and other work we needed to complete, as we drew closer to the end of the school year. His pale skin blushed rose red as the tone of his voice transitioned from lax to authoritative, shifting the atmosphere of the room. He fixed his piercing blue eyes to the slackers in the back of the class. Since I was ahead in all my classes, I just focused on the clock, disregarding his speech, and letting my mind wonder.

I was so ready for school to be over, especially because I knew my Gigi made me something good to eat before I would have to go to work. I have been living with her for a while now. My mom ran off and left me with her, without even so much as a goodbye, on my twelfth birthday... Talking about she needed to find herself or some crap like that. I haven't seen her in five years. I guess she is still on the hunt. Even though Gigi would never own up to it, I knew not knowing what was going on with her only child weighed heavy on her mind.

It wasn't long before our family's business was the whole neighborhood's business. Rumor had it that my mom ran off because she was on drugs and owed a lot of money to one of the numerous thugs in Harrow's Landing, or Harrow Park as we call it. I swear rumors move real swift in the hood. Over the years, I got into numerous fights with some neighborhood guys speaking ill about me, saying I was the bastard son of a crack addict. To this day, I wasn't sure if I was fighting out of honor or anger. On one hand, I wasn't going to let anyone disrespect me or my family, but on the other hand, it infuriated me not knowing if the rumors were true. *Is my mother on drugs? Does she owe money? What does she mean "find herself"?* Those were the questions that popped into my mind and made my blood boil with rage. I grew accustomed to coming home with bruised hands every other day until the neighborhood guys finally started leaving me alone. I wasn't sure if it was because I was winning the fights, or if Gigi was handling business behind the scenes. But either way, I was left thankful.

To add insult to injury, on top of having an absent mother, I was never granted the knowledge of who my father is. My mother never told me, even after countless times of me asking before she left. And Gigi only provided me with blank stares whenever the topic came up. *What was the big secret?* I often asked myself. Entertaining all types of random conclusions, I would sometimes write poems in my creative writing class about the day I would finally meet him. I often wondered what he looked like, what were his talents, and if we both shared a love of writing. Mr. Joyner would just rave about my work to the class, emphasizing my syntax, visual cues, and jargon; he was completely oblivious to the fact, that I was just finding literary ways to ask questions I knew either no one had the answer to, or the truth was just too unbearable.

I didn't resemble anyone on my mother's side of the family, including my late grandfather Charles. I'd only seen him in pictures; he died in the Air Force when my mother was young. My skin was slightly darker than everyone else's, and I had a noticeable patch of silver hair on the back of my head. I concluded that particular trait had to come from somewhere, if not from my father. *It's not common for a seventeen-year-old to have silver hair.* I recalled the information I learned in AP Biology.

Sometimes, I would daydream about both of my absent parents, hoping they would find me in Harrow Park and want to make up for the years they missed. Then here comes reality, never failing to be an abrupt wakeup call. *If it hasn't happened in seventeen years, why do you think it will happen now?* My mind often recited, antagonizing the small pieces of hope I have left.

2:03. "2:05, where are you?" I asked aloud, zooming in on the clock. My homeboy Rico walked past my classroom door after he glanced through the window and gave me a head nod. He continued his journey through the halls, probably skipping class as usual. I knew it was him even from a distance, not knowing too many dark skin dudes at the school with short locs and light brown eyes. We have been good friends since the second semester of my freshman year. Sadly, that's the same amount of time Rico has been skipping classes despite my numerous attempts to get him to stop. He was one of the few people that knew a little about my background and didn't judge me for it. So, the least I could do was not judge him about skipping class or the fact that this was his third year in the ninth grade.

The one time I skipped class was a life-changing moment. A little over two years ago, I skipped a class with Danielle Jenkins, my crush since middle school. Her round face, dewy soft skin, white teeth, and curvaceous body still plagued my memory. It was freshmen year, and we had been flirting with each other all through middle school and into our first year of high school. She gave me my first kiss in the gym behind the bleachers when we were playing our own personal game of Truth or Dare.

"It's your turn Wisdom," Danielle had said to me sweetly. "Truth or Dare?"

"Dare!" I had boldly replied.

"Follow me," she had insisted, grabbing my hand. "Unless you're scared," she had teased as I reluctantly traipsed behind her.

All the gym teachers had been in the main gym monitoring the basketball game that was going on. While the other students chilled on the bleachers, we snuck away. As Danielle led me through the girl's locker room, I looked around to ensure we weren't being followed. We went through the back door, which led us outside next to the field. Her grip tightened as we made our way towards the back of the school.

"What are we doing out here?" I asked, holding her hand while walking through the wet grass, as the wind ruffled our gym clothes.

"You'll see," she smirked, making it to a small grassy area behind the school. Danielle turned around after finally settling in one spot and pressed her lips against mine. She then proceeded to put my hands on her hips. I began venturing off to other areas getting me more and more excited. Somehow, during this impromptu make out session, her hands found their way to the sides of my gym shorts, attempting to slide them down. I quickly pulled them back up, breaking our lip-lock while gazing at her with bewilderment. *I know she didn't take me all the way out here, just to pants me.* I pondered.

"What are you doing?" I asked, looking around to ensure no one was outside.

"Come on, Wisdom don't act like you don't want to," Danielle teased, biting her lip.

I was slightly confused as to what she was talking about, until she took off her T-shirt, revealing her perky breasts in her black bra. I swallowed the saliva that developed in my mouth before it became drool, tasting a little bit of her cherry flavored lip gloss.

"You want to do this here?" I investigated my surroundings, now understanding what she wanted.

"Right here," she assured, grabbing me by the back of my neck. We worked our way down to the wet grass. "I can feel how bad you want this." Danielle teased, with her hand pressed against the front of my shorts.

I couldn't hide how excited I was; I had wanted Danielle since the sixth grade, but I was too shy to make the first move. It looked like she wasn't scared to go after what she wanted. So, against my better judgement and everything in my head screaming stop, I was overwhelmed by the feeling of being wanted. Besides, I couldn't risk being talked about as the guy who was too scared to get some, among other things my peers already said about me behind my back. I felt like I was at a crossroads, between Go-For-It Lane and

Dude-This-Isn't-Smart Road. Then I decided to take a strong left turn on Go-For-It Lane, obliging her request and giving her what we both wanted.

And just like that, there we were in the wet grass in the back of the school making like, love, and lust. To this day, I'm still confused on what to call it. Our bodies flopped weirdly around on the cold ground until she stayed still long enough for me to get the rhythm of it. I stared in her eyes as a gentle breeze blew dandelions across her face, looking like a low budgeted version of the love making scene from *Jason's Lyric*. That was until a security guard and one of the assistant principals, Mr. Jones, found us around the back of the school with more than just grass stains on our clothes. Looking back, we probably should have accounted for the cameras that were outside. Talk about amateur porn.

We were escorted by security to the head principal's office, getting looks and laughs from our classmates who were in the hallway making their own inferences while Mr. Jones called our parents in the main office. I can't forget the look on my Gigi's face, when she made it to the school wearing her short styled "I'm-going-out-in-public" wig. If looks could kill, someone would surely sing "I shall wear a crown" at my funeral.

We all were stuffed in the principal's office— Danielle, me, Gigi, and both of Danielle's parents— as we attempted to explain what had happened. Danielle's parents were so shocked that they instantly placed the blame on me for what had transpired. They would not believe that their precious baby girl could be capable of such acts. Danielle sat in silence while her parents drilled me with questions, even going as far to accuse me of rape. They were quickly getting under my skin. Before I could even defend myself, Gigi cursed Mr. and Mrs. Jenkins out from one end of Norfolk to the other. My face reddened with shame and embarrassment. The principal, Mrs. Sims-Jackson, somehow calmed the feud between

Gigi and Danielle's parents. She then called for Mr. Jones to escort Danielle and me out while she conversed with our guardians. Mr. Jones called on his walkie-talkie for the security guard, Mr. Lawrence, to take me to another back room in the main office and he escorted Danielle to another. I looked back at Danielle, our eyes locked in the narrow hall of the main office.

"Come on, young man!" Mr. Lawrence demanded, opening the door to the back room, and closing it behind me.

I sat in the cold metal chair in the tight room and waited for my sentence as if I was on trial. Minutes later, the door swung open. Gigi stood in the doorway holding my school clothes and bookbag from the gym locker room with a look of disgust. She threw them at me aggressively. Mr. Lawrence looked away.

"Come on, boy!" she growled as I got up and followed her out into the hallway.

"Good luck," Mr. Lawrence stated, shaking his head as I followed Gigi out of the main office.

I think I'd rather take my chances in jail than with Gigi, I thought to myself, trailing behind. Once we got outside, Gigi's pace picked up. My anxiety started to rise as we walked closer to Gigi's old burgundy Cadillac. It wasn't like my grandmother to bite her tongue, so her silence was extremely unsettling.

Gigi unlocked the car and broke her silence. "You're suspended for a week. You were going to have a tribunal hearing and an investigation, but looking at the tape it was obvious that she was the aggressor," Gigi informed me as we got in the car. "You better be glad there were cameras. Yo' ass could have been locked up for rape! What were you thinking?!" Gigi shouted. I sat there in silence. "I asked you a question," she stated through her clenched teeth.

"I don't know," I shamefully replied.

"That was obvious," Gigi agreed. "If you think with your head on your shoulders instead of the one in your pants, you wouldn't be in this mess. How yo' momma name you Wisdom, and you go and do some dumb shit like this?" she asked rhetorically, starting the car. The engine began to roar, almost matching her tone. "Act like your name!" she griped. "Got me sick to my stomach looking at your ashy ass on camera. At least you eventually got the stroke right," she insulted, finally putting the car in drive, and zooming out of the school parking lot.

As we made it to the stop light in front of the school, Gigi dug through the center console of the car and grabbed a fresh pack of Newport's and a lighter.

"Gigi, I thought you quit?" I asked. Gigi cracked open the box and grabbed a cigarette, foot pressing heavy on the gas as soon as the light turned green.

"I did until today," she replied. "You better be glad I didn't hit up Roscoe for a joint. Shut your mouth before I punch you in it," Gigi threatened with a cigarette hanging from the side of her mouth. She lit it up in one hand while steering with the other. I was too scared to even reply, so I wisely remained quiet during the drive, doing my best not to inhale the smoke engulfing the vehicle.

That week off school felt like the longest week of my existence. First, Gigi took me to the hospital and made me undergo tests to ensure I didn't have any STDs. Gigi's mind was fixed that Danielle was fast and probably "bumped bodies" with plenty of other guys, even though I believed it to be the first time for the both of us. After the tests came back negative, she gave me a punishment far worse than any beating she has ever given me. Silence. I had lost her trust, and the only things I was permitted to do were daily chores, homework, and reading until I made it back to school. Anything that resembled a screen was snatched away, and her silence was far worse than anything else, especially because I was constantly looking over my shoulder, waiting for one of those heavy hands to meet my face.

Once I got back to school, Danielle and I were the talk of Lancaster High. I kept getting looks, points, and whispers from everyone I came in close contact with. I was a freshman in high school, and I already had a bad reputation. First, I was a crack addict's bastard son, now I'm the guy caught doing "two-person pushups" in the back of the school. Our peers even endowed us with nicknames: Grass Stains and Jungle Booty. *How original*, I sarcastically thought. My class schedule was changed upon my return to school to ensure Danielle and I didn't have the same classes. Probably because of her parents' complaints. But since it was the beginning of the school year, it didn't affect my grades which left me thankful. My counselor, Mr. Taylor, gave me a new P.E. period and changed the Culinary Arts class I had with Danielle to Intro Art. I would see her sometimes in the halls passing by as we went to class, but she just kept her head down and did her best not to cross my path. Yet not a day went by that I didn't think about her.

Months went on. Until one day, I found a note left in my locker from Danielle. I was so happy to see it recognizing her penmanship. She was the only person I knew that made a complete circle over her lower-cased "I's" and points on the mounds of her lower-cased "M's." Just seeing my name on the note and having any communication with her at all left me elated. I carefully unfolded the piece of paper and began reading what the note said, feeling my own breath leaving my body for a moment as I recited her words: *"I'm pregnant."* The phrase jumped off the crumbled paper, leaving me in a critical state of mind. I continued reading, coming into cognizance that Danielle was pregnant, and on top of that, her parents were forcing her to put the baby up for adoption. When I finished reading the note, I crumbled the piece of paper up and shoved it into my pocket.

I wore an expressionless face as if I was unfazed and went to my history class. Even though I didn't outwardly express it, my mind began firing off questions like fireworks on the Fourth of July. The tardy bell rang just as I made it to class, sitting down in my usual seat. Ms. Kirkland instructed us to complete the warm-up while she took attendance. The class was rowdy as usual as Ms. Kirkland began calling out names in her distinct New York accent.

"Cayden," Ms. Kirkland called out.

"Here," he replied.

"Tyshawn," she voiced.

"Here," he replied.

"Felicia," Ms. Kirkland called.

"Here," she replied as my hands began to sweat.

"Wisdom," she called. But I was left mute. "Wisdom!" Ms. Kirkland repeated, scanning the room until our eyes met.

I couldn't even hold it together long enough to get through the class period. I instantly got up, grabbed my bookbag and walked out of Ms. Kirkland's class feeling so overwhelmed with emotion, I couldn't even think straight. "What am I going to do?" I asked myself, trying not to cry in the middle of the hall. I slid down the lockers onto the school's dirty floor. Ms. Kirkland found me in the hall with my back pressed against the lockers. Without even stating a word, she stood me to my feet and escorted me to the nurse's office. She said to the nurse that I wasn't feeling well and prompted me to call my Gigi to pick me up. It was almost like she already knew what was going on. Then Ms. Kirkland left me in the nurse's office to go back to her classroom.

After sitting in the nurse's office for half an hour, the main office called informing the nurse that Gigi was there to pick me up. I timidly walked from the nurse's office to the foyer looking at Gigi through the big glass window outside of the main office. Gigi looked at me intensely as we quietly walked from the main office to her old Cadillac in front of the building. I got in the car, and before the door even shut all the way, I began bawling my eyes out, revealing everything to her in my tearful language she tried her best to interpret.

"Danielle is pregnant, Gigi." I managed to finally get out clearly. "Her parents are making her give the baby up for adoption."

I sat there and cried not knowing what would happen next. I just knew Gigi would blow a gasket. Yet she took in a deep breath and calmly asked, "What do you want to do?"

Shocked, I sat up and wiped my face, surprised at her level of calm. I weighed out the options in my head and hesitantly asked, "Can we keep it?"

"Keep what?" Gigi's eyes widened, staring at me.

"The baby," I murmured, frightened to give her eye contact.

"Boy, what?!" her voice boomed. "You don't know the first thing about raising a child! Why would you want to do such a thing?"

I took a second before bravely looking at Gigi, who was becoming overwhelmed with the news. I voiced from the heart, "I know how it is to grow up not knowing if your parents love you, or who your father is…" I paused, clearing my throat. "I don't want the same for my child."

"If it's even yours," Gigi murmured.

"It's mine, Gigi," I said defensively.

Gigi took a second to look at me and sat back in the driver seat. The car was so silent, I could literally hear the gears turning in her head as she sat back looking at the ceiling that was apparently providing some sort of insight. After a few minutes, she sat back up and took in another breath before blurting, "You will have to get a job while going to school. This will be your responsibility." She continued, "2 a.m. feedings. It's all you. I will take care of the baby while you are in school. I'll ask Ms. Corrine to babysit, in an event where we both must work, and *you* will compensate her for babysitting. I will apply for a three-bedroom place in Harrow Park for Section 8. Weekends will be spent either working or taking care of your child. Man acts lead to man responsibilities. Do you agree to these terms and conditions?" Gigi asked in a serious and authoritative tone.

I smiled, "Yes, ma'am."

"Good," Gigi replied, starting the car. "I'm too young and fine to be someone's great-grandmother," she said, driving down the street.

It had taken everything in me not to jump for joy in the car. I knew it was a risk asking Gigi to take in another child. She shouldn't even have been responsible for me, but I couldn't knowingly let another person grow up with the same questions I had.

Later that day, Gigi contacted the school and set up a meeting with Danielle's parents and the principal regarding the news. After it was confirmed that Danielle was pregnant and their plans for the baby, Gigi concocted a deal with Danielle's parents. Upon a paternity test, if the child was mine, Gigi would be granted custody. And if the child was not mine, they would put the baby up for adoption.

As the months went on, I grew used to seeing Danielle in the hallway wearing baggy clothes and sweatshirts to hide her bump. Rumors began to spread, as our peers watched us trying not to interact with each other. It was so hard to not say anything, but since we got ourselves in this situation, we couldn't be mad at the consequences. I could hear my Gigi, "I don't care what you do, but you better not talk to that girl. Don't even gather up the spit in your mouth to spit on her if she was on fire." And I'm sure her parents said the same thing since we both did our very best to avoid each other.

All my free time was spent working and reading up on newborn babies. I didn't even have the time to worry about what people were saying. Thankfully, due to Gigi's connections, she landed me a job at The Oink Shack in Berksdale, a neighboring neighborhood to Harrow Park just a few miles away. The owner, Mr. Lee, lowered the working age to fifteen and helped me get a work permit. I went to school the next day excited about checking another thing off the list that Gigi needed for me to bring my child home, totally missing the fact that Danielle wasn't in school until the end of the day.

I was on my way to get on the bus to go home, when I saw Gigi's Cadillac flying from the main street to the front of the school. *What is she doing here?* I pondered. Her car's horn alarmed everyone as she parked in the front of the long bus line. All the bus drivers blew their horns back at her for blocking them in. I ran to the car to see what was wrong. Gigi leaned over and opened the passenger door.

"Danielle is having the baby!" Gigi said, as I got in the car.

"Now?" I asked in disbelief.

"Yeah, now!" Gigi slammed her foot on the gas, flying from the front of the bus line and onto the main street. "Buckle up," she instructed as she swerve through traffic all the way to Pope General Hospital.

Once we got there, we were told of Danielle's location at the reception desk. We rushed to the elevators and made it to the third floor. Getting off the elevator, a lullaby played in the hallway. We looked around aimlessly trying to figure out where the music was coming from until a nurse walked by us, witnessing our confusion.

"Anytime you hear a lullaby over the intercom, it means a baby has just been born." The nurse told us, pointing us in the direction of the waiting room. We walked in, and I anxiously began pacing the floor. Meanwhile, Gigi sat down and began eating a Snickers out of her purse, unfazed by my anxiety.

Several minutes went by until Gigi snapped. "Sit down, boy!" she demanded.

"Yes, ma'am," I replied sitting next to her. I began to rock in my chair overwhelmed with emotion until Gigi tapped my hand.

"Did I ever tell you about the day you were born?" she asked, probably in an attempt to calm me down.

"No ma'am," I replied.

"I can remember it like it was yesterday." Gigi recalled sitting up in her seat. "Your mother was working at Ray's Diner on Shorewater Blvd, at the time when her water broke." Gigi said, as I looked up at her illustrating the story with hand gestures. "I can just imagine how disgusted everyone could have been eating their breakfast, while your mother's fluids flowed around the restaurant floor," she laughed as I cringed at the thought. "Your mother called me on the phone screaming and crying as I rushed to this very hospital, after her manager dropped her off. I went to her room, and she was in there making those nurses and doctors earn their checks. She was hollering her life away, scaring everyone outside of her room." Gigi laughed, continuing her story. "Lucky, was just a little over eighteen, and I remember holding her hand and watching her push you out." Gigi graphically said, "When I saw that big ole head of yours come out with that patch of silver hair I said, 'Lord, you done gave birth to the black Benjamin Button'," Gigi joked as we cackled in the waiting room.

"Really Gigi, Benjamin Button?" I replied.

"Really!" Gigi voiced, trying to stop laughing. "I remember them cleaning you off and them putting you in my arms while your mother tried to catch her breath. I leaned down and gave you to your mother and I said, 'Lucky, you give this baby a name with some meaning," Gigi stated looking at me. "She took one look at you, caressed that patch of silver on the back of your head and said, 'his name is Wisdom'," Gigi replied, touching my hand. "Make sure you live up to it."

"Yes, ma'am," I replied, looking back at the double doors watching a couple leaving with their baby. "Well, Gigi, if I can ask, why did you name my mom, Lucky?"

"Because I found out I was pregnant with your mom when I was around five months along. I was drunk every other day, and her ass was *lucky* that she was healthy and ain't come out the womb with a bottle of Jack." Gigi joked.

The double doors opened again. This time, Danielle's parents emerged through with Danielle in a wheelchair as Gigi and I got up to greet them.

"It's a girl," Danielle's father said coldly.

Wow, a girl, I pondered. My heart began to race, thinking of all that would entail. "How are you?" I asked, gawking at Danielle whose eyes swelled with tears.

"She's fine!" Mr. Jenkins growled. "The baby is too."

"How would you know?" Danielle murmured. Tears rolled down her face. "You wouldn't even look at her."

"Shhh, Danny." Mrs. Jenkins whispered, leaning in.

"Don't 'Danny' me!" Danielle snapped. "You wouldn't even let me hold her."

"No need to hold something you'll never see again," Danielle's father interjected. "Now, let's go!"

Danielle pushed the brakes on the wheelchair and stood to her feet slightly off balanced, "Something?!" she shouted boldly with a hint of confusion.

"HEY!" Gigi interrupted, getting everyone's attention in the waiting room. "I understand emotions are everywhere, but let's not say anything we'll regret."

"How about you raise that boy over there and leave me and mine alone." Danielle's father stated with his jaw clenched tight.

Gigi looked up at Danielle's father, who towered over her. "Mr. Jenkins, let me explain something to you. I am not the one nor the two," Gigi declared. "I don't give a damn how big you are or how many muscles you got. I'll take this pen out this purse and deflate yo' big ass."

"Gigi!" I exclaimed.

"Hold it, Wisdom. I got this." Gigi continued telling off Danielle's father. "Now listen, I know it's hard to believe but I'm probably old enough to be your mother, and you will not talk to me like that! Is that clear?" Gigi asked. Mr. Jenkins remained muted. "Now, my grandson and your daughter made a huge mistake doing what they did, especially at school. We can all attest to that. But that baby back there is not the mistake!" Gigi exclaimed, pointing to the double doors. Mr. Jenkins' eyes glazed over. "Give your daughter a chance to deposit love and understanding in that baby, your grandchild..." She paused. "Let her say goodbye in the right way, Mr. Jenkins, please."

Silence fell on all of us as the attention was now on Mr. Jenkins. "Please, Daryl," Danielle's mother pleaded. "Listen to her."

Danielle's father looked back at Danielle before turning back to Gigi, as if he was really deciding if it was a good idea or not. His lips parted. "Fine," he said, wiping his eyes before the tears fell. "Go ahead."

"You two, go on and see the baby. Your parents and I will wait out here," Gigi instructed us.

Danielle sat back in her wheelchair and began rolling her way back to the nursery until I got behind her to push.

"Don't get any bright ideas, young man," Danielle's father boldly stated.

"I won't sir," I assured.

I pushed Danielle in her wheelchair through the double doors to the nursery. *I can't believe this is the closest I've been to Danielle in nine months,* I thought to myself as she instructed me on which way to turn to get to the baby.

We went into the room and saw the baby wrapped in a tight swaddle being tended to by a nurse. The nurse in there looked at us coming in, and she put the baby down in what looked like a clear shoe box.

"Oh, you must be the potential father," the nurse greeted me. "My chart says that a paternity test was ordered. Do you still need it?" The nurse looked back and forth between me and the baby.

"For my grandmother, yes," I said. "But I know she's mine." I looked at Danielle as she began to cry.

"Okay, well, before you see the baby, I will need to do an oral swab of your mouth. Our lab is downstairs, so we should have the results in a few hours."

"Okay," I replied. I sat in the only chair in the room while Danielle rolled herself toward the baby.

The nurse drew out a cotton swab and inserted it in my mouth, going down the walls of my cheeks, before putting it in a plastic bag. "Got it," The nurse said. "I have the baby's sample already. I'll be back with the results in a few hours."

"Thank you," I replied. Then she left.

I walked over to the clear rectangular structure to see the baby. I gawked at this tiny human moving her head slowly, making small grunts.

"She's yours, Wisdom. I've only been with you," Danielle said.

"I know, Danielle. I believe you." I draped my arm around her.

"But this should confirm it before the paternity test will." Danielle removed the baby's cap to reveal a small portion of silver hair standing straight up towards the front of her head. It resembled the same one I had at the back of mine.

Looks like it is hereditary, I thought to myself, fighting back tears. "She's perfect," I replied.

Danielle agreed. "That, she is."

Another nurse came in, bursting through the door interrupting our impromptu family moment.

"The parents, I presume?" The nurse inquired.

I held Danielle's hand and replied, "Yes we are."

After the introductions, the nurse gave us the run down on how to care for a newborn. Down to holding, feeding, burping, and diaper changing. After we spent a few hours with the baby, Gigi and Danielle's parents met us in the nursery. Gigi had the car seat and the bags that we had previously purchased in preparation. The nurse who took the paternity test came in directly behind our parents with the results.

"Congratulations, Mr. Davis. You are the father," The nurse informed me. I looked at Gigi with a smile, feeling like I was on a rerun episode of Maury.

"It's time to go, Danny," Danielle's mother said.

"Already?" Danielle cried.

"Yes, we must go now!" Mrs. Jenkins tried her best not to give anyone eye contact.

Danielle kissed our baby on the forehead and handed her to me. Tears rolled down her cheeks. "I love you sweet girl." Danielle whispered, touching our baby's hand that managed to come out of the tight swaddle. "Take care of our baby, Wisdom."

"I will," I assured, watching Danielle adjust herself in the wheelchair.

Danielle's dad walked up and gripped the handles of the wheelchair, beginning to back Danielle out of the room.

"Wait!" Danielle loudly voiced, getting everyone's attention. "Can I know her name?" she begged.

The whole room grew quiet, now making me the center of attention. I recalled the story Gigi told me in the waiting room. I took one glimpse of my daughter, immediately knowing the perfect name to give her. "Love," I said. "Her name is Love."

"That's beautiful, Wisdom," Danielle said as her parents began rolling her out the room. "Thank you," were the last words she spoke before the doors closed behind them all.

Gigi came closer and saw the tufts of silver hair. "Wow, she is your spitting image," Gigi observed. "Even down to that peculiar silver hair of yours," she pointed out. She kept looking at the baby. "Why the name Love?"

"Simple," I replied, looking at her. "It's what I want most in the world but know so little about."

Gigi glared at me touching my shoulder. "Well, what's her middle name? She got to have a middle name."

I pondered for a second. "How about René, after her beautiful great-grandmother?" I suggested.

"Boy, I told you; I am too young and fine to be a grandmother much less a great-grandmother. She will call me Gigi too," Gigi voiced. "Welcome to the world, Love René Davis!" I recalled the whole scene in my mind like it was yesterday.

Suddenly, it was 2:04. *One minute left,* I thought to myself, reminiscing over the past. Danielle's father, who serves in the military, received orders to be stationed in Texas. This meant relocation for Danielle and her family just a few months after Love was born. Since I was able to get their address before they moved, I sent pictures of Love once a month through mail. I wasn't permitted to contact Danielle any other way. Presently, this week was my last week of my junior year and the next to last week of school since having an A in all my classes made me exempt from most of my finals. I only had one final I wasn't exempt from, but the teacher allowed me to complete that exam this week, making it my last week of school. After such a long day, all I wanted to do was eat and see my daughter before I had to go to work.

Love's second birthday was coming up, and I was saving my money like crazy, to buy her this motorized power wheels SUV she kept blabbing on and on about in her toddler language. It was hard to save money after paying for pull ups, clothes, and shoes every other day because Love kept outgrowing them. She was two going on twenty. Love is sassy, smart, and caring, and everything I could ever want in a daughter. Every day I look at her face sleeping in her crib before I go to school; it becomes evident that I made the right choice in keeping her. The clock strikes 2:05, and the bell rings for dismissal.

"Finally!" I loudly exclaimed.

CHAPTER 2

Where do we go? How do we get there? Questions that plague our minds and invade our thoughts. Discipline is key, trust the process, expressions we tell ourselves to reach the next level. Or are they simply words that fall on deaf ears, as we are stuck pondering why we are in the same place annually. Up may be the goal, but down is unfortunately a location, too. Destinations.

All of us students flooded the bus terminals, going into various destinations, scattering across the front entrance of the school. We looked like roaches in a dark kitchen when the lights were turned on. I saw Rico in my peripheral vision, trying to mack on a girl. Yet I made it to our bus just in time to save him a seat towards the front. I sat directly in the middle of the seat and waited patiently for Rico to get on the bus. He constantly acted as if he didn't know saving a seat on the bus is like a fight for your life. I pulled out my notebook and began writing until I felt a tap on my shoulder, interrupting my creative flow.

"Slide over, man. The bus is filling up!" Jordan, one of my classmates demanded.

"Saving the seat, man," I told him. "It has to be one in the back somewhere." I pointed toward the back of the bus even though I knew there probably wasn't really a seat available.

He sucked his teeth. "Shoot, I hope so."

As Jordan made his way to the back, Rico finally came on the bus with his short locs swinging in the air, smiling harder than a politician in November. "Thanks for holding my seat, bro. I was trying to get that fine ass Keisha's number." I slid over closing my notebook for Rico to sit down in the seat I'd saved.

Our bus driver, Ms. T, cleared her throat. She gawked at Rico through the rearview mirror, slightly perturbed about his language.

Rico apologized. "My fault, Ms. T." He flashed his white smile, sitting up straight in the seat. Then he turned to me. "Dang, Wisdom. Was this the best you could do? Got me all close to the front and shi- stuff." Rico caught himself. "You know all the action is in the back."

"Bro, next time how about I have you fighting for a seat like Jordan is right now," I argued. "He is probably still looking for one in the back."

Rico took one glimpse behind us to see Jordan sitting three to a seat with one butt cheek on the seat and the other butt cheek hanging off.

"Nah, bro. I'm straight," Rico snickered. "Appreciate you." As he spoke, the line of buses in front of us began moving. Ms. T closed the doors.

"So, what were you writing, Langston Shakespeare?" Rico asked as I put my notebook in my bookbag.

"Bro, do you mean William Shakespeare or Langston Hughes?" I laughed. I knew Rico was probably serious.

"Which ever one will make you famous and get us out the hood," Rico replied.

"Us?" I questioned.

"Yeah. *Us*." Rico draped his arm around my shoulders. "Come on man, you can be the writer and do all that serious talk, and I can be the fine friend you invite to the parties, so I can talk to the hos."

I pushed Rico's arm off. "Man, I don't know about all that. What writer you know personally made it from the hood?" I asked. "I have a daughter. I can't be one of those living-in-my-car-until-my-dreams-are-fulfilled kind of people. Dreams are for people with money, not for people like us." The hot air began to pour in from the bus windows, emphasizing my statement.

"Man, dreaming is for everybody. That's why that motherfucker free." Rico replied.

"Whatever, man." I changed the subject. "So now you trying to get Keisha, huh?" I asked. "First it was Jasmine. Then Nicole. Now Keisha. And that was all this week."

Rico clutched his chest and looked at me as if he were appalled at my statement. "You make me sound like some type of whore." Rico joked. We both broke out into a hearty laugh.

"You said it, not me." I replied with my hands up, palms out in surrender.

"Hey, I love the bitches, and the bitches love me." Rico replied. A few of the girls in the front of the bus, who happened to overhear us, rolled their eyes. Ms. T on the other hand couldn't hear a thing. Once the bus started moving, the sound of hot air drowned out most of the conversations us students were having. If she was able to hear, she would have cut her eyes at Rico for one, cursing and for two, calling females the "B-word".

"Bro, don't refer to the young ladies as B's, man." I said, standing up for the females who were at the front of the bus.

"Man, you've been soft ever since you became a dad. Bet you wasn't thinking about that two years ago when you were behind the school giving back shots, now were you?" Rico asked.

"You way out of pocket for that one, bro!" I shouted. "You can find your own seat from now on. Miss me with that!"

"See, just like I said. Soft. I was just joking, bro," Rico defended himself.

"That shit wasn't funny!" I replied as the bus came to a stop at a light. The sound of the hot air paused, and Ms. T glared at me through the rear-view mirror. "I apologize, Ms. T," I said quickly.

"No, I apologize, Ms. T. It was my fault." Rico spoke up as the bus began to move again. "My fault, bro. I went too far."

"Yeah, man. You did. Don't talk about the mother of my child." I checked him.

"You got it, bro. My bad," Rico apologized, holding his fist out, waiting for a pound. "Are we straight?" he asked.

"We straight," I replied, dapping him up.

"Cool," he replied. "Now about this bitch," Rico continued. I shook my head. "Bam!" he yelled as he handed me a crumpled-up piece of paper with some numbers on it. "I got those digits, my boy."

I grabbed the crumpled paper. "Why didn't you just put her number in your phone?" I questioned.

"I don't know. I guess she likes that old school stuff," Rico shrugged.

I examined the paper and began to chuckle. "You are missing a couple of numbers, my boy," I mocked. Rico snatched the paper out of my hand to see that she really didn't give him all ten of her digits. There were only six numbers written down.

Rico balled up the piece of paper and threw it out the window. "Forget her!" he snapped.

"Young man don't throw things out of my window! Do you want me to write you up?" Ms. T asked.

"You can do that?" Rico asked Ms. T. I nudged him in the arm to act right. Rico sat back. "Nah Ms. T, my bad, I don't want no smoke." Ms. T was now pulling up near our neighborhood.

"Maybe if you stop referring to the young ladies as the B-word, they might be more willing to give you their full number." I explained.

"Man, whatever. I'm on to the next ho," he said. I shook my head again. He turned to give his attention to the girl in the next seat over. "How are you doing?" he asked. She completely ignored him, not bothering to lift her head from her phone. "Forget you too, then," Rico told her.

Ms. T finally stopped the bus right in front of our neighborhood sign and opened the door. "Alright, y'all. We're here!"

We all got up and began exiting the bus. "See you tomorrow, Ms. T." I said to her, getting off the bus and leaving Rico behind as he kept trying to make his move on some other females who were getting off. I was walking towards my house when Rico ran up beside me.

"Strike three! You're out!" I teased. We walked past the Harrow's Landing sign covered in graffiti.

"Hey, at least I'm trying," Rico said. "Who was the last female you talked to?"

"Danielle," was my shameful reply.

"Hold up, hold up, HOLD UP!" Rico dragged out, making a scene. "You mean to tell me that the only person you ever been with is your baby momma?"

"My daughter's mother," I corrected. "And yes, she's the only person I've ever been with."

"My boy, that was over two years ago and only one time," Rico exclaimed still baffled.

"Thanks for the recap, bro. I'm aware."

"Man, you backed up, that's why you so uptight." Rico squeezed my shoulders.

Laughing, I smacked his hands away. "Shut up, Rico!"

"My boy, you only had some buns once, and it was over two years ago. My guy, you a virgin adjacent." Rico sounded as if he said something intellectual.

"What in the blue hell is a virgin adjacent?" I asked, slightly amused.

"You, my guy," Rico laughed. "A person who only got some once, and that one time was a long time ago."

"Bro, shut up!" I laughed as a group of guys walked toward us. I readjusted both bookbag straps onto my shoulders and kept walking forward just in case these guys wanted to start something I needed to finish. The closer they got; I recognized them as the gang that I'd previously advised Rico to stop hanging with.

"What's good, Rico?" One of the guys greeted. I tried to keep a straight face as they surrounded us.

"What's good, Shy?" Rico replied, dapping him up.

"What's up, Brave Heart?" Shy greeted me, looking in my direction.

"Who is Brave Heart?" I asked, maintaining my emotionless face. I eyed the other guys who were surrounding us. They were wearing matching black T-shirts and Jordan's like they just took a family picture for Olan Mills.

Shy laughed leaving me answerless otherwise.

"You Ms. René's grandson, right?" One of the other dudes asked me from the group.

"How you figure?" I inquired.

"Man, it's Harrow Park, everybody knows everybody. Even niggas that barely come outside," the guy informed me. "I'm Poodie. My grandma Patrice is friends with your grandma."

"Oh okay," I quickly replied, trying my best not to encourage further conversation.

Poodie didn't get the hint. He kept right on talking. "You got some hands too. I've seen you out here on some three on one shit, putting niggas on their backs."

"That's why I call him Brave Heart," Shy revealed.

I shrugged. "Not my finest hour, but you got to defend yourself, right?"

"True shit," Poodie said, grabbing a rolled blunt out his back pocket and lighting it up.

"Well, we about to get into some shit," Shy told us. "Y'all want to come with?"

Rico was all too eager to volunteer. "You know I'm with it," he said.

"I have to go to work." I said to provide an escape for myself and Rico. Yet, Shy wasn't interested in my response.

"Man, I can get you way more money in a couple hours than you make in weeks, my dude."

"I'm sure you could, but I'll keep my job." I began to walk through the crowd. "Make that money, don't let the money make you."

"Nigga, this ain't *The Player's Club*, and yo' black ass sure ain't Diamond." Shy replied. The other dudes chuckled in unison. However, he and his crew let me pass. "When you ready to make that real money, come find us."

"I'll keep that in mind." I said sarcastically, walking a little further from the group. "Rico, are you coming?" I asked. Rico lived in the court directly behind me, but he hadn't moved in the same direction I was headed in yet.

Rico looked back and forth between me and the group as if it was a hard decision to make. "Nah, Wiz, I'm going to roll out with them. I'll catch you later." Rico saluted me. Then he turned around to face the group.

"Suit yourself," I replied, slightly perturbed.

The group began to walk down the street in the opposite direction with Rico in tow. "Catch you later, Brave Heart," Shy called over his shoulder, with a puff of smoke following behind.

My once emotionless face now sported a deep frown. I hated that Rico hung with those guys. They called themselves The Vigilantes. They went around terrorizing the neighborhood by robbing, shooting, stealing, and probably killing-- all the usual gang activity that constantly happens in Harrow Park. I wanted so much more for Rico, but I knew deep down it didn't matter how much more I wanted for him. It mattered how much he wanted for himself. And after taking a second glance at those guys, it didn't look like he wanted much. It wasn't like his mom was much help either. Rico stayed with his mom, but between her own mix of addictions to drugs, alcohol, and men, she wasn't home much to see that Rico had fallen into the wrong crowd.

I walked up the street, finally making it to my court. Before I could even step foot onto the front porch, the aroma of oxtails embraced me like an overdue hug. "Yep, Gigi is doing her thing in there," I declared, rushing up to the porch.

I opened the front door, stunned by a beautiful, brown-skinned princess running up to me. My heart literally stopped beating for what seemed like a minute. As she ran in what seemed like slow motion, I saw a full yellow ball gown with matching gloves, and a silver streak of hair perfectly tucked in a neat bun. I was stricken by her outward beauty until her tiny voice made time speed up.

"Da-ddy, Da-ddy, Da-ddy!" Love shrieked, greeting me at the door. She hugged my legs and put my knees in a chokehold.

"Hey princess," I said, picking her up and kissing her on both cheeks.

"Well, hey, Daddy," Ms. Eunice, one of Gigi's friends called from the couch. Our eyes met. She crossed her legs, looking at me seductively as she pilfered through a plate of food with a fork.

"Hey, Ms. Eunice," I said through clenched teeth.

Ms. Eunice had a bad habit of flirting with me, and she used any excuse to touch me. She made my skin crawl, so I didn't think twice when I sped towards the kitchen, holding Love tightly to get to Gigi.

"Hey, Gigi." I said as I placed Love in her highchair. Her fancy gown draped over the sides.

"Boy, why are you walking in this kitchen like your butt itch?" Gigi asked.

I peeped at the kitchen entrance to ensure Ms. Eunice was still in the living room. "Ms. Eunice likes to flirt with me, and it makes me uncomfortable." I whispered to Gigi. She broke out into a hearty laugh. "Gigi, I'm serious." I whispered again. I shrugged off my bookbag and put it in one of the empty chairs at the kitchen table.

"Boy, you can't handle all that woman," Gigi declared. "Half her body would snap your skinny butt like a Dollar Tree toothpick."

"Come on, Gigi. I'm not skinny, I have an athletic build." I defended myself as I grabbed a bag of Goldfish out the cabinet and spread some of the cheesy crackers across the table connected to Love's highchair. "Besides, I don't want no parts of Ms. Eunice."

"Boy, athletic build is the educated equivalent to skinny as hell," Gigi joked. She put a covered plate on the table at my usual seat. "The only reason you have a six-pack is because your skinny tail ain't got nowhere else for your abs to hide," Gigi laughed. "*Oh, Eunice,*" she teasingly called out towards the living room.

"Shhh," I told her. I really was not trying to let Ms. Eunice hear us.

Gigi's laugh came to a screeching halt. "Did you just shush me, in my own house?"

I saw Gigi's nose begin to flare. "I didn't mean to," I quickly apologized.

Gigi's mouth twitched at the corners. "Boy, sit down and eat this food, before I call her in here to touch you." Gigi joked, cracking herself up.

"You really think this is funny, don't you?" I replied, sitting down unwrapping my plate.

"Oh, baby it is," Gigi said. "Shoot, give me that plate. There is a whole buffet in the living room waiting for you. Go on and eat that. I'm sure ain't no one been down there since Bill Clinton was in office."

"Gigi!" I exclaimed loudly. I covered my mouth as she began laughing again. Love took turns fixating her eyes on me and Gigi before she began to chuckle herself like she knew what we were talking about. "Love, don't encourage her."

"Come on, baby," Gigi walked towards Love trying and failing to keep a straight face. "We are going to go in the living room, so your daddy can eat in peace."

"She's fine, Gigi. I want to spend a little time with her before I go to work."

Gigi didn't bother arguing. "Cool with me," she said changing course and walking towards the living room. "Oh, I almost forgot," she came back into the kitchen. "I got your trifold board you needed for your science project. It's in the pantry laying over the deep freezer."

"Thanks Gigi," I said with my mouth full of oxtails and rice.

"You're welcome," she replied, finally walking out the kitchen.

Between chews, I played with Love. We were working on her counting using the Goldfish as they made their way up to her mouth. I loved spending time with Love; she was the only one that could simply look at me and make me feel like I was doing something right. A few days away from turning the big two, she already knew majority of her colors, the entire alphabet, could count to twenty, and was almost completely potty trained. My child was a genius; if it wasn't for the age requirements, I would sign her up for Pre-K the following school year.

After I finished my plate, I washed it in the sink and lifted Love out of her highchair to give her to Gigi, so I could change my clothes. I found Ms. Eunice and Gigi chatting it up in the living room when I decided to put Love in her playpen to not interrupt Gigi's conversation. As I bent over to put Love down, Ms. Eunice watched me very intensely, biting her lip as Gigi blabbed on and on. *How does Gigi not see this?* I wondered, quickly scurrying out of the living room.

Unfortunately, Ms. Eunice wasn't going to let me go that easily. "Where are you going, handsome?" Ms. Eunice asked.

I peeked my head in through the doorway. "I'm going to change my clothes and get ready for work."

"Oh, you need any help?" Ms. Eunice asked seductively, making my eyes widen. I looked at Gigi to see if she heard what was just asked. She turned her head to Ms. Eunice. "I mean, do you need your uniform ironed or anything?" Ms. Eunice played off smoothly. Gigi sat up a little taller on the couch, still looking at her friend with one eyebrow raised.

"No ma'am," I replied, trying to leave the room a second time.

"Ah, Wisdom," Gigi called. She didn't take her eyes off Ms. Eunice.

"Yes, ma'am," I replied, peaking my head in again.

"Before you go upstairs and change, could you get a bottle of water out the fridge for Ms. Eunice?" she asked. I looked at her with confusion. "She's acting thirsty. Are you thirsty, Eunice?"

"No, René, I'm good," Ms. Eunice replied.

Gigi put her palm on the back of Ms. Eunice's hand and gave it a small squeeze. Her look now held a hint of distaste. "You sure?" she double checked.

"Yeah René," Ms. Eunice nervously confirmed. "Maybe I should go."

"If you insist Eunice." Gigi replied with fake innocence.

I began walking up the steps until I heard.

"We still on for spades tonight?" Ms. Eunice asked. Her voice echoed like she was at the door.

"As long as you bring the wine and are prepared for an ass whooping, we sure are," Gigi said.

I sucked my teeth and made it to the top of the steps. I loathed my grandmother's spades nights. It was always a bunch of loud, drunk, and snippy older women who would get white-girl-wasted and talk all night long. I secretly called it their "MAS meeting", which is an acronym for "Men Ain't Shit", which was always the topic of discussion for such late-night hours. I often wondered that since all of them had the same issue with men, maybe it was something *they* were doing wrong. But I dared not utter those words because Gigi would surely cave my chest in.

I took off my school clothes and gave them a good look through and a sniff to decide what needed to go in the dirty clothes hamper and what could be hung back up in my closet. Then I grabbed my deodorant to put under my arms before putting on my uniform. After I got dressed, I tucked my shirt in and walked downstairs to see Gigi talking to Ms. Eunice through the screen door, while keeping a watchful eye on Love, who was content playing with her toys in her playpen. I walked over to the playpen and planted a kiss on Love's forehead. I grabbed my bookbag out the kitchen, so that I could finish some schoolwork for my AP Biology final at work during my break.

"Off to work Gigi, I'll see you later on tonight." I braced myself to walk past her out the screen door onto the porch where Ms. Eunice was still standing.

"Wisdom, I'm off today, I can drop you off," Gigi said.

"I figured as much since you are having your spades night. It won't be too much trouble?" I asked.

"Boy, no. Let me get Love, and you can meet me in the car." Gigi handed me her car keys from the table by the door.

"Well, if that be the case can I get that board off the deep freezer, so I can finish my project?" I asked.

Gigi shook her head. "I wouldn't advise that. I'll be too tipsy to pick you up."

Experience told me that was indeed true. "You're right. I'll just print some pictures and info at work, and I'll finish it tonight at home."

"Cool. Go to the car. I'll get Princess Love together," Gigi replied.

"Yes, ma'am." I started to walk to the car. "Bye, Ms. Eunice." I tried my best to walk as quickly as possible past my grandmother's friend.

"Oh, wait baby, you have something on the back of your shirt." Ms. Eunice said. Unaware that she was just making up a reason to touch me, I stupidly pulled at my shirt and craned my neck to see what that something was.

"Oh, come here baby, I'll get it." I suddenly felt both her hands slowly tickling up and down my back.

"You got it?" I asked. I stood still hoping Gigi could see what was going on through the screen door.

"Almost," she exclaimed. She was now holding on to my side. "You must work out, huh?"

"A little," I replied. I patiently, yet uncomfortably, waited for Gigi to come outside.

"Mm-hmm." She moaned in my ear until a bottle of water flew past our heads. It frightened Ms. Eunice so much that she released me from her grip.

"Damn, I missed!" Gigi was holding Love in her left arm, while locking the front door behind her with her right. She was also wearing her "I'm-going-out-in-public" wig.

"René!" Ms. Eunice screamed. "You could have taken my head off, girl."

"Lord, I'm sorry. You were out here looking thirsty again, so I wanted to help you out," Gigi said. She made her way to where Ms. Eunice and I were standing. "You know I'm a caring bitch," she added.

"Well, could you care a little less," Ms. Eunice replied, holding the back of her head.

Gigi held out my daughter to me. "Wisdom, take Love in the car for me please."

"Yes, ma'am," I replied. I hit the unlock button and began putting Love into her car seat.

Gigi bent over to pick up the water bottle from the ground. She forcefully pressed it to Ms. Eunice's chest. "Drink up, darling," she commanded. "And keep your hands to yourself or catch these hands, your choice." Trying not to get caught eavesdropping, I pretended to be busy arranging Love's dress under the car seat straps. Out the corner of my eye, I saw Ms. Eunice standing there shocked. Gigi calmly strolled down the sidewalk towards the driver's side of her car. "See you tonight, darling, and don't forget the wine." Gigi said sweetly as if she hadn't just threatened Ms. Eunice seconds prior.

On that note, I finally secured Love in her car seat, and closed the door. I quickly got to the front, and I set my bookbag on the floor before putting on my seatbelt. I then leaned over and put the keys in the ignition, starting the car.

Gigi stepped into the driver's seat closing the door behind her. "You ready?" The sweetness was still in her voice. She pulled the seatbelt and strapped herself in.

"Yes, ma'am," I replied. She then put the car in gear, and we left the baffled Ms. Eunice still standing on the sidewalk clutching the bottle of water.

Looks like that's been handled, I thought to myself.

CHAPTER 3

The hustle and bustle. Is that all we are limited to? Just a cycle of clocking in and clocking out. The day drags as we petition the clock to speed up. Do the hours ever match the check? Labor intensifies with the demands of the world. Service with a smile, while the mind ponders on how to quit. Tiredness hits the body, but it doesn't equate to the tiredness of being broke. What do we do? Looks like we're stuck. Work.

Working at The Oink Shack was easy for two reasons: one, the job was simple, and two, there were hardly any people there. Once I got out of the car and waved goodbye to Gigi and Love, I saw my favorite co-worker, Courtland, in the back through the glass door. I knew it was going to be a fun night. Courtland was a year older than me and aspired to go to culinary school. Besides his ability to cook, he could also sing and act. He was the only dude I knew from the hood that knew what he wanted to do and worked towards it.

Usually, the only guys that make it out the hood did it one of three ways: they joined the military, they became a merchant seaman, or they died. Since the third choice was inevitable for everyone, I decided that I would go with the first option and join the military upon graduating. This was not because I was interested in protecting the country, but because it was structured and let's face it, it was quick money. Despite Mr. Joyner's and Rico's encouragement, becoming a writer didn't seem like a stable income for a teenage father. The facts were, I could barely afford to take care of my daughter, and Love was doing nothing but getting older. Doing four years of college and then trying to find a job in my field afterwards seemed like too big of a risk, and one I surely couldn't afford. But Courtland was built differently, and I knew he'd make it far. To be honest, sometimes I envied him.

"Big Court," I greeted him with my hand up in a short wave.

"Wizard Kelly," Courtland joked from the cutout in the wall that led to the kitchen.

Our manager, Anna, came from the kitchen to the front of the empty restaurant fuming. "You're late," she griped.

"Good afternoon to you too, Anna." I said sarcastically. Courtland balled up his face looking at her through the cutout. "Actually, I'm early. My grandmother dropped me off so I wouldn't have to walk. So, I know I shaved off a good twenty minutes."

"No, you're late," Anna fussed. "You were supposed to be here at 2."

"How?" I questioned. "I don't even get out of school until 2:05."

Anna's face grew red as she let out a huge breath. "Follow me, and we will look at the schedule," she replied. I followed her to the back office."

"Anna, I think you got his schedule confused with mine," Courtland interjected. "I was supposed to be here at 2:00, and I was."

"Nope, I read it right." Anna snatched the schedule from off the desk. "See right here. Courtland scheduled for 2:00 p.m.!" she declared pointing at the paper.

"What does that have to do with me?" I asked. "I'm Wisdom."

"Oh…" Anna paused, looking at the schedule again. "April fools!" Anna shouted. Courtland and I looked at each other in disbelief.

"It's June," I said slowly.

"You alright, Anna?" Courtland asked with concern. "Do all Black people look alike to you? Wisdom and I are two different complexions and two different sizes."

Anna's red face transitioned from angry to embarrassed. "No, I was just playing a trick on you guys."

"Okay Anna," I replied in disbelief.

"Sure, you were," Courtland said sarcastically. "We look like the number ten standing next to each other. I don't know how you mixed us up."

I laughed. "Stop it Courtland, you are not even that big, bro."

"Man shoot, when I go to the store, I shop in the BAH section, so you know I'm big," Courtland joked himself.

Anna and I both looked at him. "BAH section?" Anna asked.

"Yeah, BAH is short for the big-as-hell section. They keep it in the back of the store." Courtland explained to us with a straight face.

"Shut up, bro!" I laughed again.

"I'm just saying man," Courtland replied, going back to wiping the counters.

"Well, Wisdom!" Anna spoke with more confidence now that she knew the difference between her two employees. "If you want, you can clock in early and start cleaning the inside and outside of the windows."

"Clock in early, which means more money. You ain't got to ask me twice." I said, making my way to the front register to clock in.

"Go ahead and get started on those windows," Anna instructed. "I have been here since eleven this morning, so I'm going to take my lunch. Y'all need anything while I'm out?"

"A few thousands," I replied.

"A couple hundreds," Courtland added.

"I wish," Anna laughed on her way out the door. "Call me if you need me."

"Heard," Courtland replied.

"Alright," I added. Courtland and I both watched as our manager got in her car and drove off. "Is it time?" I asked him.

"Give it twelve more seconds," Courtland said. I counted silently. At twelve, Courtland shouted from the kitchen, "Now!"

I propped open the restaurant's door before making my way to the glowing "Open" sign in the window. I blinked the sign lights three times while Courtland did the same with The Oink Shack sign lights. After about five minutes, we had a restaurant full of hungry customers. A few months ago, Courtland and I surveyed a few shoppers in the plaza. We simply asked why they didn't come to our establishment. All the feedback was the same: they didn't like Anna. On top of her stoic personality, Anna would really skimp on our customers' food. She put more coleslaw on a barbeque sandwich than actual meat, and she did not even fill the side section of the to-go trays half full. After hearing this critique, Courtland and I started "Break Hour." It was a secret special we did, where we blinked the lights to signal to everyone that Anna was on break. Customers could now expect that we were going to give them a decent serving of food and more importantly, decent service.

While working, I took the orders in the front while Courtland prepared the orders in the back. Mr. Lee, an older Black man was the owner of The Oink Shack and former Navy Seal. He worked with Anna on the ship and brought her on board as the manager almost a year ago. Hiring Anna was the worst decision he had ever made. Anna, a White woman in her late thirties, knew a lot about how to run a kitchen on a ship, but knew nothing about how to run a restaurant in the hood. We expressed to Mr. Lee our concerns about Anna not being good for business and how sales plummeted after she took over. But unfortunately, it all fell on deaf ears, and we ended up stuck with her.

We were with our last customer when Anna returned with a Slurpee from 7-Eleven.

"You guys had a rush?" Anna asked.

"We sure did!" I declared. "Now I can go ahead and finish these windows."

I grabbed a roll of paper towels and the bottle of Windex behind the counter and walked to the door to start cleaning the outside windows. Anna made her way behind the register to clock back in and review the sales.

"Wow, you guys had over forty orders in one hour! That was the most sales we had all day!"

"Maybe we caught the shipyard rush. You know Berksdale is surrounded by three shipyards," Courtland offered, winking at me through the cutout.

"Yep, that makes sense," Anna stated. She left the register, making sure to grab her Slurpee and worked her way to the back office. I chuckled to myself.

I had just walked to the other side of The Oink Shack and begun cleaning the other set of windows when I heard a voice behind me.

"Young man," the voice called as I turned around to see a well-dressed older gentleman. "You René's grandson?"

"Yes," I replied, wondering how he knew Gigi.
He smiled. "I went to high school with your grandmother. I saw her drop you off here today when I was a few doors down. Figured you were her grandson."

"Oh, yeah. I am." I said more confidently now knowing how he knew Gigi.

"Please tell her Frog said hello."

"Frog?"

"Yeah, Frog. She'll know me," he assured, tipping his hat. "I own the suit shop three doors down."

"Gotcha, well it would explain the sharp fit." I complimented him on his royal blue three-piece suit with matching hat even though it was all of ninety degrees in the shade. *Nice to know he is a suit shop owner and not an old pimp*, I thought to myself.

"Appreciate it, young buck," Mr. Frog said. "I'll catch you later."

"Yes sir," I replied, continuing to clean the windows. I watched him smoothly stroll three doors down to his shop in The Berksdale Plaza.

After I finished wiping down the windows on the outside, I went back in and began cleaning the interior windowpanes of the empty restaurant.

"Courtland. Wisdom." Anna called, coming out to the office doorway. "Feel free to go on your break. It doesn't look like we are getting any more customers tonight." She turned on her heel to return to her desk.

"Yes, ma'am," I said as I went behind the front counter putting down the roll of paper towels and Windex. I grabbed my bookbag so that I could finish my project for my AP Biology class.

"Hey, Wizard Kelly," Courtland called from the kitchen. "You want to split a Courtland Special?"

"Sure," I agreed, quickly accepting Courtland's offer knowing how good his creations were.

I put my bookbag down, and Courtland came from the back and sat a tray on the table where my bookbag was previously. I went to wash my hands before sitting on the other side of the tray. We grew tired of eating barbeque sandwiches and ribs every other day, so Courtland challenged himself to create something new out of the same food we were selling.

"What is this?" I asked Courtland, curiously eyeing the tray.

"Something that will taste good now but mess our stomachs up later," he joked. "It's an adult grilled cheese sandwich. It's two grilled cheese sandwiches with pulled pork barbeque topped with mac and cheese in the middle."

"Man, that sound like that toilet is going to be screaming tonight," I said. "Slide that tray over."

I started scattering a few contents of my bookbag across the table, placing my schoolwork next to the newest Courtland specialty.

"What are you working on?" Courtland asked.

"My final project for AP Biology."

"Aww, I remember those days," Courtland said teasingly.

"Dude, you're a senior. You just finished classes last week," I said.

"Exactly, which means I'm done, and I'm graduating on Tuesday." Courtland celebrated, dancing in his chair. "It comes fast. You will be done before you know it."

"Yeah, I don't know if I'm ready, but I better figure it out soon, for my daughter's sake." I looked back and forth between my work and the sandwich.

"I feel you," Courtland nodded. He bit into his sandwich. A bit of cheese and pork tumbled back to the tray. "What's the project on?" he asked, with his mouth full.

"Genes, traits, and all that jazz." I replied finally taking a bite out of my sandwich. "This needs to be on the menu!" I raved between chews.

"Not with all-knowing Anna working here," Courtland exclaimed. "I wish Mr. Lee still ran the day-to-day operations, because she ain't it."

"Tell me about it," I agreed, looking over my paperwork and back towards the kitchen to ensure Anna didn't hear us. "Oh shoot," I said after rereading my project's instructions.

"What?" Courtland asked with concern.

I shook my head. "Nothing, man. You wouldn't understand." I replied, trying to figure out how I was going to complete my project.

"Try me," Courtland offered.

I let out a deep sigh. "The project is on family genes, and I need to use my family's information.

"Okay, so what's the problem?" Courtland asked perplexed.

"It has to be based off my parents, grandparents, and myself."

"Okay, I still don't see the problem," Courtland replied.

"Well, it would require me to know my father's information, and I've never met him," I shamefully revealed.

"Oh, okay well just do it based off your mother's info and pull the teacher to the side and inform them that you don't have any info on your father, "Courtland suggested. "I'm sure your teacher would understand."

"Man, that's embarrassing. I'm sure Ms. Lathrop is going to have me present it, and somebody is going to ask about the missing information," I said.

"Don't worry about them. The ones that ask petty questions are probably the ones failing anyway," Courtland concluded. "Besides, you are not the only person that will have that issue.

"Very true," I conceded, feeling a little bit better. Then I had a brighter idea. "Man, how about I just lie. I can find a picture online of some Black dude with some silver hair to be my dad and a pretty Black woman to be my mom and call it a day."

Courtland rose from his seat and picked up his tray. "Nah, bro. Don't lie. Be you and be truthful. Forget them other people," he said.

That was easier said than done. "Man, my momma had me at eighteen. I don't know who my father is and neither does my grandmother. Then, to add insult to injury, my mother pawned me off to my grandmother when I was twelve, and I haven't seen her since. And the cherry on top, I was caught playing "hide-the-dragon" behind the school that resulted in a beautiful baby I can hardly take care of, and now every time I pass someone in the hallway, they call me Grass Stains! You want me to present that?" I asked. I looked up to see during my rambling Courtland had walked away and was now behind the register.

"Yes, it's your truth," Courtland stated. "We all got a story."

"Well, what's yours?" I asked with an attitude. "Because mine is ghetto."

Courtland placed both hands on the register counter and leaned forward. "Welp, I'm the youngest of thirteen kids. I knew of my father, but he is deceased, and before that he wasn't in the picture. Most of my older siblings are old enough to be my parents, and they all have kids around my age," Courtland told me. He waved a hand at the restaurant's front door. "Honestly, one of them could walk in this restaurant today and I wouldn't even know who they were," Courtland continued. "My mother suffers from an autoimmune disease, and I take care of her, go to school, and work. So, like I said Wisdom. Everybody has a story. The only thing that matters is how you narrate it."

I took an angry bite of my sandwich. "Well, I'll tell you what, Courtland. I'm going to narrate it with a fake family I'm going to find on the internet." I told him between chews.

"Suit yourself, Wizard Kelly." Courtland returned to the kitchen while I turned my attention from my sandwich to my project. Later, I met Anna in the back office so I could print out some pictures to post on my trifold board at home. On my way back to the front, with my pictures in hand, Courtland shook his head at me from the kitchen.

When I'd finished all the corresponding writing prompts of my project, I placed all the contents and pictures into my bookbag.

Anna came out from the office one last time. "Well, Wisdom, it's time for you to clock out and head home. It's a slow night. I would ask you to stay and help deep clean, but you're a minor."

"I won't tell if you won't," I joked. Anna was unenthused. I immediately matched her seriousness. "Fine, I'll go home," I told her.

I went behind the register to clock out after throwing away the trash on my tray and putting it back in the kitchen's three compartment sink. I went back to the front and put my bookbag on my back and pushed in my chair, while Anna came out to the front to spray and wipe off the tables.

"Good night, y'all," I saluted, walking towards the door.

"Good night," Anna and Courtland replied in unison as I pushed the door open.

"Thanks for the sandwich, Big Court," I offered my gratitude before stepping outside.

"No problem, Wizard Kelly," Courtland replied. "Hey man, tell your story."

"Nah, I'm good, but I appreciate you." I replied smiling, watching Courtland shake his head one more time through the clear glass I spent most of my shift cleaning.

I began walking down The Berksdale Plaza, heading home. The flickering streetlights lit an uneven path back to Harrow Park. I toiled back and forth in my head about taking Courtland's advice. I knew I wasn't the only person that couldn't share their father's information, but I also didn't need anything else that my peers could add to their arsenal of jokes concerning me. I was tired of being the butt of every joke, no pun intended, especially after knowing that all the administrative staff and security had seen more of me than I was willing to share again. *Grass Stains, Grass Stains, yeah that's you.* The jokes bounced around in my mind until I realized I made it to the Harrow's Landing sign.

"Wisdom!" A voice cried out in the dark, but due to Harrow Park's horrible streetlights, I couldn't make out the figure. I tightened the straps on my bookbag until I heard the voice more clearly. "It's me, homie." Rico stepped into my line of sight.

I breathed a sigh of relief. "Man, I didn't know it was you," I said. "You know the lights out here are trash."

"Yeah, I saw you get into your fighting stance when you tightened up your bookbag straps," Rico snickered. "My boy stays ready to rumble."

"Just protecting myself," I said. "You're back early. I thought The Vigilantes tarried all night?" I sarcastically commented, continuing my walk home. Rico walked alongside me.

"Nah. At least not tonight," Rico replied. "Maybe tomorrow," he joked.

"Why do you hang with them?" I asked. "They're not going anywhere in life. Is that what you want for yourself? To be running the streets?"

"Running the streets?" Rico stopped in his tracks and dug into his pockets. "Dude, I'm making bank with those guys." He showed me a wad of cash, his evidence.

My eyes widened in disbelief. "Man, what you do to get all that money?"

He stuffed the cash back into his pockets. "Can't tell you all that, bro. You got to be down with the set. Come on Wiz, you trying to join?"

"And always be looking over my shoulder?" I asked. "No thanks. You can keep your illegal activities to yourself."

Rico held his hands out with his palms facing out to me. "Who said what we do is illegal?"

"If you're getting that much money in one night, you either stealing, slinging dope, or slinging yourself," I said. "So, which one is it?"

"Aye bro, chill out with that. I would have made more than that if I was slinging myself. You know the ladies love Rico, especially the older ones," he smiled. "Shoot, they love you too bro, I see how Gigi's friends be looking at you. It's probably all that silver hair you got on the back of your head."

I cringed, trying not to think about the ordeal between Ms. Eunice and myself earlier that afternoon. "Don't try to deflect. Let's put this back on you." I said, "I don't trust those guys."

"Well, I'm cool with them," Rico declared, as we made it to my court.

I took a deep breath and looked at Rico. He appeared to be so sure about the group. "Just be careful man," I warned. I held out my fist to dap him up.

"For sure, bro." Rico held out his own fist, agreeing to disagree.

"You coming to school tomorrow?" I asked as Rico began walking down the sidewalk to his court.

"We'll see," he joked. I shook my head, watching Rico disappear into the dark.

When I reached the doorstep, I dug in my pocket for my keys. I heard hearty laughs grow from the other side of the door. I guess the spades game/MAS meeting was in full swing. I opened the door, and there Gigi was, holding a glass full of red wine, surrounded by three other women with full matching glasses.

"Hey, Wisdom," the group of women sang in unison.

"Good evening, ladies," I replied. Ms. Eunice sipped her glass, purposely ignoring me and turning her head towards the TV.

"How was work, Wisdom?" Gigi asked, watching me hang my keys up.

"Slow, but it was okay," I replied. "Love sleep?"

"You know I wouldn't be down here if she was up," Gigi replied. "Now that you're here I can stop nursing this glass of wine." She immediately gulped down a full glass to prove her point.

"Damn, René. Looks like you got that same throat you had in high school," Ms. Patrice, one of Gigi's friends, teased.

"Bitch, you tried it!" Gigi snapped. The other ladies looked at each other giggling. "Now you know *you* are the throat goat and the mouth of the south."

Ms. Patrice lifted her own glass in agreement. "And you know it!" The room erupted with more laughter.

"And that is my cue," I said, walking towards the steps. "I'm going to go check on Love, Gigi." I told her, working my way to the first step. "Oh, by the way, Mr. Frog said hello."

Suddenly, all the other women let out girlish screeches and squeals.

"Giiiirrrrrlllll!" Ms. Janice, the third of Gigi's friends, dragged out.

"Come back, Wisdom!" Gigi made me walk back into the living room. "Who said hello?"

"Mr. Frog," I said. "He owns the new suit shop at The Berksdale Plaza a few stores down from The Oink Shack. He claims he knows you."

"Oh, your grandmother knows Frog, honey." Ms. Janice said, sipping her wine.

"Real well!" Ms. Patrice added.

"Are y'all done?" Gigi asked. "Nothing happened between me and old Fredrick Ogsby."

"That's because Charles whooped his ass in school back in the day," Ms. Eunice said.

"Sure did," Ms. Patrice clinked her glass against Ms. Eunice's, earning them a glare from Gigi.

"Grandpa?" I asked.

"Yep. Baby, sit down and learn something." Ms. Janice pointed to the loveseat. I sat awkwardly in front of the card table next to Ms. Eunice, who was still making a point not to look directly at me.

"You really going to tell my grandbaby this lie?" Gigi asked.

"Girl, you know this is every bit of the truth!" Ms. Janice declared. "This is what happened. So, Frog and your granddaddy Charles were close friends, and they were arguing on who was going to ask your grandmother to the prom."

"That is not what happened!" Gigi interrupted, shaking her head, while pouring another glass of wine.

"As I was saying," Ms. Janice continued, ignoring Gigi's disposition. "They were arguing about which one of them would take your grandmother to Lancaster's Senior Prom."

"Wait. Gigi, you went to Lancaster High?" I interjected.

"We all did!" The room echoed.

"So, interrupting someone when they are talking, apparently runs in the family," Ms. Janice observed. "Can I go on with the story?"

"I apologize, Ms. Janice," I replied. "Please continue."

"Thank you," Ms. Janice went on with the story. "So, they got into this huge argument in the foyer of the school by the south cafeteria, and your granddaddy swung on Frog. But he got right out of the way. Then he tried to kick Frog, but he hopped right over his leg. Every hit your granddaddy tried, Frog dodged it."

"Where was security?" I asked.

"Security?" Everyone in the room laughed like I'd told the joke of the century.

"Baby, this was back in the day. We ain't have no security," Ms. Patrice said. "Either we broke up our own fights, or a teacher would scream 'stop' in the hallway real loud, and that's all it took."

"It's this bad ass generation of kids today, that needs security," Gigi said.

"Who are you telling?" Ms. Janice agreed, continuing where she left off. "But Frog was jumping and moving, dodging every one of your granddad's hits, making him winded. Then your grandmother came up out of the sea of people surrounding the fight. Frog took a long gawk at your grandmother for so long, I guess he forgot he was in a fight." Ms. Janice became animated, standing to reenact the whole story. "Your granddaddy took one last hit and punched Frog flat on the floor, knocking him out cold. Then your granddaddy walked up to your grandmother huffing and puffing and asked, will you go to the prom with me?" Ms. Janice mimicked in the deepest voice she could muster.

"And you said yes?" I asked Gigi.

"Duh! How you think your momma got here?" Gigi asked. "And besides, I didn't want Charles to knock my ass out too, if I had said no."

The room erupted with laughter again, but the sounds of gunshots firing outside instantly broke the good mood. We all kneeled towards the middle of the living room floor, until the gunshots sounded like they were further away. Then we all sat back up in our seats, feeling a little more at ease.

"It must be Harrow Park's finest!" Ms. Eunice stated, grabbing her wineglass off the coffee table.

"Probably those damn Vigilantes my stupid grandson is a part of," Ms. Patrice said.

"Oh, you're Poodie's grandmother." I said, suddenly remembering the conversation Rico and I had with the group of guys earlier when we got off the bus.

"I'm Patrick's grandmother," Ms. Patrice corrected me. "I don't know why anyone would want to go by a name as dumb as 'Poodie', but I guess stupid is as stupid does. That's why he's not in my house now." Ms. Patrice scowled, sipping her wine. "He won't be nowhere near me with that foolishness."

"I know that's right, girl," Ms. Eunice said.

"Wisdom, how do you know Patrick?" Gigi asked, staring at me intensely.

"Rico and I ran into them when we got off the bus. He said that his grandmother and you were friends," I told her.

"Was that it?" Gigi asked.

Seeing as how it was always in my best interest to tell Gigi the truth, I continued. "Yeah, and some crap about how they can get me some money in the matter of hours, which will take me weeks to make at work. But you know I didn't take them up on their offer. Wish I could say the same for Rico."

"Rico?" Ms. Janice shook her head sadly. "Oh, that baby is a lost cause."

I defended my friend. "Nah, he'll be alright. He'll see the light eventually."

"We can only hope, but that baby's mother is never home," Ms. Patrice said. "He basically lives by himself and when his momma is home, she is either drunk or high off her ass. I feel bad for that baby."

"Well, that's why he needs friends like me. One of these days he will realize how dumb this all is."

Gigi wasn't convinced. "We can always hope and pray, but one day might be a little too late."

"Mm-hmm!" Gigi's friends hummed in simultaneous agreement.

"Don't get involved in something that will get you off track, even if he is your friend," Gigi warned.

"I won't, Gigi." I assured her. I then observed the clock. "I should probably finish my project and get to bed. I'll leave you ladies to your game."

"Okay, baby," Gigi replied. "Don't stay up too late."

"I won't," I replied getting up. "Hey Gigi, would you happen to have a picture of you and Grandpa that I can borrow for my project for AP Biology? Our final is on genes, and I would need it for the project if it's okay."

"Yeah baby, look in my closet on the top shelf in my room. It should be a navy-blue photo album; you can get a pic from there, but when you're done with your project, I want my picture back!" Gigi said sternly.

"Yes, ma'am," I replied, leaving the living room, and finally making my way up the stairs, while the loud laughs continued.

I peeped in Love's room to see her sound asleep in her crib with the night light shining on her face. Her playpen from the living room was squeezed tightly between her crib and her dresser. *I guess Gigi needed the room for her card table*, I thought closing the door. I slowly tiptoed my way to Gigi's room, ensuring that I didn't wake Love. Once I got to Gigi's room, I opened her closet door and something furry jumped out at me in the dark, making me jump back.

"Wisdom, you alright?" Gigi's voice flew up the stairs, as I hit the closet light switch.

"Yes!" I laughed. "I'm good, Gigi!" The furry object in question was just one of Gigi's wigs that fell off its mannequin head, landing on the floor. I chuckled, picking it up and putting it back on the mannequin's head that was on one of the shelves in her closet.

"You better not be tearing my shit up!" Gigi warned.

"I'm not," I assured, examining a few shelves in Gigi's closet until something shiny caught my eyes among her clothes.

I moved a few articles of clothing around, stunned by the sight of a gun carefully placed under three neatly folded sweaters laying on the shelf. *Now, I know Gigi doesn't play any games, but a gun seems to be a little outside her level of gangster*, I thought to myself surveying the weapon. I quickly put her sweaters back over the weapon, as if I never moved them. I stood on my tippy-toes and grabbed the navy-blue photo album on the top shelf, right where Gigi told me it was located. I hit the closet light switch and closed the door, working my way back downstairs.

Once I made it back downstairs, there was a knock at the door that halted Gigi and her friend's good time.

"Wisdom!" Gigi yelled out.

"I'll get it!" I stated, putting the photo album and my bookbag down at the table and walking towards the front door.

The poor lighting outside didn't assist me making out the figure in the peep hole.

"Who is it?" I asked, as the knocking continued. "Who is it?" I repeated. Again, there was no answer.

I looked back at Gigi, while she looked around at her friends. "Looks like somebody is getting fucked up." Gigi said, grabbing the empty wine bottle. Her three friends abandoned their cards and got into position for a bum rush.

Gigi slid in front of me and gave the room instructions. "On the count of three, I'm going to open this door. If you see me swing, go for what you know," Gigi whispered. We all replied with a head nod, unaware of who or what was on the other side of the front door. "One. Two. Three," Gigi said, swinging the door open.

Then Gigi gasped. The empty wine bottle fell and shattered all over the floor. I timidly looked around her to see what had her so shocked.

"Lucky?" Gigi whispered.

"Mom!" I screamed.

CHAPTER 4

Evidence is something that proves a statement to be true. Whether it's widely visible or smaller than a speck of dust, it can always be found. Sometimes you must search, and other times it greets you at the door like a long-awaited companion. There is always a piece of truth surfacing in every lie. Did I get it all? Is there anything left? Jumbles of mess we can't seem to clean up no matter the effort. Scrub all you like, spray all you want, but there will always be a speck left that will never go away. Residue.

We all stood at the door, stuck in place by what we were witnessing. It was almost as if we all saw a ghost staring at us directly in our faces. Time stood still as we all took in the view of my mother. She stood on the doorstep like she was a surprise Amazon package. She looked fairly the same, considering that five years had gone by. She was a little frailer than I remembered, yet oddly normal, thereby disregarding the rumors that Harrow Park folks brewed up. Mix emotions filled the room, and we stood in silence. On the one hand, I wanted to jump in her arms and welcome her back. On the other hand, I wanted to scream, "where the hell have you been?!", without worrying about being back slapped into tomorrow.

"Lucky! Where the hell have you been?" Gigi asked. Apparently, I wasn't the only one with mixed emotions.

"Hey, Momma," my mother offered enthusiastically with her arms open. "Wisdom," she said with the same elation.

We both stood there at the door like statues, until my mother closed her arms in defense.

"I think we're all waiting on an answer, darling," Ms. Janice said. "Like your mother asked earlier, where the hell you been, Lucky?"

My mother looked at Ms. Janice distastefully. I would assume she was wondering who Ms. Janice thought she was to check her.

Gigi waved Janice aside, "Janice, I got this!" she said. "As a matter of fact, goodnight, ladies." Gigi held the door open wide and motioned to her friends to go outside.

"Girl, you going to kick us out with this whole reality TV show unraveling right in front of us. Forget *Housewives*. I want to watch this," Ms. Patrice said.

"I said goodnight, ladies!" Gigi growled.

Ms. Eunice, Ms. Patrice, and Ms. Janice all grabbed their things and tiptoed over the shattered glass in the living room and walked past my mother, who remained standing in the doorway.

"René, you better call me later," Ms. Janice said, walking down the sidewalk.

"Me too," Ms. Eunice added.

"Me five." Ms. Patrice stumbled slightly as she walked.

"Good night, ladies." Gigi repeated, watching her friends walk to their respective courts in Harrow Park.

"You going to let me in, Momma?" My mother asked. She looked at Gigi sheepishly.

Gigi glared at her daughter intensely before looking back at me as if I was the deciding factor. She let out a huge breath and took a few steps back. "Come in, Lucky," she murmured, closing the door behind her. "Wisdom, can you grab me the broom and dustpan out the kitchen?" Gigi asked.

"Yes, ma'am," I replied, following her directions, and immediately returning to the living room, where my mother stood looking around. "You want me to clean this up, Gigi?"

"Nah, baby. I got it." She took the broom and dustpan out of my hands. She nodded her head in her daughter's direction. "Talk to your mother." Gigi left us to our own devices as she began sliding broken glass across the floor into the dustpan.

As I walked up to her, I found that I had no words to say. I had written this very encounter in my notebook numerous times, but I couldn't believe this was happening. *Did I manifest this?* I wondered, examining my mother. She wore a black T-shirt with a black blazer, a pair of distressed blue jeans, along with black heels which seemed odd to me. I wasn't sure if she was going for a casual look or a semi-formal one. Her hair was still full of thick curls that shaped her face with a couple added silver strands, and her skin was still fair. It was like looking at a slightly younger version of Gigi.

"Hey, Wisdom!" My mother greeted me again. She wrapped me in a huge bear hug, trapping my arms. I could smell a hint of vanilla as she held me. "Look at how big you've gotten, you're taller than me now," My mother observed. She then let go to study my face. "Is that a mustache?" she asked.

I chuckled awkwardly, "Yeah…"

"Lord, not you having a deep voice, too," my mother replied still taking in my appearance. "You're working now?" she asked running her hand on the shoulder of my uniform.

"Yeah…" I had no other words to say.

By this time, Gigi had swept up the last pieces of glass and was now gathering the empty wine glasses off her card table and taking them to the kitchen. After a few minutes, Gigi came back into the living room with a bottle of water and told my mother and me to have a seat. We settled on one side of the room, while Gigi sat herself in her favorite spot on the sofa.

"I'm so glad I was able to find y'all. I see you moved from the two-bedroom court to the three-bedroom court," my mother said, taking in the state of the house. "Everything alright?"

"Well, we needed the room," Gigi said in her clipped, matter-of-fact tone.

"And Section 8, let you do that?" My mother asked, surprised. Gigi scowled. I knew she was trying to keep herself from going off.

"Well, in a way—"

"Yes!" I interrupted Gigi. I was not ready to tell my mother about Love. Gigi gawked at me. I returned her stare with a nervous head nod, hoping she wouldn't say anything.

"Well, catch me up," my mother said brightly. "Tell me what's been going on?" Gigi's eyes rolled, and I decided to take the lead.

"Well, I'm working. I made honor roll for the third year in a row. I took up writing. I'm pretty good at it, at least that's what my teachers tell me. That's pretty much it in a nutshell," I replied. Gigi took the pause to clear her throat. Loudly. My momma gazed back and forth between us. I tried my best to fill the uncomfortable silence. "What about you, mom?"

"Yeah, what about you, Lucky?" Gigi asked, crossing her legs and arms. "What have you been up to for the past *five years*?" Gigi put a hard emphasis on those last two words.

"Well, you know I've been..." My mother's voice trailed off. She stood up. "You know, around, doing me." She began pacing the floor. "You know, trying to become more stable."

"Just walk straight, honey. It ain't that hard," Gigi said sarcastically.

"Momma," my mother sighed. Her bright and cheery disposition was gone.

"Bitch, don't 'Momma' me!" Gigi growled. "Your ass been gone for five years. You left this baby with a hole in his heart he's been trying to fill ever since you left. So, I'm going to need a little more than, 'I've been doing me.' Where the hell you been, Lucky?" Gigi snapped.

"Momma," my mother tried again.

Gigi pulled herself from the sofa and drew herself up to full height next to her daughter. "Five years, Lucky! FIVE YEARS!" Gigi screamed.

Love interrupted the show with a squeal that filled the whole house. My heart began to race, and I hoped my mother would somehow ignore it.

My mother turned her head toward the direction of the stairs. "Is that a baby I hear?"

"Bitch, you got a lot of nerve coming in here asking questions, like you ain't been gone for half a decade." Gigi said, walking away towards the steps. "Wisdom, talk to your momma," Gigi instructed. "I'm going to check on Love before I bash your momma's face in." She made her way to the second floor. "Gigi's coming, baby."

"Love?" My mother questioned me as I tried to slow my heart rate down. "Who is Love?"

"My daughter, Mom," I murmured hesitantly.

"Daughter? You got a daughter?"

"Yes, ma'am."

"You mean to tell me I'm a grandmother? Damn, I'm only thirty-five, and I'm somebody's grandmother," my mother replied, scratching her head.

"Wow, is that all you are worried about?" I asked.

"Of course not." She spoke defensively, as if she were trying to convince herself as well as me. "I'm just surprised, that's all. Where is the child's mother?"

I scratched my own head trying to figure out the best way to answer her question. I settled for keeping my response short and limited on the details. "She's not in the picture."

"Wow, really? What kind of low-down mother don't take care of her own child?" My mother asked, continuing to pace the floor.

"Shit, you tell me," I said under my breath.

My mother's feet halted. "What did you say?" she asked with her eyebrows raised.

I leaned forward in my seat and met my mother's gaze. "You heard me. What kind of low-down mother don't take care of her own child?"

"Little boy, you know nothing about what I went through," my mother said.

"Well, why don't you fill me in, Ma?" I replied. "You have no idea how many times I've defended you when the neighborhood guys told me you ran off because you were on drugs."

"Drugs?" Her eyes widened with bewilderment.

"Yeah. Drugs. And not the cheap shit, the good shit. Meth, cocaine, angel dust, heroine, all that." I explained, my voice slowly creeping up in volume. My mother stood in the living room with her mouth gaped open. "I've heard you were a prostitute. I've heard everything from everybody but you! So, I'm asking you the same thing you asked me. 'What kind of low-down mother don't take care of her own child?'"

"Wisdom. Wisdom, my sweet baby boy. I love you, but don't get it twisted," my mother pointed a manicured nail at me. "Your tone is about at a ten and I'm going to need you to bring it down to a two."

"I'll bring it down, once you answer my question," I replied.

"Oh, so you think you a man now because you got a baby, a few hairs on your face, and a little bass in your voice?" she mocked.

I lifted myself from the couch. "Man, miss me with all that." I waved a hand dismissively at her and walked towards the stairs. "If you don't want to tell me the truth, you know where the door is," I said without even so much as a backwards glance. My mother suddenly rushed behind me and used her full body weight to push me to the wall of the steps. She clenched my shirt collar tightly.

"So, you gone walk away from me when I'm talking to you?" My mother hissed. "You want to know the truth? Fine. Here it is. I never wanted kids."

I yanked my shirt from her grip. "Excuse me?"

She stepped away from me. "That's right. I never wanted kids," she repeated. "I spent twelve years of my existence trying to find my way in life with a child attached to my hip." My mother turned away and began pacing again. "Don't get me wrong. You were an easy baby and an even calmer kid, but I didn't know what I wanted to do with my life, and it was unfair to you to have a mother who couldn't hold down a job. I was so low and depressed until my homegirl Sharon brought this big ass RV to your twelfth birthday party at the arcade in Military Circle Mall."

"I remember that." I stated. "She let me and a few of my friends play in it for a while."

"After y'all went back into the arcade, Sharon told me how she blew all her savings on that RV and said, 'Luck, let's go see the world'..." my mother paused her pacing. She stared in my direction, not quite meeting my eyes. "Her offer was so tempting, but I couldn't subject you to that kind of lifestyle. You needed to be in school. You needed to have balanced meals and shit. You needed structure, and most of all, you needed discipline. You needed everything I couldn't give you. So, you know what I did?" she asked with a sad smirk. Tears began to form in my eyes. "I packed your ass up, gave you a note to give to your Gigi, kissed you on the forehead and took Sharon up on her offer. We explored all of America and experienced more than just Norfolk, Virginia," my mother continued. "Wouldn't call myself a prostitute or drug addict like Harrow Park so vividly painted, but I like to call it being free. And since you so grown, I guess you're grown enough to know the truth. I did what I wanted, I slept with who I wanted, and…" she said, walking up to me once more. "I stayed up at night not giving a single fuck about you." She pushed the center of my forehead with her index finger. "There is your answer," she griped. "You have no idea how I've protected you."

"Protected me?" I ground out. "You?"

"Damn right. I protected you!"

The tears were now rolling down my cheeks. She stood in a stance that welcomed a physical altercation. I wasn't sure what I was about to say to her. I was only able to utter two words. "Thank you," I replied, watching my mother's disposition change.

"Thank you," she repeated with confusion.

"Thank you for realizing that your egotistic, stoic, hypocritical, selfish ass wasn't fit to be a mother, and giving me to someone that you knew would take care of me," I said. "For that I am eternally grateful." My mother scowled at me with distaste, but I continued. "You know, I was thinking. After I graduate high school, I would join the military. Not because I want to, but because it will allow me to take care of Love, my daughter. A person who didn't ask to be here but is my responsibility to care for." I pointed at my chest. "That is what real parents do." I then brought myself nose to nose with her. "Take notes."

My mother's hand brushed across my face, slapping me so hard that I fell back against the wall. Gigi made it down the stairs just in time to keep me from retaliating.

Gigi ran in front of me, blocking me from proceeding, knowing I wouldn't dare move her. "Boy, that is your mother!" she shouted. "You better not ever raise a hand to her or any woman. Do you hear me?" Gigi asked.

"Yes, ma'am," I replied. I touched my sore cheek, feeling my pent-up aggression circulating my body.

"You know you were raised better than that," Gigi said.

"I know," I replied somewhat shamefully.

"Thank you, Momma," my mother said. She gave me a dark grin over Gigi's shoulder.

"That's why I'm here." Gigi winked at me. Then, she turned around and punched my mother right in the nose. My mother fell backwards into the front door. I stood in shock as I watched my mother's nose gush with blood. She tried her best to catch it in the palm of her hands before the red fluid dripped on her black shirt.

"Momma, have you lost your mind?" My mother asked in a nasally tone, pinching her nose.

"No, I haven't." Gigi held out her hand to help my mother to her feet and opened the front door. "I believe you have overstayed your welcome and it's time for you to leave, Lucky."

"For what?" my mother asked.

"Five years' worth of absence, and thirty-five years' worth of bullshit," Gigi replied. "This child is a blessing, and every day I didn't see you, he reminded me that I did something right. He is sweet, he is caring, he is smart, he is protective, he is genuine, and despite having an absent mother, he's a great father, and all I could ever ask for in a child," Gigi concluded. I leaned against the staircase wall, catching my tears with the back of my hand.

CAVON D. MILLS

"I was a mistake to you Momma?" my mother asked in a nasally voice. She pinched her nose to stop the bleeding.

"Not at all, Lucky," Gigi replied. "I thank God for you every day, and one day I hope he can deliver you from all that bullshit you just stated earlier about this child."

"So, I ain't shit to you?" my mother asked, still pinching her nose. Her eyes were also beginning to swell.

"No, baby. You're worse than shit. Shit has a purpose. Come back when you find yours." Gigi pushed my mother through the doorway. My mother stuck her foot, preventing Gigi from closing the door all the way. "You want to keep that foot, Lucky?" Gigi threatened.

"Before I go, I thought you should know that Greg is out," my mother told her. Gigi's body stiffened. She stood at full attention. It was clear this information had some effect on her.

Who is Greg, and why does that name make Gigi so nervous? I thought.

"Good for him," Gigi replied. "Now get your *free* ass off my porch before you drip blood on my shit." Gigi mocked. My mother only stared. Gigi slammed the door and locked it behind her.

Gigi turned around and for a moment we only looked at each other as we tried to make sense of all that had just happened. My heart was pounding a mile a minute, and my eyes grew heavy with more tears I tried to fight.

"Who is Greg?" I sniffed, breaking the silence.

Gigi shook her head. "Some old hoodlum you ain't got to worry about."

I dragged myself from the stairs. It became clear that I was losing the battle against my manly pride. Tears streamed down my face, and I crashed to the couch weeping heavily. Gigi sat beside me. She wrapped her arms around me and held me tight. She smelled like straight Stella Rosa. "I'm so sorry baby, I'm so, so

70

sorry." Gigi tried to comfort me. I tried my best to stop crying but was left unsuccessful.

"I can't believe that's how she feels about me," I said sniffing. "I never did anything to her."

"I know," Gigi replied, not letting me out of her grip. "There are a lot of simple people in this world, and your mother is unfortunately one of them."

I sat up to wipe my face, and Gigi's grip loosened from around me, and she went to check on Love. I couldn't fully grasp the fact that my mother deliberately told me in my face that she had never wanted me. I sank back into the couch cushions and allowed my mind to replay the past fifteen minutes. None of the many stories of my mother's return in my notebook concluded like this. I guessed that was the danger of imagination. Imagination causes you to view things too far outside the scope of reality. If reality was a meal, I was certainly served a third and a fourth helping all in one night.

"Are you okay, Wisdom?" Gigi asked, interrupting my thoughts.

"I'm fine, Gigi," I said wiping the remnants of the tears from my cheeks. "How is Love?"

"I got her back to sleep."

"Good. Didn't need her hearing that foolishness anyway."

"Yeah baby, you need to get to bed. You've had an extraordinary evening," Gigi confirmed.

"That's one way to put it," I replied, standing. "But I must finish my project. After that, I'll call it a night."

"Baby, maybe you shouldn't go to school tomorrow," Gigi advised. She put a warm hand on my sore cheek. "You've had a long night, and I can drop your project off at the school and send an email to your teacher."

"Nah, Gigi. I'm cool," I assured her. "Trust me. I'm good."

Gigi looked at me up and down carefully. "Okay, but if there is some shit with you tomorrow morning, you better stay home."

"Copy!" I replied, walking to the kitchen as Gigi walked up the stairs.

"I'm going to bed!" Gigi yelled from the top of the stairs. "Don't stay up too late."

"I won't, Gigi," I replied. "Goodnight."

I scattered my bookbag's contents on the table for my project. Then I opened my grandmother's album book, searching for a good picture of Gigi and Grandpa. As I searched, my mind jumbled the advice Courtland gave me at work with what transpired in the living room with my mother. There was no way I could share my real story after tonight's fiasco. I took the pictures I had printed at work and trimmed off the excess printer paper. *If I can't have the family I wanted, mind as well create it*, I thought to myself, grabbing the scotch tape. I stuck a good picture of Gigi and Grandpa Charles at the top. I inserted my Google searched pictures directly under my neatly written flash cards that provided a brief description. Lastly, I put my most recent school picture at the bottom, thus creating a family for a more palatable presentation.

After I finished organizing and decorating my trifold board, I placed it on top of the deep freezer in the pantry. I put all my supplies back in my bookbag and cut off all the lights downstairs. I then double checked to see if all the doors were locked before heading upstairs. By the unusual sound of snoring, I knew Gigi had to have been either really tired or mildly drunk since I could hear her snores all the way in the hall at the top of the steps. I peeked into Love's room, just to ensure she was still asleep before I ventured off to my room. Finally, I grabbed some underclothes from my dresser and walked in the bathroom to wash away one hell of a night.

CHAPTER 5

Responses are the things our ears desire while our hearts rule in a favor not understood. Ears hear one thing while the heart can hear something totally different. Overriding perception and canceling out logic. Desperation allows the imagination to wander while anxiety festers its ugly head. Do we really accept what was said? Or is the heart just as selective as the ears? Picking out only what is palatable. Which one should we listen to? Which one do we accept? Answers.

Sleep was my old friend who didn't bother to visit me. All night, I wrestled with the covers, replaying my mother's surprise visit in my mind. By the time my eyes decided to close, and my body decided to rest, my alarm went off. The sun barely peaked from behind the clouds, plastering every wall in my room with a peach-colored hue. I sat on the edge of the bed and allowed my feet to hit the cold floor. The smell of bacon went past my nose, waking me up even more, standing me to my feet. It wasn't like Gigi to be fully awake before 6 a.m., so the pleasant smell definitely alarmed me.

I walked to Love's room and opened the door to see her empty crib, and I instantly flew downstairs, with the strings from my balling shorts waving in the air. I ran into the kitchen to see Gigi over the stove and Love alternating her hands to her mouth, chomping on two pieces of bacon at once.

"Goo' mo'nin, Dad-dy." Love gave me a greasy grin as I walked over to her and leaned in for an even greasier kiss.

"Good morning, Love," I replied. "Good morning, Gigi."

"Good morning, Wisdom," Gigi turned around. Her wig was tilted a little too far back, showing her natural short curls.

"Did you go somewhere this morning?" I asked.

"Love got up a little early, so we went to the store to pick up a couple of groceries," Gigi said. "Why do you ask?"

"Well, you only put a wig on your head when you're going out, but that's not your usual, 'I'm-going-out-in-public' wig," I observed, sitting at the table. "And it's close to falling off your head."

Gigi snatched the wig off and glanced at it after putting the spatula down. "Lord, I done put on my 'going-to-the-doctor' wig. I was wondering why I kept feeling a breeze." She turned the wig over a few times in her hands, eyeing it more carefully. "Looks like it's time to retire this one." Gigi threw it in the trashcan. "Rest in peace, Melissa."

"Gigi, you really name your wigs place names and people names?" I asked.

"Sure do. That's how they last," Gigi said, washing her hands in the sink as I shook my head.

Gigi went back to the stove and began fixing me a plate. She dragged her feet in her slippers to the table and positioned the plate in front of me. My eyes widen, surveying the French toast, cheese eggs, and bacon fried slightly limp just the way I like it. My mouth salivated.

"Not complaining one bit, Gigi, but what's up with the breakfast?" I asked.

"Well, Wisdom, to be honest after last night, I just felt like we both needed a little breakfast. And since drugs and alcohol are off the table for you..." Gigi joked. "Mine as well. Eat."

"No complaints here." I replied with a mouth full of eggs while also drowning my French toast in the King's syrup Gigi already had on the table.

Gigi suddenly slapped the table. "Boy, I didn't see you pray over any piece of food!"

I dropped my fork, closed my eyes, and silently prayed over my food. Then I picked up my fork again to eagerly finish up where I left off.

"If you still plan on going to school today, you better hurry up. It's going on 6, and you know Ms. T will be out there at 6:30 on the dot," Gigi said.

I scarfed down the rest of my food in seconds. "All done," I replied, walking my plate to the sink to wash it.

"Boy, I'm about to start calling you tape worm; you finished that quick?" Gigi joked.

"You know it," I replied. Gigi shook her head. "You need me to walk Love down to Ms. Corrine's house while you get ready for work?" I offered.

"No, I'm off today," Gigi said.

"Again, Gigi? That's three days in a row." I replied, putting the clean dish in the dish drainer.

"Boy, don't worry about me and my pockets. Now get your narrow butt ready for school!" Gigi shouted.

"Yes, ma'am," I replied, walking straight up the stairs to the hallway. I grabbed a washcloth from the linen closet next to the bathroom. My feet slid against the cold penny tile. I ran the water and waited for it to warm up, flicking it with my fingers as if doing so made the water heat up faster. Once it was warm, I washed my face and brushed my teeth. After that, I sat on the toilet for a few minutes just in case a morning bowel movement decided to present itself. I then threw on some deodorant, put on a random outfit from my closet, and flew downstairs, knowing there was no one to impress towards the last week of school. I checked the time on my phone to ensure I was on schedule to make it to the bus stop, since it usually took me around seven to eight minutes to make it to the front of our neighborhood. There was just enough time to grab my trifold board off the deep freezer in the pantry.

"You finished that project last night?" Gigi inquired.

"Yes, ma'am," I replied, putting my bookbag on my back.

"Well, let me see it," Gigi insisted. My heart began beating fast as I thought about my alterations.

"I'll show you after it's graded, Gigi," I replied. "You know it's bad luck to show your project before you present it."

"Boy, if that ain't the dumbest thing I have ever heard." Gigi replied. Gigi leaned with one hand on the sink and the other on her hip. Love began laughing in her highchair, engaged in our conversation as if she knew what was going on. "Boy, we Black. We don't believe in luck; we got Jesus and Al Sharpton. Now let me see your project."

I looked at the clock on the stove. "Gigi, I'm running late for the bus," I deflected.

"Are you sure you can handle school today, after last night?" she asked.

"I'm fine, Gigi," I sighed heavily.

"Alright, if you say so. Just know this, if I got to put on a wig and a bra and slide up to that school to pick you up because you couldn't get it together... That's going to be your ass."

"Understood, Gigi." I replied, walking to Love to give her a kiss and then up to Gigi.

"Boy, don't put your mouth on me," Gigi joked. "I ain't been able to trust those lips since yo' freshman year."

"Really?!" I rolled my eyes. "Your Gigi got jokes today, Love." I gripped my project board and walked towards the front door, leaving Love giggling in her highchair.

"Bye, Da-ddy," Love said in her sweet voice.

"Bye, Love. Catch you later, Gigi." I secured my bookbag on my back and walked out of the front door, closing it behind me.

I walked down the sidewalk, inwardly patting myself on the back for being able to talk my way out of showing Gigi my project. I didn't know what she would have said if she saw it, but I knew we both were too frazzled to have that conversation this morning. I made it to the bus stop where a group of us waited in anticipation. I was so glad that this was technically my last day of school. I only had to present my project for AP Biology, and the rest was covered. I looked up and down the street for Rico, hoping he would make it in time as Ms. T pulled up at 6:30 on the dot, like clockwork.

Knowing how quickly packed the bus could get, the bulk of us flocked in the street preparing to get on the bus before Ms. T even parked. As soon as Ms. T stopped and opened the doors, we stormed onto the bus as if we were escaping poverty. I held my board directly in front of me at arm's length distance from the next person in line to ensure I didn't bend it. I took my seat towards the middle as the others kept loading on. I looked out the window, keeping hope alive for Rico to be on his way. However, once Ms. T closed the doors and began driving down the street, Rico's absence was confirmed.

"Anyone sitting here?" a girl asked, swaying slightly in the aisle of the bus.

"No," I replied. I moved my board to my lap. "Please, have a seat."

"Thank you. Your name is Wise, right?" Her long braids hit the back of the seat as she sat down.

I chuckled a bit. "Wisdom," I corrected her. I extended my hand looking up to see her face.

Her face flushed red in embarrassment. "I am so sorry," she replied, shaking my hand. I felt her soft skin with the pad of my thumb. I inhaled the smell of citrus as she shook her head, reeling in embarrassment for messing up my name.

Wow, she is gorgeous, and she smells so good, I thought to myself, before I realized I was still holding her hand. "It's cool. And your name is?" I asked, releasing her hand.

"Aliyah," she replied, just as Ms. T merged onto the interstate.

"Are you new out The Park?" I asked.

"What Park?" she asked. I let out a hearty laugh. "What's funny?"

"I'm sorry. I can tell you're new to the neighborhood. That's all," I said. "Harrow's Landing, the neighborhood we live in, we call it Harrow Park. Basically, any affordable housing neighborhood is nicknamed The Park."

"Oh, I didn't know that." Aliyah replied. "Thanks for the info."

"No problem, I'm here to assist."

"I just moved out here with my aunt. I went to Patrimony High in Newport News until last week," Aliyah said.

"Wow, so, you had to go to a new school and live in a new neighborhood at the end of the school year?" I sympathized. "I am so sorry."

"You don't know the half of it," Aliyah's previously bubbly tone was now a serious one. "I at least thought we got away from some of the violence in my last neighborhood, but the gunshots last night were definitely a welcoming gift."

"You'll get used to it," I said. "It was probably The Vigilantes or one of the other numerous gangs around Harrow Park."

"You seem so unfazed by it," Aliyah observed. Her initial embarrassment subsided. Now she gave me direct eye contact. "How does one get use to gunshots?"

I shrugged. "Think of it as a doorbell to company you don't feel like having and just roll over and go to sleep." I said nonchalantly.

"Well, you're just a wealth of knowledge, aren't you?" Aliyah teased.

"Something like that. I guess that's how I got this silver hair and the name." I pointed to my silver patch on the back of my head.

"Oh, that's how you got it," Aliyah stated sarcastically.

"Oh, you got jokes. Okay, Ms. Aliyah."

"I'm just playing," Aliyah nudged me. The embarrassment was definitely gone. She was smiling. "It's cute."

Now I was the one blushing. "Thank you," I said. I turned my attention toward the window and tried to think of what to say next. I kicked myself in the head for not taking the time to put on a decent outfit. Now there *was* someone to impress at the end of the year. As I looked outside, I noticed we'd made it to Lancaster High. Our fifteen-minute bus ride felt like fifteen seconds.

The bus pulled up at the back of the school. Everyone began getting up standing in the middle of the aisle, before Ms. T could come to a complete stop. As if they were all in such a rush to get a quality education.

I nodded at my new seat partner. "Hopefully I'll see you around school, Aliyah."

"Count on it," Aliyah replied, getting up and getting in the line of people. Behind her, I caught sight of the small patch of grass where Love was conceived; it was now covered in dandelions. My mind flashed to Danielle.

"Stay focused, Wisdom. Stay focused." I whispered to myself. I needed to snap back into reality. *You are a teenage father, that girl ain't interested in you,* I wrote off in my mind. A small part of me was still holding out for Danielle. I patiently waited until everyone was off the bus before I got up, walking carefully with my board to ensure I didn't mess it up before my presentation.

"Have a good one, Ms. T," I said, getting off the bus.

"You too, sweetheart," Ms. T replied. She closed the door behind me and pulled off.

I walked up to the school and noticed there were two single file lines entering into the building slowly. *Must be a random search day,* I thought, following the shorter of the two lines into the building. Mr. Lawrence and Ms. County, the security guards, were selecting every fifth person in line to search. I was sure they had already confiscated numerous vape pins, sandwich bags of marijuana, and lighters. So many students I knew personally smoked, among other things, in the restroom while class was in session.

"Go on, Mr. Davis," Mr. Lawrence instructed. "I know you don't have anything, because your grandmother doesn't play."

"Not at all," I agreed. "Good morning," I added. I gathered my thoughts in the stairwell, trying to remember if it was an even bell or odd bell day. *Even,* I remembered as I walked past the second floor. I decided to hike all the way up to the fourth floor to Ms. Lathrop's classroom to see if I could drop off my project, so I wouldn't have to lug it around the whole day. At the last flight of the stairs, I let out a sigh, breathing hard. *You would think after three years, those steps would get easier to climb,* I thought, walking around the corner to Ms. Lathrop's doorway.

Ms. Lathrop seemed to be in a great mood, so I thought it was a great time to ask if I could store my project. "Good morning, Ms. Lathrop," I gave her my best smile.

"Good morning, Wisdom," Ms. Lathrop replied. "You need to drop off your final project?" she asked, looking at my large board.

"Yes, ma'am, if that's okay with you?" I asked.

"Sure, it is." She smiled and pointed to the wall on my right. "Go ahead and put it in one of those shelves in the last cabinet on the wall."

"Yes, ma'am, thank you," I replied.

I walked into the room, did as instructed, and turned around to surprisingly see Aliyah sitting at a desk waving at me. Her hazel eyes locked me in as I waved back. She then put her attention to the materials on her desk. I studied her as she wrote in her notebook. As she wrote, she fought her long box braids that kept falling in her face. Her caramel complexion seemed to glow in the florescent lighting, trapping me in even more as if she already didn't have my full attention. My intense focus on her made me ignore all my other surroundings; I stumbled straight into the corner of a desk and almost fell over. A couple of students in the class began to cackle when I stood up straight, too afraid to turn around. I made my way towards the door trying to play off the five seconds of embarrassment I just endured.

"All set?" Ms. Lathrop inquired.

"Yes, ma'am," I replied.

"Good," Ms. Lathrop replied, tucking her blonde hair behind her ears. "Now don't run into anything else until I see you next block," she teased.

"Everybody got jokes today," I laughed, walking down the hall towards the steps. I winded my way through the crowd of students in the hallway walking with no sense of urgency, finally making it to the stairwell to go down to second period.

Come on, Wisdom, get it together, I thought. *You can't be stuck on her. Can you? Stay focused.* I coached myself until I heard my name breaking my concentration.

"Wisdom!" I heard the authoritative voice. I looked around searching for its owner, until I saw Mr. Joyner walking out of the third-floor entrance onto the steps.

"Good morning, Mr. Joyner. Everything alright?" I asked, referencing his tone.

"Good morning, Wisdom. Everything is fine," Mr. Joyner confirmed. "You just saved me a trip. I was just about to go to Ms. Bracy's class to get you."

"Get me for what?"

"Well, that is what I must talk to you about," Mr. Joyner said. "Please come to my classroom for a sec. I'll write you a pass to Ms. Bracy's class if you're late," Mr. Joyner insisted.

"Okay," I said, reluctantly following Mr. Joyner, unsure if I was in trouble or not.

Mr. Taylor, my guidance counselor and Mr. Kelly the school's college ACCESS advisor greeted us when we entered Mr. Joyner's otherwise empty classroom.

"Is this an intervention?" I asked nervously.

"Sort of," Mr. Taylor said, adjusting himself in the tight desk/chair combination. "But the good kind."

"Is there such a thing?" I countered.

Mr. Kelley nodded. "In this case, yes."

"Please have a seat, Wisdom." Mr. Joyner said. I took off my bookbag and anxiously sat down, still not understanding what this so-called "positive intervention" was all about.

"Please don't feel nervous, Wisdom. This is just a discussion about your future," Mr. Taylor said.

"Okay," I replied.

"Wisdom, I asked Mr. Taylor and Mr. Kelly to join me to possibly encourage you to go to college," Mr. Joyner began to explain.

"Not this again!" I replied annoyed. "Mr. Joyner, I told you I have a daughter; college ain't for me."

"You know people who usually say 'college ain't for me' usually hold a very low GPA, not a 4.7 cumulative average in their junior year," Mr. Kelly said. "College *is* for you, so what is the real roadblock?"

"Love," I answered.

"Wait, so you're not going to college because of some girl?" Mr. Taylor asked incredulously. "There are plenty of girls at any college. You can take your pick," he said.

I laughed. "Not some girl. My daughter, Love. She needs stability. And four years of college with no source of income? That ain't it."

"That's the hang up? Almost all schools are offering work study while you go to school. You can work and send money home to your grandmother and daughter. It's a win-win," Mr. Taylor offered.

"Not for Love," I said. "Love ain't doing nothing but getting bigger, and what would I look like going off to college and sending home a few hundred dollars every month? That's not enough."

"I can understand that." Mr. Kelly sympathized. "I got two boys at home and trust me, it's never enough. But what I can say is that you are giving your daughter a chance to watch you work towards a goal and succeeding."

"He's right Wisdom," Mr. Taylor agreed. "There so many young men like yourself: they're so fear oriented when it comes to finances, they neglect their own dreams and admirations. Imagine Love having a father who made six figures, who was happy in his career, and was still present in her life."

I shook my head in disbelief. "That sounds too good to be true."

"It's possible if you work for it," Mr. Taylor said. "What do you do in your free time?"

I laughed. "I don't have much of that. But I like to write."

"Interesting, like poems and short stories I presume?" Mr. Taylor inquired. Mr. Joyner and Mr. Kelly shared a knowing smile.

"Yeah," I replied, now taking a good look at all their faces. "What are y'all up to?"

"And you never thought about being a writer, working in journalism, becoming an author, or teaching English?" Mr. Taylor pried, ignoring my question.

I shrugged. "Sure, I have but I need money, and the military can give me that."

"Listen, Wisdom," Mr. Kelly interjected. "I'm not saying the military isn't a great career path, but there aren't many jobs in the military that will cater to your love of writing. Don't you want to do what makes you happy?"

"I guess," I replied.

"You guess?" Mr. Kelly questioned.

"Yes," I stated hesitantly.

"We'll take it," Mr. Kelly replied. "Mr. Joyner, take it away."

Mr. Joyner went behind his desk and pulled out a thick folder from one of the drawers. He walked back to my desk where I was sitting and put the folder in front of me. The folder was stamped "Columbia University".

"Columbia University," I read aloud. "Isn't that an Ivy League school?"

"It sure is, Wisdom," Mr. Joyner confirmed. "I went to school with their English Department Chair, and I sent him a few of your writing prompts. He believes you are exactly what their English department needs."

"Columbia University, in New York?" I exclaimed.

"Okay, I know it's a little far, but for an Ivy League school on a free ride? Might be worth it," Mr. Kelly said.

"A free ride?" I couldn't believe what I was hearing.

"With your grades, we can take a shot at it," Mr. Taylor said.

"This is just my junior year. Why the push now?" I asked.

Mr. Kelly leaned forward. "Well, there is an early admissions window ending this summer, and you can be accepted before you even start your senior year."

"Y'all are really sweating me on this." I stated, wiping my forehead for emphasis.

"That's because we believe in you, even when you don't want to believe in yourself," Mr. Taylor replied. "How about this: we all work with you to get a plan going. We will do our best to get you in on a free ride. Then, we will ensure you are in a work study program that will pay you to go to school and you can work on the side." Mr. Taylor continued, "We can get room and board taken care of while providing frequent visitation for your grandmother and daughter. If we can get all of that for you, would you at least consider?" Mr. Taylor asked.

It still sounded too good to be true. "If you can do all that, I'll do more than consider," I replied. The late bell rang as if signaling the end of our conversation.

"My man," Mr. Taylor stood up to shake my hand. "Let's get to work, Joyner."

"Way ahead of you. I emailed Ms. Bracy and told her you were up here with us. She's cool with it. She said you're done with her work and the class was just watching a movie anyway," Mr. Joyner handed me a laptop. "Here is the application to Columbia University."

"We are all here to help you," Mr. Kelly said. "After you finish that, I'll help you with the FAFSA and get you some scholarships and grants."

"And I'll call your grandmother to get her personal information, so we can get this done today," Mr. Taylor walked over to the phone.

I looked at Mr. Joyner, Mr. Kelly, and Mr. Taylor, flabbergasted. "Am I really worth all this trouble?"

"Yes!" The room echoed.

"Man, fill out that application, and we'll help you with the rest," Mr. Taylor instructed.

As we all got to work on our various tasks, I couldn't help but replay this entire conversation over and over in my mind. I couldn't believe that all three of these men would dedicate this much time for me. I had never envisioned myself going to school because I was so hell-bent on making sure Love would be taken care of, that I never considered another alternative. College... Me. Ivy League... Me. I couldn't believe it.

I took my time going through Columbia University's lengthy application, making sure I dotted every "I" and crossed every "T". Once I completed it, I handed the laptop to Mr. Kelly, who looked it over with Mr. Joyner, making sure everything was in order. After my college application was submitted, Mr. Taylor gave Mr. Kelly my Gigi's personal information so that we could complete the FAFSA. After that, we moved on to completing scholarships. Over an hour later my eyes burned from constantly looking at the computer screen.

"And just like that," Mr. Kelly said. "You're done!" I let out a sigh of relief. "The easy part is done now," he declared.

"Easy!" I screamed, earning a laugh from all three men. "Lord!"

"You better thank Him when you get in," Mr. Taylor said, walking to the door. He nodded at my English teacher. "Appreciate you, Joyner. Thanks for looking after my boy."

"Thank you for coming and helping me convince him," Mr. Joyner replied.

"Anytime," Mr. Taylor said. "Let me get back to my office. Y'all take it easy." He walked out into the hallway.

"I need to get back too," Mr. Kelly said, getting up. "Thank you again, Mr. Joyner. You know, we make a good team. We should ambush students more often," he joked. Mr. Kelly patted me on the back. "Y'all be cool."

"Alright," I replied. "Happy now?" I turned to ask the only other man left in the room.

"Ecstatic! Wisdom, you deserve this. I just wish you could see that," Mr. Joyner replied.

"I hear you, Mr. Joyner," I replied. "We'll see."

"That's all I can ask for." The bell rang again.

"Dang, I've been in here for a whole class period," I realized. I stood to my feet and grabbed my bookbag.

"You sure have," Mr. Joyner agreed. "But you are worth it. Don't forget that."

His other students started trickling in. That was my cue to leave or else risk being late to AP Biology. "I'll try, Mr. Joyner, thank you," I said. "Let me get to Ms. Lathrop's class."

"Alright, Wisdom," Mr. Joyner replied as he set up his smartboard for his incoming class. I walked down the hall and up to the fourth floor, slightly relieved that I now had one less flight of steps to Ms. Lathrop's class. I made it there with minutes to spare and went to the cabinet to grab my board. I then sat at my desk patiently waiting for class to begin, watching the other students flock in as the late bell signaled to all the teachers to begin their instruction.

"Alright, first things first. I need everybody to turn in your textbooks," Ms. Lathrop said. "You have until next week, but for some of you this is your final week in school, so please turn them in today or tomorrow, especially those who are presenting final projects this week." Ms. Lathrop grabbed her textbook log.

I opened my bookbag and grabbed the textbook to turn it in. Instantly feeling my bookbag's weight difference. I walked up to the front where Ms. Lathrop checked me off on her log.

"Hey, Wisdom. Since you are up, how about you present your project first?" Ms. Lathrop suggested.

"Cool," I replied, walking to my desk, and grabbing my trifold board. I returned to the front of the classroom and opened my board, revealing my palatable family to the class.

"You can begin when you want." Ms. Lathrop said, trading her textbook log for her gradebook clipboard.

"Alright, class. Well, I will be presenting my final AP Biology project." My announcement was interrupted by someone knocking hard at Ms. Lathrop's door.

"Hold on, Wisdom," Ms. Lathrop said. She raised her voice to be heard on the other side of the door. "Come in!"

"Good morning. I'm sorry for the interruption, Ms. Lathrop." Ms. Nixon, one of the other science teachers, greeted. Her puffy hair pressed on the door. "Mr. Ork had to leave early, and we had to split his class. Do you have room for five students?"

Ms. Lathrop surveyed the room and reluctantly conceded.

"Thank you so much," Ms. Nixon said. "Come on in, y'all. And sit towards the back."

A group of students came in with a loud commotion even though they were small in number.

"HEY, HEY, HEY!" Ms. Nixon shouted, getting their attention. "Y'all will not come in here and be interrupting this woman's class. Get it together!" The commotion died immediately, and the five students made it to their seats quietly while Ms. Nixon scowled at them from the door. "Thank you, Ms. Lathrop," Ms.

Nixon said in her normal inside voice, taking her hand off the door.

"No problem," Ms. Lathrop replied. "Wisdom, please continue."

"Alright, again, I am here to present my final AP Biology project focusing on genes, dominant traits, and recessive traits, using my family as an example." Someone snickered in the back.

"Is everything alright?" Ms. Lathrop eyed one of the students.

"We straight, Teach," one of the guys from Mr. Ork's class rudely said. But he merely began to whisper.

"Wisdom, please continue," Ms. Lathrop instructed again.

"Well, in my project I covered three generations and compared traits that were passed down, starting from my grandparents to my parents, and my parents, down to me." Laughs grew in the back again. Ms. Lathrop eyes wandered towards the commotion. "Aye yo. We got a problem?" I asked.

"Yeah, I got a problem," a guy said.

"Gentlemen!" Ms. Lathrop voice was full of concern.

"What's up?" I asked, ready to move on with my presentation.

"My problem is you, Grass Stains," he mocked. My eyes widen. "You thought we forgot?" he smirked.

"Ohhhhhhh," the class dragged out in unison, trying to escalate the situation.

"I believe your mistaken, sir," I said.

"Man, I ain't mistaken nothing. You in here trying to sound all intelligent and shit. You ain't nothing but a Park nigga," he declared.

"Language, young man," Ms. Lathrop warned.

"So, let me get this straight my dude," I said. "You're threatened by a person who speaks with subject/verb agreement?"

"Bitch, I ain't threatened by shit," he growled.

"Jayden, calm down!" One of the other students from Mr. Ork's class urged. "You are going off for nothing."

"Please watch your language, young man," Ms. Lathrop urged.

"If I don't?" Jayden questioned boldly.

"Jayden, is it?" I asked. "Bro, you need to chill. Please remember you are a guest in this classroom."

"Bitch, you the guest. You must don't know who the fuck I am," Jayden stood to his feet.

"Obviously someone who is rude, by not letting me finish my presentation," I said.

"Man, fuck you and your weak ass presentation." Jayden walked up the aisle between the desks to me. Ms. Lathrop nervously reached for the classroom phone off her desk to contact security.

"Young man, please sit down," Ms. Lathrop's voice held a little tremble. She held the phone tightly, and her usually pale skin reddened with nervousness. "I need security to room 407." Ms. Lathrop finally said into the mouthpiece.

"Yeah, I'm up here now," Jayden antagonized me. "What you trying to do?"

I felt my fist tightening up as I looked at him in his eyes, unfazed by the show he was putting on for the other classmates. I couldn't even come up with a good reason he had beef with me. I'd never met him before today. He reeked with the smell of marijuana; it became more pungent as he stepped closer to me, invading my personal space. *Maybe it's laced with something*, I thought. In my musing, Love crossed my mind along with the opportunity to go to Columbia University. The thought made me unclench my fist, remembering the promise I made to her.

"I'm trying to be a better man for my daughter's sake." I said, trying to ignore his strong odor. "So, I'm going to ask you to please get out of my face."

"Fuck you and your daughter, bitch." Jayden hacked up a loogie and spit in my face.

The room fell quiet. My heart began to race a mile per second. Anger filled my body and began to overtake me until all I saw was red. My mouth salivated with the taste of rage, feeling his saliva roll down the side of my cheek. Next thing I knew, I grabbed a textbook from the stack on Ms. Lathrop's desk and slung it at Jayden's head as hard as I could. I landed three more swings to his face as his thick spit dripped off my face. Then I tackled him to the ground. Lab tables and desks moved from the force of our weight. Once I got to a good position, I began punching him in the face repeatedly. I found myself unable to stop, until I felt my body become airborne, snapping me back into reality.

I was in security's grip. My vision began to clear, and I saw the boy's blood gushed everywhere. My hands were covered in his blood. The class was all standing on chairs and the lab tables silently recording the fight on their phones. Mr. Lawrence put me back on my feet and escorted me out the room.

Once we got to the hallway, Mr. Lawrence addressed me. "Now I know if you were fighting, it must have been for a good reason. What happened?"

Before I could answer, Ms. Lathrop marched out from the classroom to make her statement. "It was definitely the other student's fault," she said. "He antagonized Wisdom as he presented his project. He spoke negatively about Wisdom's family, and then he spat in his face," Ms. Lathrop said.

"Sounds like he deserved the ass whooping he got," Mr. Lawrence declared.

"Mr. Lawrence," Ms. Lathrop replied, shocked, grabbing her chest.

"Ms. Lathrop," Mr. Lawrence replied nonchalantly, looking at her up and down. "Please email a statement to the principal."

"I will," Ms. Lathrop stated, her attention on Ms. County who was now escorting Jayden out of the classroom. Mr. Lawrence stood in front of me as a security. Jayden's face was unrecognizable, and he left a trail a blood from Ms. Lathrop's class down the length of the hall.

"That's what you get, Jayden," Ms. County told him. "I hope you learned your lesson." He dragged his feet mumbling. Ms. County called back to us over her shoulder. "I'm escorting him to the nurse, then to AP Jones. I'll meet you downstairs, Lawrence."

"Copy," Mr. Lawrence replied. I could hear the other students clamor loudly in the classroom, hyped about the fight. I hung my head in shame.

"I did all that?" I asked Mr. Lawrence after Ms. County and Jayden made it to the stairwell.

"Yeah. That was all you, Doc," Mr. Lawrence said. "Come on. I got to escort you to boss lady."

"Yes, sir," I replied. *Gigi is going to kill me,* I thought to myself, as I was escorted to Mrs. Sims-Jackson's office.

Gigi had already been contacted by the time I made it down the stairs. Mr. Lawrence left me in the office after I gave my statement. "May I wash my hands, and my face?" I asked Mrs. Sims-Jackson, sitting in a chair as she began typing up some paperwork. I was sure the forms were for me.

She looked at me from behind her desk with her glasses tilted on her nose. "Yes, you may. The restroom is next door," Mrs. Sims-Jackson said.

"Thank you," I replied, walking next door to the tight one-person restroom.

I watched the clear water turn red as I scrubbed my hands in the sink. I began replaying the fight repeatedly in my head trying to figure out how I could have handled it better, especially after just applying to an Ivy League school. When the water was clear again, I took a paper towel and added a little hand soap with a drop of warm water to wash the side of my face in irritation, reliving that particular moment again. I threw the paper towel away and wiped out the sink with another piece of paper towel before leaving the restroom and returning to Mrs. Sims-Jackson's office. Thoughts bombarded my mind until I saw Gigi walk through the office door with her long wavy "Sunday" wig on and a balled-up face.

"Thank you for joining us, Mrs. Davis." Mrs. Sims-Jackson greeted her curtly.

"I didn't have much choice," Gigi replied, taking the seat next to me. "And I'm widowed, baby. It's miss. I don't want to block my blessings," Gigi said.

"Well, Amen, Ms. Davis," Mrs. Sims-Jackson corrected herself, putting extra emphasis on miss.

"Gigi-" I started.

"Wisdom, I told you if I had to put on a bra and this good hair, it was going to be your ass," Gigi reminded me. She pointed at her head. "And look at what I got on."

Mrs. Sims-Jackson sat forward at her desk and folded her hands. "Well, Ms. Davis, this isn't entirely Wisdom's fault. Ms. Lathrop had to watch another class, and a young man in that class antagonized Wisdom and interrupted him repeatedly as he tried to present his project." Mrs. Sims-Jackson continued, "The young man used strong language towards Ms. Lathrop and Wisdom, proceeding to walk up to Wisdom, and lastly spitting in his face before Wisdom even reacted."

"Did you say spit?" Gigi asked, sitting up straight in the chair.

CAVON D. MILLS

"Yes, ma'am," Mrs. Sims-Jackson nodded. "Now that student has been suspended for the maximum number of days; however, since Wisdom was technically a participant in a physical altercation, he must be suspended as well."

"What?!" Gigi yelled.

"School policy, Ms. Davis," Mrs. Sims-Jackson said with her hands up. "He will only receive one day."

Gigi let out a huge breath. "Today was his last day anyway."

"Last day at Lancaster or for the academic year?" Mrs. Sims-Jackson inquired. There was a hint of panic in her voice.

"The academic year," Gigi cleared up. Mrs. Sims-Jackson let out a sigh of relief.

Why is she so relieved? I wondered.

"He only came to present his project," Gigi said suddenly calm. "I have a picture that is very important to me, on his project. Can I retrieve that before I go?"

"Yes, ma'am." Mrs. Sims-Jackson picked up her desk phone. "Let me make a call."

"Gigi-" I tried again.

She put her hand in my face. "Don't say another word to me, Wisdom." Gigi snarled. We ended up sitting in the principal's office in silence until Mr. Lawrence came in with my trifold board and my bookbag.

"Gigi, I'll get it," I insisted. But Gigi made it to her feet and grabbed the board from Mr. Lawrence before I even had the chance to get up.

"Thank you, Mr. Lawrence," Gigi said, opening the board. I held my breath.

"Sure thing, Ms. Davis," Mr. Lawrence replied. He walked over to me and handed me my bookbag.

Gigi examined the board and removed the picture of her and Grandpa before closing it. "Thank you, Mrs. Sims-Jackson. Is there anything else you need from me?"

"No ma'am," Mrs. Sims-Jackson replied. "Although, I did want you to know that Wisdom still received an A for his project, and this situation did not affect his grades at all," Mrs. Sims-Jackson said.

"Wonderful, that's great to know," Gigi grinned. "Well, if that's it, I'm going to take Wisdom home."

Mrs. Sims-Jackson handed Gigi my suspension paperwork. "That's it. Have a great summer." With that, Gigi turned on her heel and walked out.

"You as well," I said, following Gigi out of the office.

We made it outside to the car, but neither one of us parted our lips. Her silence unsettled my nerves. I was terrified to even breathe heavy. I put on my seat belt and waited for her to say something, as she started the car and began driving towards the house.

"Love is at Ms. Corrine's house, if you were wondering." Gigi said, finally breaking her silence.

"Yes, ma'am," I replied. "Gigi-"

"Boy, if you trying to inform me about them two fake ass pictures representing your parents, you can save it. I saw it this morning before I even asked you to show me your project." Gigi revealed. My jaw dropped. "I was just trying to see if you would fess up to it."

"Gigi, I'm sorry," I apologized.

"Ain't no need to apologize. If I had your momma for a momma, I would have done the same thing," Gigi replied.

I couldn't help but let out a surprised laugh. "Really?"

"Really," Gigi confirmed. "Now, Mr. Taylor called me asking me for my personal information, talking about a FAFSA?"

"Yes, ma'am."

"So, did you change your mind about going to college?" Gigi's slightly less authoritative tone threw me off.

"I'm not sure yet Gigi," I stated looking out the window. "Just want to keep my options open."

"I can understand that." Gigi cut on the radio, but she kept the volume low. "Now about this punk that spit on you."

Here we go, I thought to myself. "Yes, ma'am," I said out loud, and I waited for her to explode.

"Did you whoop his ass?" Gigi inquired calmly, as I looked up at her.

There was only one good answer. "Like he stole something."

"Then we're all good," Gigi grinned, holding up her fist. I gave her a pound, and she turned up the radio as we continued rolling down the street towards our house.

CHAPTER 6

One of the most unexplainable yet most recognizable things in the world. Everyone is deserving but unfortunately everyone doesn't obtain. It is the one thing that tips the scales between beautiful and reckless. It's uncontrollable, it's dangerous, it's unfathomable and yet we seek it diligently and unapologetically. We take the risk and allow it to consume us, despite the warnings, and being fully cognizant to all its side effects. Why must we possess it? Are we truly deserving of it? Love.

The first few days of summer break was a whole trip and a side of vacation, minus the rest and the relaxation part. Boredom and depression hit our house harder than a stray basketball in an aggressive hood game of horse. It felt uncontrollable.

Unfortunately, Gigi lost her job at the cleaners, and The Oink Shack shut down after a two-year run. These events left both of us in one of the scariest words known to man. Unemployed. Money was already a little tight, but now I could literally feel it cutting off my circulation. It was a noose on my neck making it hard to breathe. I knew Anna would eventually run The Oink Shack in the ground, but I stupidly assumed I had a little more time. Well, at least until summer was over.

We still had Gigi's funds from Grandpa's insurance policy, but that had been depleting for years since Love and I were added to the pot. Even after applying for seven jobs a piece in a five-mile radius, there were no takers for either one of us.

Funds were so tight; I began contemplating taking Love's birthday present back. I had scrimped and saved to buy the motorized power wheels SUV. But truth be told, I wanted to cancel her party all together. I tried to convince myself that she wouldn't remember it anyway, but I reached the same conclusion every time. I just didn't have the heart to do it. I just kept envisioning that little face of hers and how excited she would be. So, against my better judgement, and the lint in my wallet, I still decided to go through with her second birthday party.

I stepped outside to hang the yellow and white streamers on the porch when Gigi met me outside. "Hey, I still need to go to the dollar store," Gigi told me. "You think your manager or Mr. Lee is up there to give you your last check? Might as well do everything in one trip since it's all in the same plaza," Gigi suggested.

I took a quick glance at my phone to check the time. "Yeah, they should be up there now," I said. "Need me to grab Love and take her to Ms. Corrine?"

"Nah, baby. Funds are already kind of tight," Gigi reminded. "You know that ho will want her money even if she only watched Love for less than an hour."

"True," I replied, hanging up the last streamer and securing it with a piece of scotch tape. "I'll grab her. I just hope she don't wake up from her nap."

"Wisdom, did you forget whose child she is? You know both of y'all could sleep through Armageddon."

"Really Gigi, Armageddon?"

"Really," Gigi joked. "Both of y'all could snore the lime wash off a brick."

I laughed. "You got it, Gigi. I'll go get her."

I went in the room to see Love spread out across her crib with her mouth wide open, snoring loudly. *Do I really sleep like this?* I asked myself, staring at her wild sleeping position. I lifted her out of her crib and draped her over my right arm, allowing her head to rest on my shoulder. Her dead weight made my arm instantly go numb and she snored in my ear as I slowly walked back down the stairs.

I made it to the living room where I saw Gigi in the mirror by the door, adjusting her wig.

"You ready?" Gigi asked.

"Yes, ma'am," I replied.

Gigi grabbed her keys, and I followed behind her, locking the front door. She unlocked the car from the porch. I walked as quickly as possible to the back door of her Cadillac. I felt instant relief the moment I put Love down in her car seat and buckled her in.

"That dead weight ain't no joke, is it?" Gigi asked, getting in.

"None!" I replied, closing the back door, and getting into the front passenger seat.

Gigi started the car and took off down the street. I fought with the seatbelt to stretch around me and finally heard the click. Then I cracked the window to let in some air as Gigi cut the radio on. She was alternating between lead and background vocals when one of her songs began to play. I tried not to laugh, but Gigi's car solos always made me weak. She would squeal out notes she knew she couldn't hit but went after them anyway, losing the vocal battle between her actual alto range and the wishful soprano note. I looked back at Love to see her still knocked out. Drool was rolling down her chin. *I guess she could sleep through Armageddon*, I laughed to myself.

We pulled up to The Berksdale Plaza, and Gigi parked directly in front of the dollar store.

"You want me to take her in, or should we alternate watching her in the car?" Gigi asked.

I looked back at Love. She hadn't budged from her nap in the car seat, not even through Gigi's failed audition for American Idol. "We can alternate watching her in the car," I decided. "Besides, I want her fully rested for her party today."

"Makes sense," Gigi said, getting out the car. "I won't be long," she stated before sashaying her way into the store. I leaned over to the driver's side and pressed the button to roll down all the windows completely. I then sat in the car listening to the radio until my phone buzzed in my pocket.

I pulled it out to see a text from Rico. "What does he want?" I said aloud. It was a video link captioned *"How come you didn't tell me about this?"* I clicked on the link. It was a video of the fight between Jayden and me.

Infuriated, I cut my phone off. I knew how Rico got excited about fights, and I knew I would receive more texts. *This is probably all around the school by now*, I thought. I had no problem defending myself, but I hated that I had to. *He should have kept his spit to himself.* I struggled internally because I wanted to be a better person and a good father that Love deserved, not some lightweight boxer punching everything in sight. I also worried that it would mess up my chances of getting into Columbia University. I still couldn't believe I was even entertaining the idea of college. I was still deep in thought when Gigi walked out of the store, swinging her bags.

Gigi opened the back door and tossed her bags beside Love, who didn't move a muscle.

"I told you that baby can sleep through anything," Gigi stated, putting on her seatbelt. "Need me to drive you closer to The Oink Shack?" she offered.

"Since you are offering," I replied.

Gigi started the car and drove a few stores down to The Oink Shack on the end.

"Thank you, Gigi," I said, getting out of the car and walking up to the store.

I saw Anna standing behind the register counter. The rest of the restaurant still looked the same. Empty.

"Hey, Wisdom," Anna said. "You just missed Courtland,"

"Hey Anna," I replied. "Dang, I should have come a little earlier. I know he is about to graduate and everything."

"And you're up next year. Y'all kids grew up quick," she reflected.

"If you say so," I replied. Anna tapped a few buttons on the register and opened the drawer, pulling out a white envelope. She came around the corner, and I noticed she was wearing a T-shirt and jeans. Her sandy blonde hair was out of its usual ponytail.

"Is there a reason you are looking at me up and down?" she asked.

I shook my head. "Oh, my bad. Just never seen you in regular clothes before is all."

"Oh," she replied slightly shocked. "Well, I haven't seen you in regular clothes either or without your visor. I didn't know you had all that grey hair in the back of your head. You're just a baby," she teased, walking behind me to get a better look.

I laughed turning around to face her. "Thank you, I think…" I paused to see if she just played me or not. "I was born with it," I said. "My daughter has it too, but it is at the front of her head instead of the back."

"Oh, cool," Anna replied in a flat tone. "Well, here is your last check." She handed me the white envelope. I noticed she had written my name on it. She extended her hand to me. I shook it. "It has been a pleasure working with you, Wisdom."

"Likewise," I replied, not really meaning it. "I better go cash this and finish setting up for my daughter's birthday party."

"Well, you go ahead. I have to wait for Ms. Linda to pick up her check, and after that, I'll be gone too," Anna told me.

I took a moment to take one last good look around the restaurant, reminiscing on the two years I worked there. "I'm sure going to miss this place," I said.

"You're young, Wisdom. Think bigger and look for better," Anna advised. "There's more for you than this."

I looked around again. "I hope you're right. Have a good one, Anna." I pushed the door open.

"You too, Wisdom," Anna said to my back as the door closed behind me.

I walked outside and was making my way towards the car when I noticed Gigi talking to the suit shop owner. He was dressed in another sharp suit with a matching hat. *What is his name again?* I asked myself, trying to think of the animal he was named after. *Wolf? No. Rabbit? No. Oh, I remember.* "Hey, Mr. Frog," I called out confidently as if I didn't just have this huge debate in my mind.

"Hey there young man, how are you?" he asked.

"Doing well," I replied, getting into the passenger seat. Gigi was still looking up at Mr. Frog from the driver's seat not taking him out of her sight.

"Hey, Wisdom, we got a few minutes to burn," Gigi said. "How about you cash your check at the check cashing place a few doors down while I talk to Frog."

"You trying to get rid of me?" I joked. I looked back at Love, who was still in her car seat asleep in the same position.

"Boy, if you don't get out this car and do what I said," Gigi growled. Her tone was serious, and her teeth were clenched.

I heard that warning loud and clear. "Yes, ma'am," I said, and I got out the car with a quickness. "I'll be back," I said, looking at Mr. Frog, who was still locking eyes with Gigi through the driver side window. *Lord, forget Stella, it looks like René is trying to get her groove back,* I thought to myself. I cringed at the idea and walked into the empty check cashing place.

"Can I help you?" the teller asked rudely. She stood behind the protective glass popping her gum, looking like she didn't really want to be bothered.

I dug in my pocket and pulled out my wallet to grab my ID. Then I took my check out of the envelope. I saw it was made out to me for five hundred and seventy-five dollars. "I would like to cash this check."

I grabbed one of the pens that was outside of the protective glass and signed the back before I slid the check and my ID under the glass insert. She took my ID and glanced at me then back at the ID to ensure I was who I said I was.

She slid me back my ID. "The cost to cash this, is fifty dollars, may I proceed?" she asked, still popping her gum.

"Yes," I replied. She nodded and went to the back with my check. After a couple of minutes, a couple guys came into the check cashing place and stationed themselves by the front door. The teller came back with my cash and counted it in front of me, glaring at the guys by the door.

"If you're here to get your check cashed get in line, if not, get out!" The teller demanded, fixating her eyes on the guys who came in.

The two guys sucked their teeth and walked out as she continued to count the money. The teller ensured I had my five hundred and twenty-five dollars after she took out the fifty-dollar cashing fee. I watched intensely as she placed every bill on the table and as she slid all the money into a fresh envelope. She finally pushed it all through the glass insert with my receipt.

"Thank you," I said.

She popped her gum again. "No problem," she replied.

I was barely out the door when I found myself surrounded on both sides by the two guys who were kicked out the shop.

"Hey bro, let me hold five dollars?" one asked.

I continued walking to Gigi's car. "Sorry, I can't help you," I replied, thinking about my current financial situation.

"Man, you just got paid," the other guy added. "Help us out, little homie."

"Sorry," I repeated. They followed me to Gigi's car, only halting just short of the parking spot, glaring at me.

Gigi halted her own conversation with Mr. Frog when she caught sight of my unwanted company. "Looks like I'm going to have to fuck some shit up," Gigi stated. She unlocked her door.

"It's cool, Gigi," I said. "I'm good." I took my spot back in the passenger seat.

Gigi acted like she didn't hear me. She cracked the door open and leaned back to get out the car, but Mr. Frog pushed her door back closed.

"It's cool, René. I got this," Mr. Frog said. He strolled up to the two guys. "Hey, gents. I'm looking for a full-time employee. We start you off with good pay and benefits. Either of you interested?" The two guys gawked at him like he had asked them for their social security numbers. The two guys exchanged a look and turned around to walk away in the opposite direction. "Then keep your begging asses away from this plaza!" Mr. Frog aggressively demanded. He returned to Gigi's door. "The one thing I can't stand is a lazy nigga that rather beg for it than work for it." Mr. Frog shook his head.

"Who are you telling?" Gigi agreed. "You really hiring?"

Mr. Frog grinned. "Yeah, you know somebody interested?"

"Hell yeah," Gigi replied. "Me!"

"Me too," I added. "You know The Oink Shack just closed down."

"Wow, really?"

Gigi and I both nodded.

"Hiring age is eighteen, and we only stay open until 5 p.m." Mr. Frog told us.

"Well, never mind," I said. "That wouldn't work for me with my school schedule, and I'm only seventeen."

Gigi huffed. "Well, I'm a little older than eighteen, and it works with *my* schedule."

"A little?" I murmured. Gigi backhand slapped me in my chest. I choked.

"Well consider this your interview, Beautiful." Mr. Frog glided his hand down Gigi's cheek. "See you on Monday at 8 a.m. sharp for your first day," he said. "We'll get all the paperwork straight then."

"Frog, are you serious?" Gigi asked in disbelief.

"Dead serious!" Mr. Frog stated firmly. Gigi got out the car to hug him.

I stayed in the car watching Mr. Frog hold Gigi tight around the waist. Our eyes met, and he immediately let her out of his grip.

He cleared his throat uncomfortably. "Well René, I got to get back to work," Mr. Frog said. "I'll see you on Monday."

"See you Monday. Thank you so much, Frog," Gigi said, getting back in the car.

"Anything for you, René. And please call me Fredrick."

"Thank you, Fredrick." Gigi replied. Mr. Frog tipped his hat and walked back to his store.

"Well, congratulations, Gigi." I offered, "At least one of us got a job this week."

"Yours is coming Wisdom." Gigi replied, driving us out of the parking lot. "Besides, at least you're able to spend more time with Love."

"That's true." I dug into my pocket for the envelope of cash. "Here." I handed Gigi the envelope as soon as we came up to a red light.

"Is this your whole check?" Gigi growled, snatching the envelope out of my hand. "Boy, put that back in your pocket." She demanded, tossing the envelope in my lap. "I just got another job, today!"

"I know, Gigi," I replied. "But Love and I are the reasons you got to get a job anyway. It's the least we can do."

The light turned green as I held the envelope out again. "Wisdom, I sympathize with you. I know you've felt like a burden on me ever since your mom dropped you off..." Gigi paused, continuing to drive. "But you're not. I'm good, and we're good, and we are going to get through this temporary inconvenience. Okay?"

"Okay," I replied.

"Now put that money away and save it for the next time Love gets diarrhea and she starts having those pull-up explosions again," Gigi half-jokingly instructed.

"Yes, ma'am." I laughed as we pulled up in front of the house. Rico was sitting on the porch.

"Lord, what does this crazy boy want?" Gigi asked, getting out of the car. I put my envelope back in my pocket and went to grab Love out of the car seat when Rico walked up to us.

"Davis family, how the heck are ya?" Rico greeted us with his arms out for an embrace. His locs fell over his eyes.

"Be even better if you'd take some of these bags in." Gigi forced the bags into Rico's hands.

Rico smiled. "I got you, Gigi, I got you." He walked up to the house with the bags as I unbuckled Love, who finally began to wake up from her nap.

"Da-ddy?" Love rubbed her eyes as I picked her up.

"Yes, Princess," I replied, holding her, and closing the door behind me.

"Par-ty?" she questioned.

"Almost, Princess, almost," I replied, following Gigi and Rico into the house.

"Alright, Dad, it's almost party time," Gigi said to me, putting the few bags she hadn't given Rico down on the kitchen table. "There are four kids coming from Ms. Corrine's daycare and a couple of parents, so you better roll out that grill and get them hamburgers and hotdogs going."

"Yes, ma'am," I replied.

"Is that my favorite niece?" Rico asked Love.

"Un-cle Ree," Love squealed, still unable to say his full name. She wiggled in my arms to get to him.

I handed Love to Rico. She hugged him and grabbed two strands of his hair to play with. "Thanks Love, I needed that hug." Rico stated. "You ready to turn up at your birthday party?"

"Tur-n up!" Love screamed, releasing Rico's hair. She clenched her little fists, making us break out into a hearty laugh.

"You ready to get chocolate wasted?" Rico asked.

"Cho-co wasted," Love repeated. She shook her head wildly.

"Would you stop corrupting my daughter please?" I replied, laughing at Love's crazy face expressions.

"Please stop!" Gigi said firmly. She took Love from Rico's arms. "You ready to get dressed, Love?"

"Yes, Gi-gi," Love replied.

"Rico, go bring the grill from the back and put it on the front porch. Wisdom, make sure you get all the other stuff, the cooler, chips, pans, buns, and utensils from the kitchen." Gigi listed. "Put all of it in the front. I already put the charcoal, lighter fluid, and matches on the front porch. Can you two manage to do the set up and not burn off your eyebrows?"

"Yes, ma'am, I got you," I replied.

"I make no promises, Gigi." Rico put his hands over his eyebrows.

Gigi laughed at his foolishness. "Get out my face, boy!" she continued laughing as she went up the stairs with Love.

"You see that, Wisdom?" Rico asked. "I'm wearin' Gigi down, bro. I'm finally going to make her Christmas list!"

"Not if you don't help out like she asked," I replied, going in the kitchen to grab all the items as instructed.

"I'm all over that." Rico went out to get the grill from the back as I slid the other items to the front door and onto the porch.

We made it outside and began completing Gigi's list. I put up Gigi's card table to place the food on. I then set up to pour some of the charcoal into the grill. This party was going to be exactly what we needed. We had all the typical kid's cook-out food. Hamburgers, hotdogs, chips, cake, ice cream and Capri-Suns in the cooler. Nothing more and nothing less.

I started to light the grill when I felt Rico's eyes over my shoulder. "Can I help you?" I asked, squirting lighter fluid over the charcoal.

"Yeah, man I want to hear about this fight that was sent to me today. Why you ain't tell me?"

"Dude, tell you for what? You should have been in school." I replied, grabbing the matches.

"Man, you know I had business to tend to," he offered his usual excuse.

"Vigilante bull crap, I presume." I stepped back to drop the lit match on the charcoal. The flames roared to life.

"Yeah man, you know it," Rico smiled. "You know I'm about that money."

"Yeah, I know," I replied, as the fire began to calm down, alerting me to get some hotdogs and hamburgers on.

"Don't try to change the subject. I want to know about you and this fight. Did you get my text?"

I grabbed my phone from my back pocket. "Bro, I forgot to cut my phone on," I lied. "My bad."

Rico looked at me with distaste.

"What?" I asked, rubbing some hand sanitizer on my palms.

He crossed his arms. "If you going to lie, at least cut off your read receipts before you cut the phone off."

"Alright, man. You got me," I admitted. I put some hotdogs on the grill. "I just don't want to dwell in the past. You know I don't like fighting."

Rico made a seat on top of the cooler. "I know, I just want to know what happened."

"Man, long story short, Ms. Lathrop had to watch a few students from Mr. Ork's class. Some dude named Jayden started acting mad disrespectful towards me and Ms. Lathrop when I was presenting my project. He came up to me and spit in my face, so we fought."

"Dude did what?" Rico shouted, standing up from the cooler.

"You heard me." I grabbed the tongs off the card table to flip the hotdogs.

"That's why that nigga's whole face was gushing in that video," Rico exclaimed.

"Man, I blacked out for a second hitting that dude."

"I saw," Rico replied. "I bet his ass won't spit on nobody else."

"I hope not." I put some aluminum pans near the grill preparing to take the hotdogs off, when I looked up and saw a group of girls walking down the sidewalk. Aliyah was among the group. Our eyes met across the yard. "What's up, Aliyah," I called out.

Aliyah waved back. "Hey, Wisdom." Rico turned his head to see who I was talking to.

"Watch the food bro," I instructed, giving him the tongs before I walked down the sidewalk to meet Aliyah.

"Man, I can't cook!" Rico shouted.

"Dude it's hotdogs, figure it out," I shouted back. "And make sure you use the hand sanitizer."

"On the hotdogs?" Rico balled-up his face. "That's nasty."

"On your hands, dummy," I replied. Rico flicked me off.

I ignored him and turned my attention to the girl in front of me. "Hey, how have you been?"

She smiled. "Good and yourself?"

"Good, can't complain," I said.

"I haven't seen you in school. Heard you got into a fight."

"Yeah..." My face grew warm with embarrassment. "I promise you, I'm not a violent person, but..."

"I know, Wisdom. There are multiple videos going around the school, and I saw him spit on you in one of them," Aliyah said. "He got what was coming to him."

"I wish I didn't have to but..." I paused.

"Sometimes you gotta do what you gotta do," Aliyah replied. I looked at her surprised. It was weird how well she understood me.

I decided now was a good time to change the subject. "What are you getting into today?" I asked. I observed the few girls who walked up the street had turned around and stood waiting for Aliyah.

"Just discovering Harrow Park with a few new friends." Aliyah replied. She put extra emphasis on "Park".

"Look at you, learning," I joked. She gave a small laugh. "That's what's up?"

"What about you? Looks like a celebration up there," Aliyah nodded her head towards the house.

"Yeah, it's a birthday party," I said.

"Aww that's sweet," Aliyah stated. "For whom?"

I laugh nervously as I wondered what to tell her. I wanted to be honest, but at the same time I didn't want to scare her away. However, I decided regardless of how I felt, Love had never been a secret, and she wasn't going to start being one today of all days.

"It's for my daughter," I admitted.

Aliyah's eyes widened. "Daughter?"

I nodded. "Yeah, my daughter, Love, she turns two today."

She let out a giggle that sounded unsure at best. "Are you joking with me or are you serious? You have a daughter?"

"Yeah, I'm serious," I confirmed. "Love's mom moved to Texas with her parents a few months after she was born. They were going to put her up for adoption, but my Gigi and I got custody of her, and the rest is history."

"Wow!" Aliyah's jaw dropped. "That's an interesting story."

"Interesting?" *What did she mean by that?*

She didn't get to explain. The group of girls up the street shouted her name, trying to get their new friend back.

Aliyah looked in the direction of her friends then back at me. "I got to go. Catch you around," Aliyah stated abruptly. She walked to the group without so much as a backwards glance.

"Bye Aliyah," I replied to her back. I watched her walk with her group further up the street. I went back up to the porch, ignoring Rico's smirk as I put on some more hand sanitizer. The smell of burned food immediately caught my attention. "Bro, did

111

you even look at the hotdogs?" I asked. I knew Rico hadn't taken his eyes off me since I first left the porch.

"Man, I closed the grill. Don't that slow the cooking down or something?" Rico inquired.

"Get out my way!" I nudged Rico to the side and opened the grill to see charred hotdogs. "Really bro?!"

Rico peeped over my shoulder. "Man, that's how old people like them anyway. Every time I go to a cookout they say, 'let me get that burnt one.' See I did you a favor."

"Whatever, man," I stated getting the hotdogs off the grill and into the aluminum pans.

"Yeah man but bump the hotdogs. Who was the girl you were talking to?" Rico asked. He slapped me on the back. "She's cute, my boy."

"Oh, Aliyah," I smiled.

Rico gawked at me. "Dude, she got you like that?" he asked.

"Like what?" I asked innocently.

"Like that," he replied pointing at my smile.

"Man whatever," I replied, putting on some burgers and a few more hotdogs.

"When did you meet her? When did she move out here?"

"My last day in school."

"Oh, same day you rearranged ol' boy's face?"

"Yeah. I hope I didn't scare her off."

"Well, what happened? And don't you miss a single detail." Rico sat back on top of the cooler. "I felt that sexual tension from the porch. Y'all got my nipples all hard and stuff."

I couldn't help but laugh real loud at that one. "Bro what? Rico, you a fool."

"I'm serious, man. That was tense. Like that one time I read the Bible by myself," Rico shared, grabbing his chest like he was having a heart attack.

"First off, you read the Bible?" I asked incredulously. "And second off, how did God's word get you all hot and bothered?"

"Man, I messed around and read Songs of Solomon to myself when I was bored..." Rico paused. "Let's face it, I was getting high," Rico admitted. "And next thing you know, I was butt naked on the bed with the end of a blunt in my hand," he explained.

"Why are you like this?" I asked. "It ain't even like that. I just told her about Love, that's all. I think I scared her off."

"Oh, she'll be cool, she just needs a little time," Rico affirmed. "You know your life is a lot."

"Man, shut up and help me with these hotdogs," I demanded.

"Looks like she was trying to help you with *your* hotdog," Rico cackled.

"Enough bro!"

"I'm just saying, man," Rico put his hands up, palms out.

I stopped laughing to ask a more serious question. "You don't think I messed it up telling her about my daughter so soon?"

"Nah, man. Besides, you have a motherless daughter," Rico explained. "No baby momma drama. I'm sure Aliyah don't mind playing house."

"Bro, chill," I urged.

"All jokes to the left, bro. Just give it time. And if it's meant to be, she'll come around," Rico assured, touching my shoulder. "And if she doesn't, you know my motto."

"Skip class, forget school?" I questioned.

"No, my other motto," Rico laughed. "Say it with me."

"On to the next ho." We said together.

We were still laughing when Gigi came outside with Love dressed up in her yellow tutu. "Are you corrupting my grandson, Rico?" Gigi asked.

Rico straightened up, "No ma'am."

"Is that my favorite princess?" I asked, putting the tongs down and picking Love up to toss her in the air. "You look beautiful, baby girl."

"What do you say, Love?" Gigi asked.

"Ta-nk you, Da-ddy," Love replied.

I kissed her on the cheek. "You're welcome."

"Party people, party people!" Ms. Corrine, Love's babysitter, finally arrived with the four other kids she was babysitting. "Where is the birthday girl?"

"Right here," I stated, handing Love off to Ms. Corrine.

"I've missed you, Love," Ms. Corrine shared hugging her. Love hugged Ms. Corrine back, the feeling obviously mutual since she hadn't been to her babysitter's house in a little over a week.

"Well, she'll be back soon," Gigi said. "I landed another job today."

"Well, congratulations René," Ms. Corrine stated, putting Love down to play in the yard with the other kids.

"Yeah, girl, I'm looking forward to it." Gigi turned her attention to me. "Hey, Wisdom. How about you and Rico go get Love's gift while I man the grill and make the kids plates."

"Sure thing, Gigi," I replied. "Come on, Rico."

"What you get her, bro?" Rico asked, following me in the house and up the stairs.

"This motorized SUV," I said. "I'm glad I can finally stop hiding this big thing in my room." I opened my bedroom door.

Rico whistled. "Dang, Wiz. How you get this up here by yourself?" I wasn't lying when I said it took up a lot of space.

"It was disassembled, and I put it together in here. Now I just need help getting it out."

"Shoot, well come on then. I don't want to miss the party." Rico grabbed one end of the SUV, and I grabbed on to the other.

"You know this is a two-year-old's birthday party, right?" I asked. We backed the SUV out of my room and carefully down the stairs.

"Shut up, man! 'Baby Shark doo-doo', still go hard."

"You are so dumb, man!" I laughed, barely making it off the last step. We shimmied our way through the living room and made it back outside with the SUV in one piece.

The kids were now all at the kiddie tables set out in the front yard, eating their hotdogs. Gigi took the moment to yell out, "Look what your daddy got for you, Love!"

All the kids abandoned their plates and ran up to the porch as Rico and I put her SUV down.

"WOW!" A few of the kids voiced.

"Ta-nk you, Da-ddy," Love stated, immediately climbing into the seat of her SUV.

"You're welcome, baby girl," I replied. I barely cut the thing on before she took off down the sidewalk.

"Love!" I called out to her, as she began circling the yard.

"I'll watch her," Ms. Corrine said. "Go ahead and finish the food." She stepped into the yard with the kids.

"Thank you, Ms. Corrine," I said. I put more hand sanitizer on my hands and got back to the grill. After a little time had passed, a few of the kids' parents showed up. We prepared them a plate too. And after all the food was done and eaten, Rico, Gigi, and I sat on the porch watching Love chase her friends around the yard in her pink SUV.

"You did good, Wisdom," Gigi said proudly.

I squeezed her hand. "Thanks Gigi, I learned from the best." Rico suddenly wrapped his arm around me and buried his face in his shirt. "Are you good, bro?" I asked.

He revealed his balled-up face as if he had been crying and said, "I just love this family," he teased. I pushed him away from me, snickering.

"You sure can ruin a moment, Rico." Gigi shook her head as she got up from her seat. "How about y'all come help me with this cake and ice cream."

"No problem, Gigi," I said.

"I guess I can help," Rico joked.

We obediently followed Gigi to the kitchen. I pulled the cake out of the fridge while Gigi grabbed the ice cream out of the freezer. Suddenly, the sound of tires squealing against the pavement caught all our attention. Screams began to fill the air outside. The sound of gunshots fired off repeatedly and bullets hitting our home's brick exterior made me drop Love's birthday cake. We all hit the kitchen's cold concrete tiles, squirming around to safe locations. Gigi crawled under the table as Rico made it to the pantry. I wedged myself between the lower cabinets under the sink, left the most exposed. The smell of buttercream frosting invaded my nose. After all of ten seconds, my mind went to Love. I was now hearing her tiny little voice screaming over the noise of the shooting.

"Da-ddy!" Love screamed, snapping me out of my panic. I got up and ran in full pursuit to the front door, disregarding my own safety.

"Wisdom, get back here!" I heard faintly, as I continued.

Rico ran closely behind me and tackled me to the living room floor before I could make it to the screen door. We both heard the bullets continue to rain outside.

"Get off me!" I demanded.

"Wiz, are you crazy?" Rico insulted. I pulled his fingers back, making him scream in agony.

All I could think about was Love when I made it to my feet and burst through the screen door.

"Wiz! Rico shouted. "Wiz!"

I could barely hear anything else Rico and Gigi were screaming. It was all overridden by my fear for Love's safety. I made it to the porch to barely catch a glimpse of a dark SUV that was drifting down the street.

I scanned the area looking around where everyone had dispersed. A lifeless body wearing all black was laying out in the road. Neighbors began surrounding the person in the street, cutting off my view.

"Love! Love!" I began screaming, scanning the front yard until I saw Ms. Corrine on the ground holding her arm next to Love's empty motorized SUV a couple units down.

I ran to Ms. Corrine, silently praying for the best. I dropped down to the ground seeing if she was alright and more importantly if Love was with her.

"Ms. Corrine, you alright?" I asked, sitting her up, as I attempted to examine her arm.

"I'm fine, I'm fine!" Ms. Corrine snapped. Her bloody hands swatted me away. "It's just a graze," she said. I shook my head at her stubbornness.

"Where is Love?" I asked, turning Love's SUV back on its wheels.

"I'm not sure," Ms. Corrine replied nervously.

Ms. Corrine and I searched the entire front area. Then she suddenly began crying, making my stomach turn in knots. Ms. Corrine pointed her bloody finger behind me. I turned around hesitantly only to see Love face down in the tall grass a few feet away from our very spot.

"Love!" I yelled. I got back up to run to her and crashed to the ground again. "Love!"

I turned her body over. Blood flowed onto her tutu. She groaned in pain fighting consciousness. "Love, talk to me, baby girl, talk to me." I pressed my hand on her tiny stomach, trying to stop the bleeding from her side. "Someone call, 911!" I screamed. The tears flowed, feeling hot on my face.

Gigi now came outside, screaming from the front porch. "Noooooooo!"

"Someone call, 911!" I screamed again. A few people that were outside started calling. I continued to press my hands against her side.

Rico ran out to me, tearing off a piece of his T-shirt as he moved. He handed me the torn fabric. By this point, I was sobbing heavily.

"She's going to be alright, Wiz. She's going to be alright." Rico encouraged, as I held the torn piece of shirt against her, but the blood continued to gush.

The ambulance came flying down the street along with two fire trucks and four police cars, blocking the entire street off. Gigi flagged them down running from the front porch.

"Please help!" Gigi screamed, as a couple of paramedics jumped off the ambulance, one male and one female. Gigi ran up to us as the paramedics followed.

"What happened?" The male paramedic asked.

"There was a drive-by, and she was shot." Ms. Corrine offered. She was still holding her arm on the ground.

"Do you need medical attention, ma'am?" The male paramedic asked.

"Help the baby!" Ms. Corrine demanded. "Help the baby!"

The other paramedic dropped to the ground and began checking out Love.

"She lost a lot of blood," I finally spoke as they looked her over.

"We need to get her to the hospital, now!" The female paramedic ran to the ambulance to get the stretcher.

"Please help her!" I begged. "Please!"

"We will do all we can." The male paramedic said, picking up Love's tiny body and putting her on the stretcher. Her eyes began to slowly blink. After he secured her, he pushed the stretcher into the ambulance.

Gigi ran up to me, while the female paramedic was asking me a slew of questions. "Young man, can you tell me a little about what happened? What's the child's age? Any allergies to medication?"

"There was a drive-by. It was a dark SUV probably a Suburban, but I could hardly see it." I tried to speak clearly and calmly. "She was shot!" I cried. "Today is her second birthday," I choked out through the tears that just wouldn't stop. Rico patted me on the back as I continued. "And she has no allergies to any medication."

Police officers stormed the streets getting statements from the large group that was surrounding the lifeless body stilly laying in the middle of the street. A few more were rolling out the yellow tape, blocking other areas off. An older gentleman pulled up to the scene and got out of the police car. He was wearing business attire, so I guessed it was safe to assume he was the head honcho. He walked over to the body in the street and covered it with a white sheet.

"He's dead, he's dead!" A woman cried out. I tried to remain calm and focus on the questions the paramedic was asking me, while the other paramedics worked on Love in the ambulance.

The ambulance door suddenly opened, and the male paramedic yelled out, "She's crashing, we have to go now!"

I ran up to the ambulance in full speed, attempting to get on, but was stopped by a few of the other paramedics.

"We need the parents of the child only, young man," one of the paramedics said.

"I am the parent!" I declared.

"That is her father!" Gigi came to my defense, and they opened the doors to let me in.

"Where are you taking her?" Gigi yelled out.

"Pope General!" The paramedic said.

"Wisdom! I'll meet you there." Gigi said. She ran to her car with Rico on her heels. The doors closed, and we took off down the street. The other vehicles moved as the sirens sounded off, alerting the entire neighborhood, clearing the roads. Four people tended to Love, trying to get her to respond. I sat in the back of the ambulance feeling helpless.

"What's your daughter's name?" A female paramedic asked.

"Love, Love Davis," I replied.

They put an oxygen mask on Love's tiny face and injected her arm with some fluids. Her eyes were still blinking slow; she was fighting to stay conscious.

"That's it, we got her back," the female paramedic said. "Love, stay with us baby girl."

"Daddy is here, baby. Daddy is here." I called to her, still feeling helpless. The paramedics continued tending to her. It felt like the ambulance was flying down the street.

One of the female paramedics soon took a seat beside. She began informing me of what medications they gave Love and what they were trying to do.

"Is she going to be alright?" I asked, as the tears still flowed.

The female paramedic held my blood covered hands. "The bullet seems to be in a very bad place near her spine."

"Her spine!" I screamed. "What does that mean? Will she be, okay?" I asked again.

"We can always hope," she offered.

The ambulance pulled up to the hospital, and I watched as Love's eyes slowly closed. She became unresponsive.

"We're losing her again!" The paramedic said.

"No, Love! Come on, baby girl!" I cried out.

The ambulance doors swung open. The paramedics took the stretcher out and ran her into the emergency room. I ran close behind trying to keep up, until a nurse stepped in front of me with both hands up, blocking me out.

"I'm sorry sir, but you can't go in there," she said.

"That's my daughter," I told her.

"I understand that, but we need to let the doctors do their job," the nurse said. "It looks like she's going to need surgery."

"Surgery!" My voice was loud, even to my ears.

"Unfortunately, sir," the nurse said. "If things go bad, can we resuscitate?"

I paused, trying to get a grip as to what was happening. *Surgery. Resuscitate. Nothing is making sense anymore,* I thought to myself, becoming overwhelmed.

"Sir, I need an answer!" The nurse demanded.

"Yes!" I replied coming out of my reverie. "Please do everything you can for her."

"We will," the nurse said. "Someone will come and find you when we are done. Please wait in the lobby." She pointed at the room behind me and closed the door. Through the door's window, I could see a slew of people in white coats filling the tiny room.

I sniffed, trying to pull back the tears and remain calm. "She's going to be alright. She's going to be alright," I repeated out loud as I tried to find the nearest restroom.

I washed my hands in the sink until the blood was no longer visible. By the time I was done, the white porcelain sink had a slight red hue. I looked up in the mirror and kept rehearsing,

"She's going to be alright. She's going to be alright," doing my best to convince myself.

Before I could even make it fully out the restroom, I was bombarded by a few hospital staff members, asking questions regarding insurance and other info I didn't have. Luckily, after I confirmed my identification, they were able to see all of Love's documentation on file, freeing me from a ton of more questions I didn't feel like answering.

I made my way to the waiting room, finding a chair near the water fountain. Gigi and Rico ran through the doors to the reception desk. I waved them down. Gigi hugged me so tight, I fought to breathe.

Gigi finally released me to be updated. "What are they saying? What's going on?"

"She has to get surgery," I relayed. "That's all I know." I crashed back down to my seat rehearsing my new mantra again. "She's going to be alright. She's going to be alright." I started crying fresh tears.

"She is going to be alright, Wisdom," Gigi assured with a faint voice, sitting beside me.

Rico flopped down in the chair across from me looking distraught.

"Rico, she'll be fine," I stated, watching Rico's eyes begin to swell with his own tears.

"That's not it," Rico said, breaking down I got up and sat beside him.

"What else happened?" I asked.

"The body in the street..." Rico paused. "The one that died." Rico attempted to get out, as Gigi sat in the other chair next to him rubbing his back.

"Yeah, you know who it was?" I asked.

Rico looked up at me with his eyes now blood shot red. "It was Poodie."

I gasped, "Ms. Patrice's grandson?"

"Yeah, baby," Gigi replied. Rico began to break down again.

"I'm so sorry to hear that man," I replied. He tried to fix his face, wiping his eyes and cheeks with both hands.

"Yeah, man, but enough with that." Rico slapped his face and cleared his throat. "We are here for Love, and she'll pull through, bro. She's a fighter like her dad."

"And like her Gigi!" Gigi added.

"Yeah, she is," I agreed. "But I'm still sorry to hear about Poodie, man."

"Yeah, me too," Rico replied.

Hours went by. I watched the sun begin to set, making the sky the same peach color it looks like first thing in the morning. I got up and paced the floor until my legs felt like Jell-O, doing my best to keep my mind busy. Gigi kept begging me to sit down, but my nerves wouldn't let me. The sky transitioned from peach to a dark blue as I kept walking, hoping, and praying that Love would pull through. Gigi sat silently and rocked in her chair watching me pace, until Rico got up and joined me.

"Lord, now I need both of y'all to sit down!" Gigi demanded. "I wonder what is taking them so long."

"Family of Love Davis." A voice called into the otherwise quiet waiting room. Rico, Gigi, and I all ran to the doctor who was standing by the door. We all stood there waiting to hear the update on Love. The doctor pulled his glasses off, uttering the two words no loved one in a hospital wants to hear. "I'm sorry."

CHAPTER 7

Despair wrapped its arms around me as I wept. Welcoming me in and serving me nothing but dark impulses and regret. Joy never came to visit, so I was left in sorrow that my heart couldn't shake, and my mind didn't want to let go of. I bathed in my own tears and dried myself off with questions no one with the highest level of intellect could answer. Why? Why did this have to happen? I lowered the blinds, I closed the drapes, and I embraced what embraced me. The stranger I didn't welcome in, and the stranger that wouldn't leave. Grief.

I stayed in bed not having enough strength to get up. Trays of food towered in my room because I couldn't eat. I cried until my body grew sore from it. I felt like I had an illness that Caster Oil and Tussin couldn't get rid of. I rotated around my bed looking for new areas to sulk in. I hadn't left my room in days. I heard knocks at the front door non-stop, and I listened for footsteps downstairs, but I couldn't muster up enough care to see who came to visit. *Keep your condolences, thoughts, prayers, and chicken*, I thought to myself. I just wanted Love, and no one could give her back to me.

Everything in me knew she was gone, but I couldn't let the truth fall from my lips.

Love is… Love is… Love is dead. I came into the realization every couple of hours as if it was new information. I'd awake to go back to sleep, trying to force reality to become a nightmare, realizing they were one in the same.

A hard knock at my door made me sit up momentarily in bed. "I'm not hungry, Gigi," I said weakly, laying back down and rolling over.

"It's Rico," said the voice on the other side of the door.

"I don't want any company." I covered my head with the blanket and sheets.

My locked door swung open. "I'm not company, I'm family." Rico responded.

I sat up in the bed again. "Negro, did you just open my locked door?" I asked. Rico stood in my doorway of my dark room with a hairpin he used to break in.

"Yeah, I did," Rico confirmed. "What you gonna do about it?"

I glared at him for a second, feeling my nose begin to flare. "Nothing," I replied defeated, laying back down covering my head with my bed's comforter once more.

"Come on Wiz, this ain't you man," Rico stated. He closed my door. I felt the foot of the mattress dip as he sat at the edge of my bed. "We are all worried about you. You know Love…"

"Don't say my daughter's name!" I snapped, snatching the covers off my face.

I saw Rico's expression change. He looked like he was telling himself in his mind to calm down. He shook his head at me. "Bro, you are not the only one that lost someone. She wouldn't want you to sit here and just…"

"And just what? Mourn?"

"She wouldn't want this, bro." He pointed at me. "She'd want you to live your life."

"Well, I guess we'll never know."

"Wiz."

"How man? How can I live without her?" Fresh tears began to burn my face. The anger was beginning to overwhelm me. "How?" I pulled the collar of my shirt over my face as I sobbed.

Rico sat in silence for a bit. My guess was he was really thinking about my simple yet tough question. Then he murmured. "One day at a time, bro."

I wept in my shirt, until the odor of not leaving my room for days raised up my nose.

"Shit!" I groaned in disgust.

"Uh huh. You smelled that funk and came out of that shirt quick, didn't you?" Rico teased, making me laugh. I'd almost forgotten how it felt. "Oh shit. Did my nigga just giggle?"

I threw a pillow at him. "Shut up, Rico!"

"See, you just laughed. That is what she would have wanted," Rico said. "One day at a time, man."

"I hear you," I replied.

"How about this," Rico offered. "I'll take this garbage downstairs." Rico wrinkled his nose at the trays of food that began to collect fruit flies. "You go take a much-needed shower. Then we'll eat all that fresh food people have brought over. *Downstairs*," he emphasized.

"Man, I don't know." I looked around the room I hadn't left in days.

"I ain't taking 'no' for an answer," Rico said. "Besides, you need to do both of our noses a favor."

"You got jokes."

"Oh shit. Not another giggle," Rico teased. He threw the pillow back at me. He stood up from the edge of my bed. "I'll see you downstairs." Rico picked up the trays of food off my dresser and left my room.

A few seconds later, I pulled the covers back and put my feet on the cold floor, bracing myself to get up. I stood up slowly, feeling the full impact of my weight on my feet after not having stood in days. I instantly got lightheaded, which forced me to take baby steps to my dresser, pausing every so often to catch my breath as if I traveled a far distance. I assumed not eating for a few days, coupled with just lying in bed had taken its toll. I grabbed some underclothes and a pair of balling shorts out the dresser before I shuffled through the dark hallway to the bathroom. I closed the door and cut on the shower water. A little bit of light came in from the sides of the thick closed drapes. I removed my foul-smelling clothes and got in the tub. For a moment, I just let the hot water run down my skin, alerting me to reality a little more with each passing second. I felt weird. Everything felt wrong still being able to cognitively function without Love. I let the water run across my face and held my breath until my lungs were forced to breathe.

"One day at a time. One day at a time." I rehearsed, grabbing the soap, and attempting to wash away the grief I sulked in for days.

When I finished, I dried off and threw on the fresh underclothes and balling shorts. My bare feet scraped the concrete tiles in the upstairs hallway. I stared dead ahead, knowing I couldn't afford to glance at Love's bedroom door for a second. I turned my body and began walking down the stairs.

I followed the sound of the noise coming from the kitchen. On my way there, I noticed the bullet holes in the walls were now patched up. I threw my arms over my eyes the instant I stepped in the kitchen in an attempt to block my face from the sunlight beaming in from the opened drapes. *I haven't seen light in days,* I thought to myself, feeling very much like a vampire. The blinding moment didn't last long because I got swept up into Gigi's arms. I squinted, slowly opening my eyes adjusting to the light until it became easier to take in.

Rico sat at the table smirking. Gigi let me out of her grip only to wipe her eyes. "It's good to see you, Wisdom. Would you like anything to eat?" she asked. I glanced at the food on the stove. I also noticed the plates from my room were now washed and sat drying in the dish rack.

"I guess I could eat," I shrugged, sitting at the table with Rico, still squinting to adjust to the light.

"I'll make you a plate," Gigi said brightly.

Among other things, I noticed Love's highchair stood in its normal spot at the table. I breathed in and out slowly in an attempt to not fall apart. Gigi slid a plate of food in front of me temporarily distracting me from the sight of her chair. I took a bite of the chicken, feeling it go all the way down to the bottom of my stomach. Gigi and Rico watched me intensely.

"Can I eat in peace?" I asked, looking up at them.

"You sure can," Rico stated, getting up. "I have some business to tend to anyway."

"What is that?" I asked with my mouth full. "The Vigilantes got you working?"

"Sort of," Rico said. "Helping out with Poodie's funeral."

I slowly stopped chewing, realizing that I had never asked Rico about how he was holding up after Poodie was killed. Or even checked with Gigi to ask how she was doing or asked how Ms. Patrice was holding up. I was so locked into my own feelings that I never stopped to think about anyone else's. Rico was right, I wasn't the only one that lost someone.

I finally swallowed the food. Then I murmured, "I'm sorry," which got Rico's and Gigi's attention.

"For what?" Rico asked.

"For what, Wisdom?" Gigi echoed.

"For how I've been for these past few days," I said. "I never checked in with y'all, Ms. Patrice, Ms. Corrine, or with anybody. I've just been in my own feelings."

"It's cool, Wisdom," Rico stated, walking towards me. "It's totally understandable."

"That's right," Gigi added. "We have all lost someone, and we all mourn differently. It's alright."

"We good, bro." Rico assured. He held his fist out for our usual dap. "I'll catch y'all later."

"Wait!" Gigi shouted, walking up to Rico, and giving him a huge hug. His feet dangled in the air for a second. "Thank you. I didn't know how I was going to get his ass down here."

"It's my specialty, Gigi." Rico stated, pulling out of Gigi's grip. "I told you I was wearin' her down, bro." Rico fake whispered, giving me a wink. We all laughed. "Catch y'all later," Rico said a final time, walking out the front door.

"Later," I replied. As soon as I heard the door close behind him, I went back to eating my food in silence, feeling every little piece hitting the bottom of my stomach. I only made it through half the plate before realizing I was full.

Gigi frowned at me and my plate in concern. "That's all you can handle?"

"Yeah, Gigi." I said, rubbing my stomach.

Gigi didn't bother to argue. She just took the plate and wrapped it in foil. "Well, at least you ate something. It'll be in the fridge when you're ready to finish it." Gigi opened the fridge door. It was so stuffed, she had trouble finding a space to squeeze my plate in. She found a little room at the top, but she had to lean her weight on the door to fully close the fridge.

"Dang, Gigi. Who you trying to feed?" I asked.

"This is all the food people brought over," Gigi said. "You know how people do when someone d…" Gigi's voice trailed off. She pressed on the fridge door to make sure it was closed one last time. Then she sat down at the table and grabbed my hand. "I wanted to talk to you about the arrangements."

"What arrangements?" Gigi looked up to the ceiling as if she was trying to figure something out. It clicked in my mind. "Love's funeral arrangements," I finally said. The words that just rolled off my lips were very overwhelming.

"Yes," Gigi said, wiping away the one tear that sneaked from her eye and rolled down her face. "I didn't want to do much without your consent, so I wanted to know how you wanted to go about it."

I shook my head. "I don't know much about how to orchestrate a funeral, Gigi. How are we even going to pay for all this?"

"Well, I have an insurance policy on her that you would have taken over when you turned eighteen but…" Gigi paused again. "Either way the insurance policy should take care of her arrangements."

"You had a life insurance policy on Love?"

"Yes, and I got one on you too." My eyes widened. Gigi explained further, "I wanted y'all to be covered knowing how high everything is going up now."

I squeezed her hand. "Well, I can understand that. Where would the funeral be located?"

"I was thinking Berksdale Funeral Home," Gigi suggested. "It's centrally located, and I figured you would want it to be close to home."

"Sounds like it'll work, Gigi." I agreed.

"Mrs. Anthony, the co-owner, said we can talk to her today, if you'd like," Gigi said.

"Sure, Gigi." I said trying to stay calm. My attempt at calm failed no sooner than it had started. I slammed my hand on the table and stood up.

"What's wrong Wisdom?" Gigi asked, getting up frantically.

I pointed at the empty highchair. "This is wrong, Gigi!" I was outraged. "All of this is wrong. Love should one day have to bury me, not the other way around! How am I supposed to do this? How am I going to tell Danielle?"

Gigi walked up to me and wrapped her arms around me, keeping me in place long enough for her to talk. "We are going to get through this. Together."

"How Gigi?" I asked, feeling her tears drip on the side of my face. "How?"

She repeated the same advice Rico gave me earlier upstairs. "One day at a time," she said.

I took in a deep breath, and I let Gigi go, fighting the urge to stay in that head space. "I'm going to get dressed, so we can go to the funeral home," I said. "I'll write Danielle and her family a letter, and I'll meet you in the car in about thirty minutes. Is that okay?"

"Yeah, it's fine. Go ahead and handle your business. I'll be waiting," she said.

I walked up the stairs, doing my very best to not even point my body in the direction of Love's bedroom. I pivoted my body into a sharp left turn to enter my room. The smell of grief surrounded me; I almost vomited. I gathered my sheets off my bed into a large ball and put them by the door. I opened my curtains and let the natural light flood my room. In the process, I kept trying to remind myself to breathe. I put on some deodorant and lotion before I got dressed and sat on the bed with my notebook and pen.

It felt like it had been so long since the last time I've written, that just grasping the pen felt unusual and strange. I knew I needed time just to figure out how I was even going to write the letter. *How do you tell someone their child has died?* I asked myself. Several minutes later, I had started and stopped the letter so many times that my floor was littered with balled up notebook paper. Then the words started coming a little smoother, at least as smooth as they could, considering the content. I grabbed an envelope from my desk with a stamp and assembled the pieces, making the letter eligible for mailing. My chest tightened when I threw the paper balls into the hallway trashcan, which happened to sit next to Love's shut room door.

"Breathe, Wiz, just breathe." I coached myself as I made my way back into my room to grab my sheets off my bed and the letter to mail to Danielle.

I closed my eyes and ran down the steps holding tightly to my sheets and my letter, still refusing to look at Love's room door. I found Gigi frozen with the front door open, staring outside the screen door. I ran to the kitchen to throw my sheets in the washer before coming back to her.

"Everything alright, Gigi?" I asked.

"Yeah, I'll be fine," Gigi said. "I just wasn't expecting no one to do this."

"Expecting who to do what?"

"I think you should see for yourself." Gigi grabbed her keys and held the screen door open for me to walk onto the porch. She closed the door behind us.

We were greeted by a sidewalk memorial for Love and Poodie. Members of our neighborhood showed their solidarity by covering the area with balloons, teddy bears, and warm messages. "Wow," I said as I read some of the warm messages, thoughts and prayers everyone had for us while I was making my way to the car. I also noticed there were no traces of blood around. "I wasn't expecting this either."

"Get in," Gigi said.

I held Danielle's letter tightly, getting into the car and putting the seatbelt on. I felt my chest tighten again with the glimpse of Love's car seat behind me. I barely had time to process any thoughts concerning Love when Gigi took off down the street, stopping directly in front of the Harrow's Landing sign where the mailbox was located. I got out the car and let out a sigh before I dropped the envelope inside. Back in the car, I wondered how hard Danielle would take this news. I envisioned Danielle finding out about Love, wishing I could be there to hold and comfort her, wondering if her parents would even let her come to the funeral. My daydream was interrupted by Gigi turning into The Berksdale Plaza, which was on the opposite street of the funeral home.

"Gigi, where are we going?" I asked.

"I just have to make a quick stop before we get to the funeral home." Gigi was parking right in front of Mr. Frog's suit shop. She got out the car without so much as a full explanation. I stared in amazement. *I know Gigi didn't stop to go flirt with this man again,* I thought until I realized what day it was. Monday. *Today was supposed to be Gigi's first day of work,* I remembered, watching her go into the store.

"I hope she still has the job," I said aloud, hoping that Mr. Frog would understand the circumstances. A few moments later Mr. Frog and Gigi emerged from the store. He held Gigi's hand, guiding her to the car.

"It's okay, René," Mr. Frog comforted. "Take as much time as you need." He opened Gigi's car door and helped her get in.

"Thank you, Frog..." she paused. "I mean Fredrick," Gigi corrected herself.

Mr. Frog ran over to my side of the car and opened my door. He leaned down to hug me. He smelled like expensive cologne, which threw me off slightly. I could also feel the needle from his lapel pin against my chest.

"I'm so sorry, young man. Please know that I am praying for y'all." He straightened back up.

"Thank you," I replied. He closed the door and walked back to Gigi's side of the vehicle.

Gigi rolled down her window. "You are amazing. Thank you again."

"Anytime René," Mr. Frog sympathized. "If you ever need someone to talk to, you know where to find me."

"I certainly do," Gigi grinned, putting the car in reverse. "See you later." Mr. Frog blew her a kiss in response.

Gigi zoomed down the plaza's parking lot.

"I think Mr. Frog has a 'thing' for you, Gigi." I said, breaking the silence in the car. Gigi looked at me, waiting for a green light.

"Boy, I ain't checking for Fredrick," Gigi replied.

"Well, Fredrick is checking for *you*."

The light turned green. Gigi pressed her foot to the gas pedal. "Please," she sniffed. "With all these curves and rolls, I'll break little Fredrick."

"Be careful what you say, Gigi. He looks like he likes curves and will darn sure bite a roll," I replied. That made her laugh. The playfulness didn't last long. When Gigi finally parked in front of the funeral home, our minds came back to the reason we were there.

Our laughs ceased. We sat in the car quietly looking at the building. Neither of us moved. None of it felt right, but we knew we had to go in. I looked over at Gigi; she looked over at me. We gave each other a nod, and we both reluctantly got out of her Cadillac and began walking up to the funeral home's entrance. I made move to open the door for Gigi to go inside, but the door opened by itself with Ms. Patrice emerging with her hands full of tissue.

"Patrice," Gigi greeted.

"René," Ms. Patrice replied. They embraced each other.

"How are you holding up?" Gigi asked.

"One day at a time," Ms. Patrice replied.

Is that just a cultural thing Black people tell each other when they lose a loved one, or is that sound advice? I began to speculate.

"Wisdom," Ms. Patrice wrapped her arms around me.

"I'm so sorry to hear about Poodie—I mean Patrick." I said, hugging her back.

"And I'm sorry to hear about Love," Ms. Patrice let me go to grab just my hands. "You think they finished their investigation?"

"What investigation?"

"Well, the police have been by my house informing me about what they believed happened," Ms. Patrice said. "They haven't come to see y'all?"

"I wouldn't know," I stated shamefully, realizing all I've missed in the past three days. "Have they, Gigi?"

Gigi nodded. "They have, but they said they have no leads. That is why we got to look out for ourselves."

"You know that's right," Ms. Patrice replied. "Well, you know the streets talk." Ms. Patrice said, putting her used tissue in her purse. "When I hear something, I'll let y'all know."

"Likewise," Gigi replied.

"I'll catch you all later." Ms. Patrice began retreating to her vehicle.

"Alright, Patrice," Gigi said. "Please let me know when the homegoing is."

"Next Tuesday at 2 p.m." Ms. Patrice said, making it to her car. "I'll call you sometime this week."

"Okay," Gigi replied.

When we finally stepped into the funeral home, I found myself surprised by the grandeur of it all. I observed the white walls, marble floor, and sturdy metal accents, until a lady came walking out of some back room, interrupting my visual tour.

"Good afternoon. Can I help you two?" The lady asked.

"Hello, my name is René Davis. I'm here to speak with Mrs. Anthony concerning my great-granddaughter's homegoing service."

"Oh, yes," the lady replied. She extended her hand. "I'm Mrs. Anthony."

"Nice to meet you," Gigi stated, shaking her hand.

"And who is this handsome young man?" Mrs. Anthony asked, shifting her eyes in my direction.

"I'm Wisdom," I greeted her, extending my own hand.

"It's a pleasure to meet you," Mrs. Anthony said. "Please follow me, and we will get right to it." She had us follow her to another room. "First, let me show you the sanctuary. It can hold about two hundred guests; it comes with a piano and a TV if you want to show pictures on the screen. We have an identical one on the other side as well. "Mrs. Anthony said.

"This is nice." Gigi's tone was dry. I said nothing as I looked around the huge room. I only wondered if I even knew two hundred people personally.

Mrs. Anthony took us back into the hallway past the bathrooms to show us another room. "This is where the repast will take place if you care to have one." Mrs. Anthony motioned to us to take a closer look. She rambled on and on to Gigi. I walked around looking at the thick, fancy carpet, trying to get over the fact that we were really planning Love's funeral.

"Wisdom!" Gigi called. She pulled me back from going too far off and getting lost in my thoughts. "You, okay?"

I nodded and walked closer to her and Mrs. Anthony.

"Well, that is the extent of these areas. Let's go to the back office and talk logistics," Mrs. Anthony suggested. We then followed her down the hall into what appeared to be a conference room. "Please, sit." She pointed to the two chairs at one side of an oversized conference table. She took her place at the head of the table with a stack of papers and a box of tissues. Mrs. Anthony slid the box of tissues in front of us. "I want to first state how truly sorry I am to hear about the recent passing of your loved one. And for her to be so young, I couldn't even imagine." Mrs. Anthony's sympathy caused tears to start rolling down my face. I grabbed a tissue from the box while Gigi rubbed my shoulder.

"I'm so sorry, Wisdom. Was Love your sister?" Mrs. Anthony inquired.

"His daughter," Gigi answered for me.

Mrs. Anthony took a few seconds to really look at me. She extended her hand to mine at the table as I wiped my face with the other. "I won't lie and say that this pain will ever go away," she said. I wondered where the conversation was going. "But what I know is that God has the power to give you a peace that surpasses all understanding. And just when you find yourself at your lowest, He can pull you up," Mrs. Anthony encouraged. "We aren't meant to understand everything…" She paused. "God knows I have my own set of questions, but He will be with you to the very end."

"Amen," Gigi said, grabbing a piece of tissue to wipe her own tears.

I pondered Mrs. Anthony's words while she placed catalogs on the table in front of Gigi and me. *Peace needed to meet me three days ago,* I thought about the last seventy-two hours that led us here. The thought made me angrier than anything else. How did this drive-by even happen? Were they going after Poodie? The questions popped in my mind like ads on the internet.

"Wisdom!" Gigi interrupted my thoughts yet again.

"Huh?" I answered.

"Did you just 'huh' me?" she asked.

"Yes, ma'am," I corrected. "My apologies, Gigi."

"Mrs. Anthony asked you if there should be a color for the service?" Gigi said. "Sometimes services have a theme color."

"Yellow," I said without giving it too much thought. "Everyone should wear a touch of yellow." I stated, thinking about how much Love brightened up my day.

Gigi grabbed my hand, "Love definitely lit up a room, didn't she?"

"She sure does...did," I replied as Mrs. Anthony wrote down some notes.

"So, let me make sure I got this all written down," Mrs. Anthony reviewed her legal pad. "You want the Prestige plan with a keyboard player and the choir from your church," Mrs. Anthony went on. "Guests will be encouraged to wear some sort of yellow, and you're going to use your own pastor for the eulogy..." Mrs. Anthony paused, looking at Gigi, who gave her a head nod. She continued, "It will be a closed casket funeral, and the casket will be open at the end as guests and family proceed out into the hall. Lastly, the body will be buried at Remington Memorial Cemetery and a strong no on the repast."

"You got it, Mrs. Anthony," Gigi confirmed.

How did I miss this whole conversation? I asked myself, realizing that I really was stuck in my head.

"Good, now all I need from y'all are some pictures for the programs and an outfit you would like us to dress your loved one in," Mrs. Anthony said. "I can give y'all Tuesday at 3 p.m." She looked at her large desk calendar as she confirmed the date on her tablet. "Now, we have a service at 2 p.m. on the same day, but it's an intimate quick service in our other sanctuary, and they are not having a repast either," Mrs. Anthony said.

"Is that Patrick's homegoing?" I asked.

"Yes!" Mrs. Anthony replied with a shocked expression. "How did you know?"

Gigi and I exchanged a look as if we were both trying to figure out how much to tell her.

"I am good friends with Patrice Slater," Gigi said. "We lost our loved ones on the same day... Love's second birthday." She plucked another tissue from the box.

"Oh, I'm so sorry, Ms. Davis. I didn't mean to pry. I had no idea," Mrs. Anthony said kindly. "Would you prefer another day; we can do the following Saturday, but there will be more fees associated, due to how long the body is being preserved including the weekend rates."

Gigi wiped her face, and I placed a hand on her shoulder. "That won't be necessary. We'll take Tuesday."

"Yes, ma'am," Mrs. Anthony replied, writing it all down on her desk calendar. "Last thing," she added. "Would either one of you like to say or recite something during the homegoing? Some family members like to sing, talk, recite poems, and even dance."

"Wisdom, you should do a poem," Gigi suggested. "You're an awesome writer, and I believe Love wouldn't have wanted it any other way."

"I don't know, Gigi," I replied.

"I believe it would be a beautiful sentiment for a father to say something regarding his child," Mrs. Anthony interjected.

"I agree," Gigi added.

"Fine!" I said reluctantly.

"Great! Now again, all I need are pictures for the program, an outfit, and possible hair design that you can come up with. You'll be able to view the body this Wednesday once everything is dropped off and set up to your liking," she said. "Oh, and please send the death certificate to Lincoln Heritage, and we will send them our invoice."

"Lincoln Heritage already has the certificate, so you can go ahead and send them your invoice," Gigi informed her.

"Great! Well, everything has been outlined, if you have any questions feel free to call or email me." Mrs. Anthony said, getting up.

"Wait, what about the casket?" I inquired. Mrs. Anthony looked at Gigi. Gigi turned her head to me. "Did I say something wrong?"

Gigi shook her head. "No, not at all. It's just, the casket has already been purchased and should be here by tomorrow. There were only a few I could pick from since she was only..." Gigi cleared her throat. "There weren't many to choose from because of her stature, but I did get a pink one due to the fact that the other ones were kind of boyish." She held her breath waiting for my response.

"I understand, Gigi." I replied standing. Gigi let out a sigh of relief and pushed her chair back to stand up from the table.

"Well, everything should be good. I hope we have it all to your liking." Mrs. Anthony bid us to follow her back to the funeral home entrance.

"It is," I said.

"Again, if you have any questions or if anything should arise, please give me a call," she insisted.

This time, Gigi answered. "We will,"

"I'll see y'all later this week with those items, and I hope you all have a good one." Mrs. Anthony let us out the front door.

"You too," Gigi replied, and I just nodded.

Mrs. Anthony closed the door behind us, and Gigi and I walked to the car in silence.

"I hope I didn't overstep?" Gigi seemed a bit unsettled. I just looked at her. "I just didn't want to put any extra pressure on you, that's all," she explained.

"Gigi, I completely understand." I stated, watching relief go across her face. "I haven't been much help lately and I appreciate you doing the bulk of this by yourself," I said. "I'm sorry I wasn't more help."

"Baby, anyone who went through what you went through can understand." Gigi said, starting the car. Then she reached over to rub the back of my head.

Gigi began driving down the street cutting on the radio, silently listening.

We passed a mailbox and another thought occurred to me. "Guess I got to send another letter to Danielle and tell her the funeral date."

"Wisdom, you've taken some huge leaps today," Gigi said. "Let me handle that, and you handle your speech for this fune—Love's service," she managed to get out as we pulled up to our house."

I opened my door. "Are you sure?" I asked.

"I'm sure," Gigi replied, getting out.

We walked up to the porch when I saw a group of guys down the street near Ms. Patrice's house. I squinted hard still slightly adjusting to daylight. The Vigilantes were putting a wreath on Ms. Patrice door. It matched the one someone seemed to have placed on ours while we were out handling our business.

"Well, that was sweet of them," Gigi said as she opened our front door.

I agreed. I turned around towards the street. "I'm going to tell them thank you."

Gigi quickly caught hold of my hand. I turned around to look at her, wondering why her grip was so tight. Gigi let out a sigh and brushed her hand across my face. Her eyes and voice were full of concern. "Please be careful."

"Yes, ma'am," I replied, realizing how shook she became. Gigi went in the house while I walked down the street to see The Vigilantes.

"Brave Heart," Shy acknowledged me and dapped me up. The other guys closed rank, surrounding their leader and me.

"What's going on, bro?" Rico asked, coming up behind Shy. "You good?"

"As good as I'm going to get," I replied. "I just wanted to thank y'all for the wreath. I guess it's safe to assume y'all did the memorials too."

"Yeah, man we got to look out for family," Rico said.

"No doubt," Shy added.

Ms. Patrice's door creaked open. We all turned around.

"If y'all don't get the fuck from in front of my house!" Ms. Patrice yelled through the screen door.

"We come in peace, Ms. Patrice." Shy assured, as the other guys nodded in agreement.

"They got us memorial wreaths," I said, pointing to the yellow flowered wreath on her porch.

Ms. Patrice opened her screen door and walked outside to the porch. She glanced at the wreath for all of twenty seconds before she picked it up and slung it at The Vigilantes.

"I don't want shit from y'all!" she screamed. "Y'all the reason Patrick and Love are dead in the first place!"

"Lady, that's not true!" Shy yelled.

"I'm sure it is!" Ms. Patrice put her hands on her hips. "I heard it in the streets. Some damn turf war between y'all and The NK7s, right?" she argued.

"Rico, what is she talking about?" I asked. But Rico was speechless. "What is she talking about, Rico?" I asked again.

"I'll tell you what I'm talking about," Ms. Patrice continued. "A few members of a gang called The NK7s used to deal near the old Scott's Market before they started tearing shit down over here. A few of them relocated, and The Vigilantes started dealing right over the rubble—"

"Ms. Patrice, you don't know the whole story!" Shy interrupted.

"Oh wait, Wisdom. It gets better!" Ms. Patrice said. "Then one of The NK7 members tried letting them know that Scott's Market whether up or down was their spot, but they didn't want to move." Rico started to sweat. Ms. Patrice continued, "So, they called up their leader, and they began chasing them through the streets, shooting at them, and that's how we both ended up with these damn wreaths at our doors!" Ms. Patrice yelled. "It's all their fault!"

I looked at Rico. The other guys were mute. "Rico is that true?" I asked.

"I was with you and Gigi, bro. I don't know the whole story," Rico stated, looking at Shy.

Shy didn't bother to lie. "Yeah, it's true." My heart sunk. "But there is more to the story," Shy tried to explain, "We didn't know that they were going to do that to Poodie."

My blood began to boil. "Are you serious? They said it was their spot!"

"Wiz, chill!" Rico urged.

"Chill?" I yelled. A few neighbors were now coming outside to see what the commotion was all about. "Y'all are the reasons my daughter is dead, and you want me to chill?"

"They just said it's more to the story, bro," Rico defended his so-called crew.

"Man, you really doing this right now?" I asked. "They are the reason Love and Poodie are dead, and you're defending them?"

144

"Man, calm down!"

"Calm down?" I yelled. "You really got me fucked up!" I brushed past Rico and walked up to Shy. One of the other guys stepped in front of him. "Answer me this!" I said furiously. "Is the fact that you wouldn't leave that spot the reason why Love and Poodie are dead?"

"It's not that cut and dry, Brave Heart. Here is the whole story—" Shy started.

"Nigga, I don't care about chapter one, two, or three. Let's skip straight to the climax! Is that the reason Love and Poodie are dead?"

"Wisdom!" Rico grabbed my arm, but I slapped his hand off me.

"Answer me!" I demanded.

"Yes," Shy murmured. I swung at the guy in front, hell-bent on working my way to Shy.

"Chill, Wiz. Chill!" Rico grabbed my shirt. Ms. Patrice ran off the porch.

Rico held my arms as I relentlessly kept trying to go after Shy. "Let me go, Rico!" I growled, continuing to pull myself out of his grip. The guy directly in front of Shy punched me in my chin, making me fall to the ground. They all began to surround me. I jumped up and threw my weight into the middle of them, falling to the ground again. When I looked up, my face was staring down the barrel of a gun. One of The Vigilantes had pointed the weapon directly between my eyes.

"No!" Rico shouted, diving in front of me with his hands out. "Everybody just chill!" he yelled. Seeing the gun, the nosey neighbors decided to step back into their houses.

Click, click. We all heard it. Everyone's eyes widened. "Put that shit down before I blow your brains all over this block." A voice growled from behind The Vigilante that pointed his gun at us.

The guy lowered his weapon. Rico and I stood to our feet to see Gigi with her gun pressed to the back of the guy's head. The Vigilante dropped his gun, and Gigi instructed Ms. Patrice to pick it up.

"Wisdom, go in the house!" Gigi commanded.

"But Gigi—" I began. She cut her eyes at me.

"Go in the house, now!" Gigi growled, and I began to walk across the street to our house. "Patrice, you can hand me his gun," she said. As I walked away, I watched Ms. Patrice hand the other gun to Gigi. She then pointed both guns at Rico's crew. "You ever point a gun at my grandson again, I'll rain hell down on all y'all. You got me?" Gigi threatened.

"Yes," a few of the guys mumbled.

"Yes, what?" Gigi growled through her clenched teeth.

"Yes, ma'am," the guys said. I bore witness to it all from across the street, purposefully ignoring the 'go in the house' directive.

"Now, as you know we have been through a lot in the past three days. Y'all may be sad that you lost a gang member, but we lost family members... Blood." Gigi declared, putting the guns down. "We are not the same."

"Tell them, René!" Ms. Patrice added, stepping back onto her porch.

"Now, get out of here before the police come," Gigi ordered. "My gun is registered. Are yours?" Gigi asked. The Vigilantes looked at each other and began walking down the street. Gigi huffed, "I didn't think so."

Rico did not follow the others. Instead, he walked across the street towards me.

"Wisdom, didn't I say go in the house!" Gigi shouted, turning around to face me.

I turned to walk to the house when Rico tapped my shoulder.

"Wiz... I," Rico mumbled, getting choked up on what to say.

I wasn't trying to hear it any way. "Fuck you, Rico." I left him on the sidewalk, running straight into the house, slamming the front door behind me. I punched the center block wall in the living room and crashed down to the floor. "Fuck!" I cried.

CHAPTER 8

Tears burning like flames streaming down my cheeks, unable to be extinguished. My breath blows so hot with hopelessness, that kind words can't even form on my lips. I attempt to keep everything in, doing my very best not to explode. My thoughts alone begin picking at me, dancing in my head until I react. What's wrong? A simple question without a simple answer. My forehead heats with blame, while my body runs hot with regrets. Nothing can cool me off, and nothing can keep me calm. Rage.

I took a long look in the mirror, fighting with my pale-yellow shirt that kept crinkling up at the bottom even after ironing it twice with starch. "I hate dressing up!" I declared, putting on my beige suit coat and buttoning the first button to hide the wrinkles. I grabbed my phone off my nightstand and cut it off before shoving it in my pocket. I knew I would need it as a distraction later, and I wanted to ensure that the battery remained fully charged. I did a mental checklist ensuring I had everything. *Phone, wallet, keys, and notebook.* I grabbed the last three items off the bed before leaving my room.

The hallway was dark with all the bedroom doors closed. Yet, I was able to make out my sunshades I'd purposely placed on the banister rail the night before, ensuring I wouldn't forget them. I needed them just in case the expressionless face I'd been rehearsing for this day wouldn't hold up against the weight of my grief. I cowardly walked towards Love's room, tiptoeing in the hall as if someone could be disrupted. I took a deep breath before opening the door I hadn't touched in almost two weeks.

I sat down in the rocking chair beside her crib and looked around. Her room appeared the same. Nothing was out of place. I realized that when I sat still long enough, I could almost hear her laugh again. I closed my eyes and rocked back into the chair, remembering all the joy she brought me.

"Love if you're listening, tell Daddy what to say," I whispered, hoping her spirit was lingering. It had been a whole week since we'd arranged the service, and I still hadn't written a speech or even a full sentence. Nothing sounded right, and nothing fit the moment. Every time I thought about what happened and what was taken from me, I became enraged. I couldn't sleep, I couldn't eat. Someone needed to pay for what happened to Love.

My mouth salivated with the thought of vengeance, totally distracting me from why I was in her room to begin with. I sat up in the rocking chair looking at the ceiling, reminding myself to breathe, attempting to remain calm. "Talk to me, baby girl." I said, trying to surpass my frustration.

"Wisdom!" Gigi's voice floated up the stairs. "We are leaving in five minutes!"

I sucked my teeth. "Alright!" I replied. I looked down at the blank page in my notebook. "I'm coming!" I said, getting out of the rocking chair, and walking to the door. I turned around to take one last glimpse of her room. "Improv it is," I said, closing her door behind me.

Clenching my notebook tightly, I grabbed my shades off the banister and walked down the stairs to meet Gigi in the living room. She stood in the middle of the room wearing a yellow dress and matching hat on top of her new "Sunday" wig.

"Boy, ain't no sun in here!" Gigi exclaimed, as I was putting on my shades.

"You sure?" I joked, looking at her up and down in her yellow outfit.

"Boy, did you just try me?" Gigi asked me. She examined me carefully. "You might want to button the second button on that suit coat to hide those wrinkles." I looked down to see a portion of my shirt exposed. She sucked her teeth. "Talking about me, and your shirt more wrinkled than Eunice's chest."

"Really Gigi, you are going to go there?" I scratched my head. "You got it."

Gigi grabbed my hand looking at me in my eyes as if she could see them through the dark shades. "We're going to get through this, Wisdom."

"I don't see how," I murmured, looking back at her through the dark lenses.

Gigi let out a huge breath. "You ready?"

"I'll never be ready."

Gigi clutched her keys and opened the front door. Light flooded the living room. "Me either," she said.

Gigi locked the door behind us and paused on the porch to look up to the sky. "It would be a bright sunny day today, wouldn't it, Love?" she then looked at me. "She was really the light of our lives, wasn't she?"

I looked at the memorial a few feet away from Gigi's Cadillac. It all still seemed so unreal. "Yeah, she was..." Even my voice sounded far away to my own ears.

The sound of the Cadillac doors unlocking brought me back to the present. When I opened the door, I saw that Love's car seat was gone. I got in uneasily, closed the door, and grabbed my seatbelt. I took a hard look at Gigi. Her hat was rubbing against the ceiling of the car.

"Gigi, where is Love's car seat?" I asked.

"It's in the trunk," Gigi said, looking straight ahead. "Every time I looked in my rearview, I would see…" Gigi choked up. "It's in the trunk."

I gave Gigi's shoulder a squeeze as she started the car, and we took off down the street. I fought the urge to sob. Not even the sound of the wind pouring in from the windows could fully override the silence that filled the car. Neither one of us parted our lips; we both realized that there was nothing comforting we could possibly say to each other. Nothing would lessen the blow of where we were going and why we were going there. The thought of it made my eyes water behind my shades.

The funeral home's parking lot was flooded with cars when we pulled up. Seeing all the cars and the people making their way into the building got me wondering if the letters we wrote made it to Danielle and her parents on time.

I was the one to finally break the silence when Gigi parked in a spot in the front reserved for us. "Gigi, who are all these cars here for?"

"I'm not sure," Gigi rolled the windows back up. "You know Patrick's funeral is today as well."

"Yeah, that's right," I stated, unbuckling my seat belt. "But I thought Mrs. Anthony said it would be a small ceremony like ours?"

Gigi shrugged. "I guess they had more than they anticipated."

"I guess so," I replied. Honestly, I was not expecting many people to show up for Love's funeral.

Gigi unlocked the car doors from the driver's side. "You ready for your speech?" she asked.

I clenched my notebook tight, knowing I was left unsuccessful in writing anything. "As ready as I'm going to get," I said.

"Well, let's go in." But words didn't match her actions. She remained in the driver's seat looking out the window.

I felt a sense of dread wash over me. "Do we have to?"

"I wish we had another option, Wisdom, but in this case, we don't." Gigi said. "How about we get out on three."

"Alright," I agreed.

Gigi began the count. "One." I grabbed the door handle. "Two." Her voice was firm, and I waited for the next number, half hoping she would just give up. "Three," she breathed at last. We both got out the car and closed the doors behind us.

The pathway seemed unnaturally long as we boldly walked up to the funeral home doors. Once we opened them, the grandeur of the foyer was oddly overshadowed by Rico sitting on a bench in the hall. He wore a yellow Polo shirt tightly tucked into the waist of his black pants. He stared at us as we came through the doors.

"I'm going to go find Mrs. Anthony," Gigi said. "Go over there and talk to your friend."

My jaw clenched. "I ain't got nothing to say to him."

"Wisdom, I know you're upset, and you have a right to be, but Rico is not to blame for what happened." Gigi wasn't having it. "Talk to him," she said firmly. "I'll be back shortly."

"Fine," I huffed.

I walked up to the bench. Rico stood to his feet. "What's up, bro?" he greeted me hesitantly.

"Rico," I replied coldly.

"Man, you still mad? It's been a whole week."

"You say that like it means something!" I raised my voice. "I got a calendar!"

"Wiz—," he tried.

I cut him off and used my anger to hurl each word in his direction. "Love is gone, and no matter how much I pray, how much I cry, how much I vent, or how much I complain, she ain't coming back!"

"I understand that." Rico's voice was low, nearly a whisper in an attempt to bring me back to calm. "But I had nothing to do with that, I was right there with you when it happened," Rico reminded me. "That day I lost my niece and a friend, and I'll be damned if I lose a brother, too. You got to let this go, man."

"Bro, I can't let it go. I can't let it go, until whoever did this is dead."

"You mean in jail?" Rico clarified for me.

"I said what I said, Rico." I grit my teeth. There was no tremble in my voice. "I just can't believe you are defending them."

"Wiz, as much as you try to blame The Vigilantes, you know as well as I do that, they didn't kill Poodie or Love," Rico said.

"Watch it, Rico," I warned, hearing my daughter's name fall from his lips.

"No bro, I won't! And I'm willing to get my ass beat in a funeral home until you hear me." Rico stepped up to me, glaring at me. "Poodie was running from The NK7s," he stated. "Your anger is valid, but it's misplaced. They are who you should be mad at, not The Vigilantes."

"Man, I ain't trying to hear that."

"Because you know I'm right. And I know how much you hate being wrong. I promise I'll tell you the whole story after the funeral, but The Vigilantes aren't to blame. I wouldn't still be with them if they were…. You know that, right?"

I lifted my shades for a second to wipe my eyes. "I don't know what I know anymore, Rico."

"You are my brother," Rico confirmed with his fist out. "You know I wouldn't compromise that."

"Oh shoot, my boy using words like compromise." I half-joked, dapping Rico up. "Alright, vernacular."

"You ain't shit, Wiz." Rico replied, bringing me in for a bro-hug.

"About time!" Gigi declared coming around the corner with Mrs. Anthony. She wrapped her arms around us both and brought us all in for a group hug.

"I told you, Wiz, I'm wearin' her down." Somehow, I was able to laugh.

Gigi let us out of her hold. "Rico, you can ruin a wet dream and a loose bra."

"Are you coming on to me, Gigi?" Rico teased, rubbing his chest. Gigi took one of her heavy hands and smacked him on the back of the head. "My bad, Gigi, let me stop playing with you. Since I know you're packing now," Rico said, rubbing his head.

Gigi patted her purse. "You got that right. Mad heat."

The sanctuary doors of one of the chapels suddenly opened and people started pouring out. "It looks like all of Harrow Park is here," I said. Then I noticed they were all heading into the second chapel across the hall. "Wait, isn't that where Love's service is going to be?" I asked, pointing at the chapel.

"I think so," Gigi said. "Mrs. Anthony!" she yelled over the crowd. Mrs. Anthony walked through the sea of people to get to us.

"Yes, ma'am," Mrs. Anthony answered.

"Why are all these people going into that chapel? Gigi inquired. "I thought this one was set up for Love?"

"It is, Ms. Davis," Mrs. Anthony said. "They are all here for y'all."

"What?" Gigi asked in disbelief.

"Yes, ma'am," Mrs. Anthony replied. "Do I need to get security or call the police?" Mrs. Anthony wrung her hands nervously. "I thought you knew."

"No, you don't need to do that. I'm just surprised that's all." Gigi was still trying to believe what she was seeing when Mr. Frog emerged from the sea of people and approached her.

"Well, hello there," Mr. Frog tipped his hat to Gigi. He was wearing a cream three-piece suit with a yellow bow tie and matching handkerchief.

"Frog! Why do I feel like you did this?" Gigi stated with her hand on her hip.

"I didn't do anything but make a few calls," Mr. Frog explained. "These people came out in support of y'all. And a group of young men have done a little orchestrating too. And again, everybody else can call me Frog, but I want you to call me Fredrick." He took Gigi's hand, lifted it to his lips, and gave it a kiss.

Gigi let out a girlish giggle. "Well, Fredrick, you never cease to amaze me."

I used my elbow to nudge Rico in the ribs. "Bro, did you and The Vigilantes have something to do with this? I asked.

"See, I told you we weren't all bad, but bump that. Did he just hit on Gigi?" Rico whispered. "I mean like, in front of us?"

"You better believe it," I replied.

"And you cool with it?"

"Man, they are old. It's harmless."

"You say that now. But when you find them on top of each other, sweating, using asthma pumps, and wearing life alerts, you remember this conversation."

"Bro, chill!" I tried desperately to get rid of the image Rico's ignorant comments conjured. My shout made Mr. Frog and Gigi look back at us.

"What's going on gentleman?" Mr. Frog's sudden attention made the both of us straighten up. "How are y'all holding up?"

"Doing the best, we can, Mr. Frog," I said. "Thanks for asking."

"I understand that." Mr. Frog lightly touched my shoulder. "I'm still praying for y'all."

"I appreciate it," I replied. The last group of people were coming out of the chapel. I saw Ms. Patrice at the end of the processional. She was holding on to a woman's arm. The other woman was carrying an urn. Ms. Janice and Ms. Eunice followed out behind them waving at us as they went into the other chapel for Love's service.

"Patrice," Gigi called, waving her down.

Ms. Patrice walked over, bringing the woman who held the urn with her. She hugged Gigi. "René, how are you? You remember my daughter, Paris?"

"Of course, I do," Gigi recalled. "She went to school around the same time as Lucky. How are you holding up, sweetheart?"

"Doing my best to stay sane," Ms. Paris replied. She lifted the urn for Gigi to see. "Just can't believe this is all that is left of my child." With that, she began to weep.

Gigi touched the back of Ms. Paris' hands. "Trust me. We know how you feel, darling. Lord knows I wish I could take the pain away." Ms. Patrice wrapped her arm around her daughter, who continued to sob.

"We must get going, René. If you're up for it, I'll check on you, later today." Ms. Patrice gave Gigi's hand a light squeeze goodbye.

"Only if you're up for it." Gigi replied. Ms. Patrice and Ms. Paris walked in my direction.

"Wisdom, I'm praying for you," Ms. Patrice offered. She cut her eyes at Rico, but she said nothing else.

"Thank you, Ms. Patrice," I replied. Then we watched Ms. Patrice and Ms. Paris make their way to the exit.

"You saw that, right?" Rico asked the moment they were out of the building.

I nodded. "Even Stevie Wonder saw that, my guy."

"She had security escort The Vigilantes out of Poodie's funeral," Rico said.

I raised my eyebrows behind my shades in surprise.

Rico continued his update. "Yeah, bro. They came in and asked us to leave, but I told them I was here for another funeral, and they let me stay in the lobby."

"Wow bro, I'm sorry to hear that." I stated. I saw Mrs. Anthony was now making her way towards us.

"Family, are y'all ready to usher in?" Mrs. Anthony asked, bringing me back to my own reality.

Gigi took a large breath, and she hooked her arm in mine. "Let's go."

"I'll meet y'all in there." Rico suggested. He began walking to the door of the sanctuary.

I stopped him. "For what? She asked if the family was ready to usher in. You know you're my brother."

Rico's eyes glaze over. He looked away for a moment and cleared his throat. "Alright, alright," he replied. He rolled his shoulders obviously trying to keep his cool.

"You stay too, Fredrick!" Gigi instructed, grabbing Mr. Frog's arm.

"Anything for you, René," Mr. Frog replied, kissing Gigi's hand again.

Finally, the doors opened and revealed a packed sanctuary. Pastor Isaac gestured his hands for everyone to stand up as we began to proceed down the burgundy carpet that lined the middle aisle. I was so glad he agreed to eulogize Love, especially because my work schedule at the time wouldn't permit a Sunday service. Gigi and Love were the only two from the Davis household that made it to church regularly, so his willingness to still go through with the service was much appreciated.

All eyes gawked at us. I eagerly looked for Danielle amid the large crowd until I noticed Aliyah, standing in one of the pews. She gave me direct eye contact and a head nod, and it seemed like we were having a conversation that no one else understood but us. *What is she doing here?* However, the more I looked around, I slowly realized that almost the whole neighborhood was here. We made it to the front row, and it all started to sink in. Pastor Isaac gestured for everyone to sit down. The room remained silent like a TV on mute.

Pastor Isaac started the service. I surveyed the tiny pink casket that made up the front center of the sanctuary, covered in yellow flowers. An elderly usher passed out programs. Love's face beamed at us from the front cover. Her name was scrawled in bold cursive letters at the top. The matching birthdate and expiration date at the bottom left me fuming. The choir rose to sing a song I could not really hear. All my senses were too overwhelmed by anger. Someone truly took the most important thing from me. *How could someone be so careless?* My eyes flit between the cover of my daughter's obituary and her casket. *On her birthday of all days.* My right knee started bouncing slightly, as I tried my best to keep everything in. I wiped my eyes behind my shades with the tips of my fingers before the tears could even fall.

Rico leaned over. "Wiz, you good?" he whispered.

I couldn't answer him. I sat there shaking my leg, taking in one breath at a time. Gigi's hand began to rub circles on my back.

"Wisdom, are you alright?" Gigi asked, as I looked straight ahead, unable to answer.

I could hear Rico and Gigi, but I couldn't respond. I was afraid that any words I had to say might not be anything pleasant.

"Wisdom, Wisdom." Gigi called out. She glanced at Mr. Frog in a silent plea for help. The choir sat down, and the Pastor made it back up to the podium.

"We will now have a few words from Love's father, Wisdom Davis," Pastor Isaac told the congregation. My head snapped up.

"Wisdom, are you okay?" Gigi whispered.

"Wiz, you good?" Rico repeated.

I just stood to my feet, clutching my notebook. I then turned around to look at them and gave them a head nod. I put my notebook down on the pew where I had been sitting and slowly walked up to the pulpit. I still didn't know what I was going to say.

Pastor Isaac patted me on the back and went to sit in one of the large wooden chairs behind the podium, leaving me to address the massive crowd, who were all wearing some shade of yellow. From my spot at the podium, the congregation looked like a swarm of bees. I scanned each face hoping to see Danielle, but my eyes landed on Aliyah again. For some reason, this made me feel centered. So, I took a deep breath and greeted them. "Good afternoon."

"Good afternoon," the room echoed.

"My name is Wisdom Davis and I…" I paused, stumbling on what to say next. I took off my shades, embracing my vulnerability.

"Take your time, son!" Pastor Isaac voiced from behind me.

"It's alright, Wisdom," Gigi added from the first pew.

I took another deep breath. "And I am, Love René Davis' father," I managed to get out. "To be completely honest, my assignment was to write some sort of speech or poem to honor the memory of my daughter, but after a week, I was left unsuccessful." I paused again, and the room remained quiet. "To be honest, I spent most of that week in bed trying to force this horrific tragedy to be a dream," I declared. "But it isn't...My barely two-year-old daughter is gone, and as much as I want her to, she isn't coming back. So, if you would, please allow me to just say a few words from the heart."

"You have the floor, sir!" Pastor Isaac assured.

I took what seemed like my one thousandth deep breath and looked up at the large crowd, attempting to lower my anxiety.

"The day dimmed as your life diminished, taking your rightful place among the sky. How is it possible for someone so young to hold such a role in life? You were light in a different form. One with skin, one with flaws, and one with vulnerabilities. Every minute I raised you, and every second I got to know you was life changing. Your smile was infectious, your laugh was contagious, your eyes were heartfelt, and your presence was desired. Light eventually must go out, but it always returns. The rain may block, and the winds may blow, but nothing can keep me from your touch. So, shine bright and become what I've known you to be, exactly what this dark world needs. Radiance."

The audience roared at the completion of my poem. I retreated behind my shades and timidly walked down the steps from the pulpit to my seat, doing my best not to look in anyone's face. Gigi embraced me as the sanctuary continued to clap. Only the squeak of the sanctuary door could be heard above the applause, stealing my thunder and making everyone look back out of curiosity. The claps faded. Mumbles and nosey whispers started to fill the room. I turned around, letting Gigi go to see what had everyone's attention.

It was Danielle. She wore a yellow dress and oversized black shawl that draped over her upper body. Time stood still for a moment. I viewed her, her silhouette framed by the sanctuary doorway, like it was my first time seeing her at all. I walked towards the back as Pastor Isaac made it back to the pulpit continuing the service. I walked up to her, looking at her in her eyes for the first time in two years.

"Danielle," I said warmly.

"Wisdom," she returned coldly.

I stuck my hand out, but she ignored it as she began to cry. Her body shook in her effort to fight the tears. "It's okay, Danielle." I replied. I went in for an embrace, but she put her hand out to stop me. She lifted her head and pulled herself together.

"I'm fine," she whispered. She tried to take a seat in the last row, almost ignoring the fact that I was standing there.

"No! The family sits at the front," I said firmly. Are your parents here?"

"It's just me," Danielle sadly confirmed.

I stuck my hand out again. "Please join us at the front," I begged. "You are her mother."

She didn't fight it anymore. Tears streamed down Danielle's cheeks as she took my hand. I held on tightly and guided Danielle to the front, observing how full her face had gotten since I saw her last. Eyes began burning the sides of our faces as we walked to the front. The path up the aisle felt like it was a mile stretch.

Pastor Isaac was still speaking when we finally made it to our designated pew. Rico slid over to give us some room. The sight of Danielle left me both surprised and angry. Surprised, she was there and mad that her parents didn't show up to their own granddaughter's funeral. I couldn't believe that Danielle had flown here from Texas by herself. My rage kept shifting from Danielle and back to Love; the rest of Pastor Isaac's sermon fell on deaf ears. Before I knew it, the undertakers strolled to the front and began taking the flowers off Love's casket. I looked at Gigi.

"They're going to roll her out into the foyer and allow us to view her." Gigi whispered, already knowing what I was about to ask.

They rolled the tiny pink casket into the foyer. Pastor Isaac gave the benediction and gestured for us to proceed out. I let Gigi and Mr. Frog go ahead. Rico walked behind Danielle and me. I watched Danielle remain frighteningly reserved with her arms folded tightly, while her oversized shawl dangled off the sides like she was freezing cold.

When we walked into the foyer, the mood changed drastically. Gigi stepped closer to the now open casket. When she got to the top of the casket, she lost it upon seeing Love's face. Mr. Frog held her up as she sobbed. I felt the tension on my neck as Mr. Frog and Gigi went ahead and Danielle and I stepped up to see our daughter.

I snatched my shades off to see her clearly. She rested peacefully in her favorite yellow princess gown, with her white stockings and matching yellow baby doll shoes. Her cheeks were slightly blushed, and her normally wild hair was tamed, pinned up in a bun. Her silver strand of hair was curled, perfectly placed and falling down the right side of her face. I took a deep breath, pulling Danielle close to me with my free hand. I tightly clenched my notebook with the other. Danielle began to sniffle.

"I'm so sorry, Danielle," I whispered. My eyes dripped with tears that fell onto the outside of the pink casket.

Danielle snatched herself out of my grip, "You should be sorry!" she suddenly screamed. "How could you have let this happen?"

"Excuse me?" I asked, straightening up. Danielle took a few steps away before turning around to face me.

"It's your fault my daughter is dead!" The whole sanctuary began to crowd the door to see what the fuss was about.

"Danielle, there was a drive-by, this was some gang mess, it wasn't my fault," I tried to explain.

"And where were you when my daughter got shot, huh?"

Rico took that as his cue to jump in. "I know this bitch didn't..."

Danielle's eyes widened. "Bitch?" she repeated.

"Chill, Rico!" I demanded.

Rico blew his hot breath on the back of my neck and began pacing.

I looked up at Danielle. "You have some nerve coming up in here blaming me for Love's death!" I declared. "You ain't been here in two years, ain't respond to not one of my letters or pics I've sent, and you got the nerve to blame me!"

Danielle's face grew red. "But you—,"

"Shut up!" I demanded. The whole funeral home went silent. "Where was I when Love got shot? That was your question, right? Well, here is the answer, I was getting her birthday cake out the fridge while she played in the front yard with her friends, being supervised, by her babysitter I like to add, when it all happened," I said. "So, don't you dare come here asking me where I was for five minutes when you've been an absent parent for our daughter's entire short life!" I shouted.

Danielle slapped me so hard, I leaned towards the casket. I caught myself before I bumped it off the stand.

"Have you lost your mind?" I shouted, standing up straight and gripping the side of my face.

Rico rushed forward. I dropped my notebook and grabbed him with both hands before he made it to her.

"Oh, you are really lucky, girl!" Rico jumped in my grip. "Really lucky!"

I only turned around when I felt it was safe to release Rico. Danielle stood there with her shawl opened. A round belly protruded under her dress. "Are you pregnant?" I blurted out. She quickly covered herself back up with her shawl. "Are you?" I asked again. Danielle looked up at me shamefully as Gigi made her way to us.

"Answer him!" Rico demanded. "Pregnant or not, it don't make me no never mind." Rico punched the air behind me, getting into a boxing stance. "These hands are bisexual and rated D, for 'don't give a damn'."

Danielle's face transitioned from shameful to confident. Her hands ventured to the top of her belly, and her face revealed a sinister smirk, making my skin crawl.

"Are you?" I shouted.

"Yes, I am!" Danielle stated boldly.

You didn't wait for me. My chest tightened with the thought. I stared at her, too shocked to move. *Did I mean anything to you at all? Maybe it was wise that I got that paternity test.* I recalled that conversation with Gigi. *If you're going to low ball me, Danielle, watch me go lower.* "Are you going to keep that one?" I asked aggressively. Danielle looked up at me as if my words cut her even though she provoked me first.

"That is enough, you two!" Gigi declared. "Not here, and definitely, not now!"

"But Gigi, she—" I said.

"THAT IS ENOUGH!" Gigi's voice filled the entire funeral home. "This is y'all's daughter's funeral for God's sake. Stop it! Both of you!"

Danielle wrapped herself back in her shawl and walked up to the casket. She kissed Love's forehead. "Rest well, baby girl," she whispered. Then she folded her arms, and walked straight to the ladies' room, leaving the drama she sprouted behind.

I looked at Love again. If I didn't know any better, I'd swear she was just sleeping. I leaned in and kissed her cheek that was surprisingly cold. "Daddy loves you, Princess." I whispered over her body. Then I bent down to pick up my notebook from the floor and walked right into Gigi's arms. "I'm sorry, Gigi. I'm sorry," I cried.

"It's okay, baby," she replied. She held my head close to her chest as I wept. At this point, I didn't care to put my shades back on.

Rico stood near us while all the people began to proceed out, filling up the grand foyer. I felt another hand on my back while I continued embracing Gigi. I turned around, surprised to see Aliyah, standing there with her arms open for a hug.

I leaned down and let her wrap her arms around my neck; my arms encircled her waist. "I'm so sorry," she whispered in my ear. I felt overly comforted by her embrace. "I'll be sure to send up a few prayers for you!"

"Thank you," I said. I released her from the hug, but I held on to her hands, amazed that she still decided to speak to me after that whole Danielle incident.

A woman walked up behind Aliyah and cleared her throat. Aliyah jumped a little at the sound and let my hands go. "Oh, Wisdom, this is my Aunt Yolanda," she introduced us.

"It's a pleasure to meet you, ma'am," I said, extending my hand.

"Pleasure to meet you too, Wisdom," Ms. Yolanda replied. She shook my hand. "I'm so sorry about your loss," she sympathized. "I know I don't know you or your family well, us being new to the neighborhood and all, but Aliyah kept insisting that we come."

"I appreciate y'all for coming," I replied.

"But please know you and your family are in our prayers," Ms. Yolanda said.

"Thank you so much, ma'am."

"No, thank you. Now I can put a face with a name." She saw my puzzled look and clarified, "Aliyah talks about you a lot."

Aliyah blushed with embarrassment. "Okay, Aunt Yolanda. Let's go somewhere else," she stated, pulling her aunt's arm. "Catch you later, Wisdom," Aliyah told me as her aunt waved goodbye.

"Catch you later," I replied, watching them take a few steps towards the front of the funeral home.

"Wisdom, who was that?" Gigi asked.

"A girl I know from school," I said.

"Well, that was some embrace," Gigi observed.

"Wasn't it?" Rico teased.

"She's just a friend from school, Gigi." I stated, wiping my face as the rest of the people finished viewing Love's body.

Mr. Frog stepped up. "Y'all want one last look before they get ready to take her to the grave site?"

"We should," Gigi suggested. "I'll get Danielle."

"Why?" Rico asked, making Gigi scowl at him. He backtracked fast. "My bad, Gigi, do your thing."

"Fredrick, watch them for me," Gigi instructed as she walked to the restroom.

"Yes, ma'am," Mr. Frog replied, intensely watching Gigi walk away.

Rico cleared his throat walking up to Mr. Frog. "What are your intentions with my Gigi?" Rico said, causing Mr. Frog to gawk at him with confusion.

"What?" Mr. Frog questioned.

"You heard me, Mr. Ribbit-Ribbit," Rico teased. "What are your intentions with my Gigi?"

"*Your* Gigi?" Mr. Frog let out a hearty laugh.

Rico squared his shoulders, "Yeah, my Gigi."

Mr. Frog's smile revealed his gold tooth. "I have much respect for your Gigi," he assured us. "We were very good friends when we were in school, and we're good friends now. That's it."

"Uh huh, you expect me to believe that?" Rico asked, sizing Mr. Frog up.

"Yeah. I'm too old for games, young man."

"You may have the old part right, but you look like you play a mean game of spades, tic-tac-toe, Monopoly, and all that," Rico blurted.

"Shut up, Rico!" I demanded, trying not to laugh.

Mr. Frog raised his eyebrows coolly. "Excuse me?"

"Just playing, OG," Rico said with his hands up. "Just got to make sure my family is straight." He shook Mr. Frog's hand as some sort of truce before I moved him out the way. There were things I wanted to say to the man trying to impress my grandmother.

"I appreciate you for doing all this, Mr. Frog. We weren't expecting this many people," I said.

"Any time, young man, any time..." Mr. Frog's voice trailed as his attention was no longer on me, but rather back on Gigi as she emerged from the restroom with Danielle.

Danielle walked up and looked at me square in the eyes. My stomach turned in knots, and I wondered what was next until her lips parted. "I'm sorry," she offered weakly.

My anger melted and my arms couldn't do anything but go around her. I hugged her, and I almost forgot she was pregnant until I felt her hard belly against mine. "It's okay," I answered sincerely.

Mrs. Anthony walked up to our huddle. "We are getting ready to transition to the grave site in about ten minutes," she informed us. "Did y'all want to see her one last time before we closed the casket?"

"Yes!" We all chorused and walked to the casket as a unit. So, we stood there looking at Love in her tiny pink casket. The undertakers stood behind it patiently waiting for their directive to move to the next step in the process. Then Gigi gave the undertakers a curt head nod. They closed the casket slowly. Clearly, we needed more of a warning because suddenly everyone in our group began to sob. Mrs. Anthony stood alongside us. She waited calmly for us to fix our faces.

Once we had ourselves somewhat together, she kindly told us, "The hearse should be coming around soon." With that, she left us and walked towards her office urging the crowd that still lingered to make their way out the front doors.

"Thank you, Mrs. Anthony." Gigi stated before the funeral director got too far.

Rico glared at his phone before tapping me on the arm. "Yo, Wiz, can I see you outside for a second?" Rico inquired.

"Right now, bro?" I asked wiping my face.

"Yeah. It won't take long, I promise," Rico assured.

"Alright." I was feeling too vulnerable to argue. I pressed a light finger to Gigi's arm. "Gigi, we'll be right back," I told her before following Rico outdoors.

"Hurry back!" Gigi instructed.

I walked with Rico around the side of the Berksdale Funeral Home. The sun beamed down on us. I slid my shades back on and wondered what was so important. "Bro, what's going on?" I asked. I had a sinking feeling in the pit of my stomach.

"Just follow me," Rico advised.

It seemed our final destination was the back of the funeral home. There The Vigilantes were huddled in an empty parking space, surrounded by a puff of smoke.

"Rico, what the hell is this?" I inquired.

"They have some important news," Rico said.

"More important than my daughter's funeral?"

Rico who bowed his head in shame and didn't answer. Instead, the infamous Vigilante leader decided this was his time to step in.

"Look man, I'm sorry about the whole misunderstanding last week," Shy stated. He walked up to me like he really knew me.

"Which part? Getting my daughter killed?" I pointed to the other guy from the gang who stepped to me on Ms. Patrice's porch. "Or was it having that big block looking dude put a gun in my face?"

The same dude with the gun glared at me. He pulled himself up to his full height and started to take a step towards me. Shy pushed him back. "Whoa Black, chill big dog!" he demanded. The guy named Black listened and took a reluctant step back, keeping the glare on his stupid face. When he was sure Black was good, Shy addressed me again. "Hey man, I told you there was more to the story. And you stepped to me first, Brave Heart."

I ignored his point, spitting on the ground. The strong smell of marijuana encased all of us, and I wasn't that interested in explaining to Gigi why we smelled like weed when we got back to her. This little meeting needed to be over quick. "Alright, so what's the important news?" I asked, trying to get to the point of all of this.

"Well, first I want to tell you what really happened that day Poodie, and your daughter were killed." Shy opened, piquing my interest. "Poodie was told by me to move out of NK7's territory. We knew them old heads wanted all the smoke, so I advised him against staying there. Yet, Poodie still decided that he was going to slang there."

"Slang?"

"Sell drugs," Shy explained and added air quotes for emphasis like I was slow. "That day he was there in their territory, and one of The NK7's members started chasing him with their SUV and shooting at him all through Harrow Park. Which led to the drive-by near your crib." Shy hung his head a bit. "And that's what happened. Poodie ain't want to listen, and now—"

"Him and Love are dead." I interjected, finishing his sentence. I felt overwhelmed and annoyed. "That's the big news you had to tell me?" It was the same story that Ms. Patrice had told us that day on her porch. *What was his point?*

Shy lifted his head. "Nah, Brave Heart, that's the story behind what happened. What we got to tell you is that we know where The NK7's spot is located."

"Good, you should give it to the police," I said.

"Man, the police don't give a damn about what we find. They just look at it as two dead niggas in the hood." Shy said. He dropped the bud of his joint to the ground.

"Watch it, Shy!" I growled. "That's my daughter!"

"Man, it's the truth. You know it, and I know it."

"So, what are you proposing?" I couldn't help but ask despite wanting to get off the subject all together.

Shy looked at me carefully. He adjusted his stance and stood with feet apart folding his hands over his stomach. "You want justice for what happened to your baby girl, right?"

My eyes widen in disbelief. "Damn right!"

"Then assist us in taking them down," Shy stated.

"What do you mean 'take them down'?"

"Finding out who killed Poodie and Love and taking them out, execution style." Shy said it like it was so simple.

I shook my head. "Dude, they are The NK7s, man, that suicide," I said. "You would need a plan for that."

"Exactly." Shy agreed. "That's why we'll need a smart-ass nigga, like you."

"To do what?"

"To join us." Rico replied. Shy nodded in agreement.

"What?" I yelled. "The Vigilantes?"

"Yeah, Brave Heart. You said you want justice for your daughter. This is how you'll get it," Shy said.

"Yeah Wiz," Rico agreed.

The idea and their confidence made me feel uneasy. "Man, we should just give this information to the police," I told them.

Shy lost his patience. "Brave Heart, the police don't give a fuck, bro!" He stepped forward and pointed a finger at my face. "Get that through your head. They been had this info, and they've done nothing about it. We on our own, so are you going to join or not?"

I contemplated Shy's offer as he stood there. *I want revenge for Love, but I don't really want to be affiliated with a gang.* I weighed the pros and cons. I looked up at Shy as if I didn't just have a huge battle in my mind. "I'll assist only under one condition," I stated.

Shy rolled his eyes in annoyance "Here we go with the shit," he said.

"I want to give this information to the police," I said. Shy blew his breath, and the other members sucked their teeth. "Hear me out. If they don't do anything within two weeks, we'll come up with a plan and take our own justice." I held out my hand. "Deal?" I asked.

Shy looked at my hand a few seconds before he gripped it with his own. "Deal!" he replied.

CHAPTER 9

The rain flooded the streets as the water washed away everything in its path. The waters have a vague memory of severing ties between loved ones, only accepting partial blame. Once enough time has passed, it becomes easy to forget all that was lost, or so they think. Love has a way of making you remember things that could never be erased, even if all the evidence has been washed away. Memories may fade, but a piece will always remain in the heart. Who is the guilty party? The one who commits the crime or the one that destroys the evidence. Everything points to the rain as the wrongdoer. However, the rain isn't the only one that is guilty. Culprit.

It rained nonstop since Love's funeral. I started to believe it was an ocular demonstration of my mental state, but there probably was an actual forecast of some sort. There was nothing but dark clouds for weeks. It was like the sky couldn't do anything else but provide a rerun of the same episode every day. Gloom. I vaguely remembered how the sun felt or even looked. Yet all of that seemed miniscule as I combatted the memory of watching my daughter's casket being lowered into the ground, and totally losing it in front of everybody.

Truth be told, part of me wanted to go in the ground with her. Life began to seem pointless without Love, in a mental, physical, figurative, and actual sense. Days seemed long and nights were never-ending. A little over two weeks had past and everyone seemed to have moved on but me. Gigi started working at Mr. Frog's shop and even started her MAS meetings again. Rico was still running the streets with The Vigilantes, and I couldn't forget about Danielle being pregnant with someone else's baby. *A baby that she would probably keep.* I rolled over in bed and tried to force my mind to figure out if I was more relieved or envious.

I felt stupid for even thinking that one day we would find each other and pick up where we left off, but I guess that was far-fetched like all the other writings in my notebook. It was obvious that she had moved on. I didn't ask her again about her plans for the baby. For one, it wasn't the right time; for two, I was afraid of her answer. In a way, she could replace Love and me with a whole new family. A fresh start with no baggage.

Danielle flew back to Texas directly after the funeral. Gigi was gracious enough to drop her off at the airport, while I ensured she got to her gate safely. It surprised me that she didn't have any bags after she shared with me that she literally only came for the funeral. Days later, we found out that Danielle's parents didn't even know she was in another state. Turned out, Danielle's parents went to check on Danielle's grandmother who lived in Arizona when Danielle used her dad's credit card to fly four hours to get to Virginia. Gigi received a nasty call from Danielle's dad like we were to blame. Disregarding their disposition, Gigi hung up the phone, not even having enough energy to deal with him. I guess we both realized since Love was gone, so was our connection to them.

After we got home from the funeral, I immediately told Gigi the information that was shared with me regarding Love and Poodie's possible killer and their involvement with The NK7 gang. Gigi turned around and called the detectives to give them the information. The detectives said that they were going to look into it, and the feeling of ease came upon us knowing that the authorities were aware. But then a little over two weeks had gone by, and all we heard were crickets. We called again, but we were just encouraged not to call anymore. They claimed that it was still an ongoing investigation. It was hard to admit, but it looked like Shy and Michael Jackson were right: *They don't really care about us.*

All I could do was mope, until one day Gigi had enough. She burst into my room first thing in the morning. "Wake yo' ass up!" Gigi demanded, interrupting my last few minutes of sleep.

"Gigi! What's going on?" I asked. I blinked a few times, trying to get my eyes to adjust. When my vision cleared, I saw the clock on the nightstand showed 7 a.m.

"You've been in this house for weeks; you need to get out and do something," Gigi instructed. She snatched the covers off me. The aggressive breeze on my skin mimicked the wind and rain that was currently blowing against my window.

"Gigi, Hurricane Katrina's little cousin Keke is outside, and you want me to go out there in that?" I pointed to the window.

"Yes," Gigi said, as I looked at her in total confusion. "I am going to work. You should go to the mall, go hang with some friends, do something young people do. Just don't—"

"Just don't what, Gigi?" I interrupted. "Just don't what?"

Gigi stared at me for a minute. Then she sat next to me on the bed with a slightly labored sigh. "Grief is a part of life. At the end of the day, you sitting here stuck in this rut doesn't do anything for the person that has departed," Gigi explained.

"What are you saying, Gigi?" I asked, wiping the crust out of my eyes.

She huffed. "You loathing in sorrow ain't doing nothing to celebrate Love. You staying depressed ain't doing nothing to celebrate Love." Gigi's voice intensified. "You not eating, you not sleeping, you not caring about your future ain't doing nothing!" Gigi shouted. I gawked at Gigi. Her eyes were glazing over. She took a deep breath. "So today," she calmly stated. "You're going to get back to taking care of you. You're going to get up, get dressed, and you're going to leave this house. Come hell or high water, literally," Gigi declared.

"Gigi—" I started, but she wouldn't let me finish.

"I'm taking your keys. You can't come back until I get off work," Gigi said.

"Gigi, that's eight hours!"

"Sounds like a full day for you then. You got thirty minutes to meet me downstairs. Your keys are already in my purse, so don't even try anything." She got up from my bed and walked towards my door.

"Really?!" I screamed. Gigi had only made it halfway out of my room into the upstairs hall. It took her zero seconds to turn right around and burst into my room a second time.

"Who are you screaming at?" I leaned back from her as she stepped closer to the bed. She continued, "The next time you scream in this house, you better have the holy ghost. You understand me?"

"Yes, ma'am," I replied, nodding my head regretfully.

"You got twenty-eight minutes," Gigi warned. She walked out of my room and slammed my door. I sat at the edge of my bed trying to get my mind together. "Twenty-seven minutes!" Gigi screamed from downstairs, not even a full minute later.

I sucked my teeth and got up to go to the bathroom to take a quick shower. *Where am I even going to go at seven in the morning?* As the shower ran, I could still hear Gigi counting down to a number I couldn't recognize while the water was on. I hurried, trying to hit all the hot spots and practically flew out the tub to brush my teeth. I swiped on deodorant and jumped into my underclothes in the fleeting minutes I had left in the house. I went to my room and patted lotion on my body and dabbed a little Vaseline on my lips. A glimpse in the mirror showed that my hair had grown out to a point where even a brush couldn't make it lay down flat anymore. I rubbed my hands through it in hopes it looked like something, knowing my silver patch of hair wasn't ever going to cooperate.

"Fifteen minutes!" Gigi's voice roared through the house.

"Man, she is trippin'," I mumbled under my breath. I periodically glanced at the door to make sure she didn't hear me.

Considering the rain that continued to pour outside, I grabbed my black jeans and a random shirt from the closet. Then I pulled out a black hoodie just in case I was left unsuccessful in finding a place to squat for eight hours.

"Thirteen minutes!" Gigi called. I sucked my teeth again and quickly put my clothes on.

After I got dressed, I surveyed my room for things I would probably need. I grabbed my bookbag and emptied out the loose pieces of paper from the school year. I tossed in a phone charger, my notebook, a pen, and some random clothes from my dresser just in case the rain decided to get more carried away during my journey of wandering. I shoved my phone and wallet in my pockets and threw the bookbag on my shoulder before flying down the stairs.

"Seven minutes!" Gigi screamed from the couch, as I made it to the last step. "Look at you, with minutes to spare," she said as I walked into the living room.

"Yay," I sarcastically replied.

Gigi got up. "Don't get dropped, Wisdom," she threatened and walked past me to go into the kitchen. When her back was turned, I peeped at the key rack to see if she really took my keys. All the hooks had nothing on them. She was serious about getting me out of the house.

Gigi came around the corner with her purse, lunch bag, and a plastic bag that she handed me.

"What's this?" I asked, grabbing the bag.

"Two breakfast sandwiches and a couple bottles of water," Gigi said, walking towards the front door.

"Gigi, you're really serious? Why today of all days?" I asked.

"It's time for you to start living again, Wisdom." Gigi replied, opening the door.

"Gigi, I know you see that rain out there," I stated, pointing outside. The same rain began to pick up as if to emphasize my point.

"I do," Gigi said. "The news said it should stop by 9 a.m. Let's go."

"Gigi," I groaned.

She was having none of it. "Wisdom, this isn't up for debate. Let's go!"

Annoyed, I walked past my grandmother onto the front porch as she grabbed her umbrella and closed the door behind us, locking the dead bolt with her key. I put my hood on my head. Gigi looked at me for a second before she leaned in and kissed my forehead unexpectedly.

"I love you," she stated. I dodged eye contact looking at the rain instead of her soft brown eyes. "See you when I get off," she said. She opened her umbrella and walked out in the rain to her Cadillac while I remained on the porch fuming.

Gigi got into her car. She looked at me for a second before she started the car and adjusted the windshield wipers to pull off. She left me on the front porch with nowhere to go. The wind began picking up, and I knew I couldn't stay on the porch for much longer, especially when the rain started zigzagging. I stood stoically, letting the drops of water hit my face.

Since no store around Harrow Park was open this early, I began walking aimlessly, examining my court's attached brick houses, and tightening the strings on my hoodie to combat the wind and rain. I couldn't help but notice a few airless balloons were laying in a puddle tied by limp string to the tree The Vigilantes put Love's memorial on. It seemed that the rain had taken away all the other memorabilia, too. *Yep, not just everyone but everything had moved on,* I thought. My aimless stride led me to the court in the back of the neighborhood. I knew Rico probably wasn't up, but I also knew I couldn't just stay outside all day, especially in this weather. On my way to Rico's house, I spied someone on their front porch, a few houses down from Rico, with what looked like a large sketchbook. *Must be a dedicated artist.* I began to get a little closer.

I paid no more mind to the person on the porch as I continued walking towards Rico's house. I needed my head on a swivel just in case there was some foolishness that could pop off.

"Wisdom," I heard a voice call. I turned around to face whoever it was. It seemed to be coming from behind the large sketchpad. I think I knew that voice. I frowned and squinted to see through the rain.

"Aliyah?" I replied. The person brought down her large sketchbook, revealing her face peeking out from a gray hoodie.

"Hey," she smiled. Her cheeks were blushed, and I wondered if such a response was due to me or the weather.

"Hey," I replied, walking towards her porch.

"What are you doing out here?" We both asked at the same time. My hearty laugh melded with her light giggle.

I shrugged. "My Gigi wanted me out of the house. And yourself?"

She held up her sketchbook. "Just doing a little art." Aliyah closed her sketchbook and set it aside. "She wanted you out this early in the rain?" Aliyah asked. She pushed back her hood, releasing her box braids.

"Apparently," I laughed. "I guess she was tired of me moping."

"Well, your moping is definitely justified."

"Thank you." I was relieved to finally run into a person that seemed to understand how my grief worked. "Well, I'm out because I have to be, why are you out here so early?" I inquired.

"Early will I seek thee," Aliyah quoted.

"That sounded really biblical," I stated with a nervous chuckle.

"It is," Aliyah confirmed. "I could never sleep past 7 a.m. Probably because my aunt works in the medical field and she's not very quiet in the morning."

"I can relate," I replied. "My Gigi likes to sing and give a whole concert in the morning."

"Can she sing?"

"Not well." We both laughed again.

"Yeah," Aliyah said, as she pushed a braid behind her ear. A moment of silence fell between us. We both fixed our eyes on the rain and then back on each other.

"So, you're a bible scholar and an artist?" I asked trying to break the awkward silence.

"I do what I can," Aliyah replied. "I am an artist, but I don't know about bible scholar. I just do my best to live by God's word."

"Oh, so you're one of those?" I teased.

"One of what?" Aliyah asked defensively.

"You know," I replied. I noticed Aliyah's hands working their way to her hips. "A church girl," I explained, trying to clear everything up.

"Not Beyoncé's version, but you can say that." She joked, cocking her head to the side. "You have something against church girls?"

"Not in the least," I said. "I actually wished I could attend church more regularly, but after Love died I just..." I paused. "You know," I said lamely, looking down at the ground.

"I get it, my aunt took me to church every Sunday after my mom passed. It actually was a big part of my healing process."

I looked up at her. "I am so sorry to hear about your mom," I said. "I had no idea."

"It's alright. You didn't know," Aliyah replied. It was her turn to look down. "How are..." She paused, taking a second to think. "Never mind."

"What were you going to say?"

"I just wanted to know, how are you? Since the whole..." Aliyah paused again, while I pieced together her question. "You know?" she inquired, dodging eye contact.

"I'm making it."

"I'm sorry for asking," Aliyah offered.

"Actually, I'm glad you did," I said. "It makes me feel like she's remembered."

"She will always be remembered," Aliyah replied. "And she will always live on in your heart."

"Sounds like you know that from experience."

"Yeah, I do." Another awkward silence fell between us.

I stared at her sketchbook. "You mind if I see some of your art?" I asked, changing the subject and breaking the silence again.

"Sure," she picked up her sketchbook. "You want to sit?" Aliyah asked, pointing to the chair next to her.

"Is it okay with your aunt that I'm on your porch?" I asked nervously.

"Well, well, let me find out you're a gentleman," Aliyah joked. "Asking permission to sit on people's porches and whatnot."

I laughed. "I see you got jokes. But yes, ma'am, I'm a gentleman, through and through."

"Well, the porch is a 'yes', but the house is a strong 'no', especially when she's at work," Aliyah said seriously.

"Noted," I replied, sitting next to her.

She handed me her sketchbook. "Alright. 'I'm an artist and I'm sensitive about my shh—.' You know the rest," she declared as I opened her book.

"Alright, Ms. Erykah Badu," I said. As I examined the pages, I felt the heat of Aliyah's eyes on my skin. "These are amazing," I said, flipping through the pages in her sketchbook.

"Really?" Aliyah asked incredulously.

"Really," I assured.

"Well, I heard you are a writer, but I haven't read anything of yours," Aliyah said.

"Who told you I was a writer?"

"Word travels fast."

I smiled. "So, you've been asking about me?"

"Boy, get over yourself," she blushed. "I heard you recite a piece you wrote for your daughter; it was beautiful."

"Oh, yeah," I replied. I'd almost forgot she was at Love's funeral. "I was just asking." I gave her another smile as I tried to play it off. I handed her sketchbook back, and I took off my bookbag to get my notebook out. "Looks like you're in luck," I stated, handing my notebook to her.

Aliyah took the book and ran her fingers over the front cover. "Are these your writings?"

I nodded. "A few of them."

"Okay, well how about you look at mine while I look at yours," she blushed again. "The books, I mean," she clarified.

"Alright," I agreed. She handed her sketchbook back to me, and we exchanged our works right there on the front porch.

Silence once again fell between us. We both became engrossed in the other's chosen form of art.

Aliyah was the first to break this round of silence. "Wow, this is really beautiful," she breathed.

I looked up and leaned over to see the page she was talking about. "What is?" I asked. She didn't give an answer. Her soft hazel eyes met mine, and I suddenly realized just how close I was to her. I felt the tension growing as we met each other's gaze. My heart started pounding, and I began to feel overwhelmingly anxious. Sebastian from *The Little Mermaid* was singing, "Kiss the girl" in my head, taking over my emotions. I leaned in and found myself in a position I've never taken before. Assertiveness.

So, I went for it. With my eyes closed, our lips met, and for a second time stood still. I couldn't even hear the rain. Then she jumped up, dropping my notebook.

"I am so sorry," I stammered. She turned her back towards me. I tried to do damage control regarding the situation. "I must have read that moment all the way wrong. Please forgive me," I said, standing up.

"No, you didn't read anything wrong," Aliyah said. "I just wasn't expecting it, that's all."

"Do you not like me?" I asked.

"No," she said quickly.

"No?"

She whirled back around to face me; her eyes were wide with concern. "No—I mean, I *do* like you," Aliyah said. "A lot."

I laughed nervously. "Well, that makes me feel better."

"I just think now is not a good time," Aliyah shared. "We both have a lot going on, and I think we should slow walk this thing until we figure out what it is."

"That's very mature of you," I offered.

Her eyes flickered to mine, and she tilted her head to the side. "You're not mad, are you?"

"Not in the slightest." Just to show her that I meant it, I held out my hand to shake on it like we were making a deal. She took my hand with a nervous giggle.

After a couple seconds, Aliyah let my hand go with another blush. She picked up my notebook and handed it to me. I returned her sketchbook. "I guess I should go in," Aliyah stated. "Are you going to be alright out here?"

"Yeah, I'll be fine," I said, walking her to the door.

"Okay, well thanks for the kiss— I mean the chat." Aliyah's whole face reddened, embarrassed with her slip up.

"Well, thank *you* for the chat *and* the kiss," I replied.

Aliyah smiled. "Bye," she said in that shy, high pitched voice girls often use when they flirt. Then she closed the door.

I put my notebook back where it belonged before slinging my bookbag on my back and grabbing my plastic bag with the breakfast I hadn't touched. I began strutting towards Rico's house, feeling like a new man, not even bothered by the wind or the rain. *Aliyah is definitely a welcomed distraction,* I thought as I knocked on Rico's door. I didn't know if Rico's mom was home or not, or how she would feel about me coming to their house so early, but I literally had nowhere else to go. After a couple of minutes with no answer, I knocked again.

Rico opened the door with his eyes blazing red. His locs laid in random patterns across his face. He wore a wrinkled yellow polo shirt and some khakis. His eyes widened like he was surprised to see me.

"Nigga," he greeted breathily. He looked to the left and right of me. "Why are you knocking on my door at the butt crack of dawn?"

"Gigi put me out of the house."

"What?" His eyes grew even wider.

"Just until she gets off of work," I explained. "She got tired of me moping around the house."

"Shit, I can understand that." Rico said. "But she could have at least waited for a clear day."

"Exactly," I replied. I looked Rico up and down. "Why are you dressed like you getting ready to play golf?"

"You got jokes, huh?" Rico asked. "You were knocking on my door this early in the morning. I thought you were the police," Rico said. "Got me hiding my stash for nothing. Come on in!"

"Stash?" I questioned, entering his house. I thought better of it and realized that I didn't actually want to know the answer. "Never mind," I told him, closing the door behind me.

"Good morning, Ms. Fisher!" I yelled out, walking into the messy living room.

Rico yawned. "She ain't here," Rico said as he walked into the kitchen.

"Is she ever?" I murmured.

"What you say, bro?" Rico asked from the kitchen.

"Nothing." I replied, pushing a small pile of clothes over on the couch before I sat down.

Rico came back to the living room with a black tank top and some balling shorts, sliding his ashy bare feet across the concrete floor. He sat on the pile of clothes on top of the accent chair.

"I see you got out of that Tiger Woods get up," I observed, as he turned on the TV.

"Shut up, Wiz," Rico cackled. "Had to bro, you got a nigga thinking you were the cops. I had to dress like a civil citizen, so they wouldn't raid the house.

"Man, that's why you need to let this Vigilante stuff go," I said.

Rico adjusted himself in the chair. "Hold up. Who crib we in?"

"You got it," I replied, getting off the subject.

"Appreciate it," Rico replied, leaning back again. "Besides, you need to join. Probably be the only way you get some justice for Love." Rico stated, flipping through the channels with the remote. "Heard back from the detectives?"

"Yeah," I replied dejectedly.

"Yeah, and what they say— better yet, what they do?" Rico antagonized.

I shrugged. "Nothing."

"That doesn't surprise me." Rico continued to flip through the channels. "How have you been holding up?" he inquired.

"'One day at a time', right?" I quoted, looking straight ahead at the TV.

"That's all we can do, man." Rico paused his channel surfing to lean forward again. He gave me a strange stare. "Bro, what's on your lips?"

"What do you mean?" I ask.

"You have some red lip gloss on, my dude?"

"Nah man," I replied, wiping off my lips with the back of my hand. "It's probably from the jelly I had on the breakfast sandwich Gigi gave me," I said, playing off my encounter with Aliyah. Whatever it was she and I had, I wasn't ready to share details with anyone, including Rico.

Rico accepted my answer, not bothering to press me further. "Oh okay. Well, eat up, my dude. You look a little skinny." He sat back in his chair again, finally landing on a channel that he was interested in.

I laughed. "Forget you, bro. I got two in here if you want one." I held up my plastic breakfast bag for him to see.

Rico clapped his hands for me to toss him a sandwich. "Shit, I'll never turn down a meal from Gigi." Together, we unwrapped the aluminum foil from each of our sandwiches, and for a split second, everything felt normal. Chilling at my bro's house eating and watching TV felt long overdue despite being such a simple thing. After a few minutes of eating and watching TV on Rico's clothes covered couch, I started to feel sleepy. The "itis" snuck up on both of us. I found my head rolling back on the couch cushions and my eyes growing heavy. We slept until Rico's alarm rang, waking both of us up from our catnap.

Rico dug in his pocket for his phone to cut his alarm off.

"Let me guess," I said. "The Vigilantes."

"Wiz, we really ain't that bad," Rico defended. He stretched and stood to his feet.

"You ain't all that good either," I said.

Rico waved his hand dismissively. "Whatever, man. I'm going to get dressed." He left the living room and walked upstairs. I looked at all the clothes strewn about the living room, confused as to why he was going all the way upstairs to get dressed when it looked like every piece of clothing he owned was downstairs.

After a few minutes, Rico came back down the stairs and met me back in the living room.

"You trying to come with?" Rico asked.

I sat on the couch in silence for a short second to think. "Not really, but I ain't got nowhere else to go."

"Well then, let's roll." Rico opened the door to usher me outside.

I tossed the water bottles that were left in my grocery bag in my bookbag and met Rico on the porch. He stood in the doorway patting himself down, ensuring he had his phone, keys, and wallet before closing the door. I looked up at the sky. Although, the rain had stopped, the grey clouds still hovered over us ominously.

We started walking down the court, and I saw Ms. Corrine leaving her back door to take out some trash.

"Hey, Ms. Corrine," I greeted.

"Hey Wisdom. Hey Rico." She stopped on the sidewalk to wait for us to get closer to her.

"Hey, Ms. Corrine," Rico said.

Ms. Corrine just nodded at him before wrapping her arms around me in a tight hug she seemed to know I needed. "It's good to see you, baby," she said.

"It's good to see you too, Ms. Corrine," I replied.

"I'm sorry I didn't come to the funeral," Ms. Corrine offered. "I just couldn't..." Ms. Corrine paused, shaking her head and taking a deep breath. "I just couldn't see that baby like that."

I took a deep breath of my own, touching Ms. Corrine's shoulder. "I completely understand. It was hard on everybody."

Ms. Corrine wiped her eyes quickly with the back of her hand before the tears had the chance to fall. "Anyway, I need to get back to these kids," Ms. Corrine said. "Please thank your grandmother again for the toys she dropped off." Ms. Corrine replied before walking back to her house.

Toys? "What toys?" I said aloud.

"Oh shit," Rico muttered under his breath.

"Love's old toys," Ms. Corrine said, as my blood began to boil. "She didn't tell you?"

"Let me get this straight. Gigi. Gave you. My daughter's toys?" I asked, trying to make sense of it all.

Ms. Corrine's face dropped, and she gave me a nervous head nod.

Rico placed a hesitant hand on my shoulder. "Hey Wiz, I need you to breathe," he suggested.

"Breathe!" I exclaimed. "Breathe!" I yelled again, walking down the sidewalk away from Ms. Corrine's house.

"Where are you going, bro?" Rico asked, following behind me. There was a hint of nervousness in his voice.

"Mr. Frog's suit shop," I said. "Gigi, is way out of line for this." I turned down the sidewalk to the front of Harrow Park.

Rico ran to catch up to walk beside me and try to talk me down. "Bro, I understand you're a little upset right now, but maybe you should calm down before you go up there."

"Calm down for what?" I shouted. "She just gave my daughter's stuff away without telling me." I picked up my walking pace. I needed to see my grandmother. Now. Yesterday even.

"She should have talked to you, bro. I agree with that, but you need to calm down before you talk to her," Rico advised. He was now walking backwards in front of me to slow me down.

I stopped at the Harrow's Landing sign at the front of our neighborhood, doing my level best not to cry, as I looked down the street.

"Breathe, Wiz," Rico urged.

"Is that Gigi's car?" I questioned, squinting in my struggle to see down the street.

"Nah, bro," Rico replied, grabbing my arm.

I snatched myself out of his grip. "Dude. Yes, it is," I stated, marching towards the house.

"Wiz, you have to calm down first," Rico begged.

"I am calm!" I shouted.

"You got a funny way of showing it," Rico replied, walking beside me.

Once I got closer, I confirmed that it was Gigi's Cadillac, examining the burgundy paint up close.

"I told you that was Gigi's car," I said, walking up to the porch.

"Wiz, don't go in there like this," Rico warned.

I ignored him and walked up to the door. I patted my pockets for my keys, before remembering that Gigi took them. I wiggled the doorknob just to check, and to my surprise, the front door was unlocked. I opened the door and saw no sight of Gigi when I entered the living room.

"Bro, you need to chill," Rico whispered, following me into the house.

I rolled my eyes and continued barreling my way through the house. "Gigi!" I called out. There was no reply. I walked into the kitchen, leaving Rico in the living room. The kitchen was empty too. "Gigi!" I called out again. I walked back to the living room.

"She is not here, bro. Let's go," Rico urged again.

She's probably in the bathroom, I concluded. "Stay here," I told Rico.

I walked up the stairs, noticing some sort of squeaking sound the closer I got to the second floor. Once I made it, I noticed the bathroom door was wide open and there were a pair of dress shoes in the middle of the hall. *Is Gigi trying to surprise me with some church outfits?* A loud squeal echoed from Gigi's room, interrupting my thoughts. Worried, I grabbed the doorknob and pushed her bedroom door open. The squeaks I first heard coming up the stairs intensified. My eyes widened in absolute surprise. Gigi was lying on the bed with Mr. Frog pressed on top of her while she moaned in satisfaction.

"Gigi!" I screamed.

"Wisdom!" Gigi yelled. She pushed Mr. Frog off her and reached for her covers to keep herself from being exposed.

"Oh shoot!" Mr. Frog tugged at the other end of the covers. They both struggled to keep every part of them under wraps.

I ran down the stairs, fighting the urge not to vomit.

Rico was still in the living room. "Bro, what's wrong? What's with all the screaming?" he asked.

I pushed him toward the front door. "Man, let's get out of here!"

"Wait. Let me explain, young man." Mr. Frog came into the living room with nothing on but a fedora.

"Oh shit!" Rico screamed. "Eww!"

The vomit I was trying to hold down was slowly moving its way up. "Put some clothes on, man!" I demanded. Mr. Frog pulled his hat from his head to cover his private parts. Rico and I turned our backs towards him.

"Nooooooo," Rico dragged out. "The wrinkles, all the wrinkles."

"Shut up, Rico!" I snapped, as I tried my best to think of anything that could burn the vision from my memory.

"Frog, get your naked ass back upstairs!" Gigi ordered, coming down the steps with her clothes looking like they were put on in a hurry. Her blouse was wrinkled, and her "work" wig was slightly twisted and pushed too far back, revealing her bald cap.

Mr. Frog quickly ran upstairs while Gigi tried to catch her breath to explain herself.

"I'm about to be sick as hell," Rico voiced, making vomiting noises.

"Shut up, Rico!" I demanded again. I turned my focus back on Gigi. "So, this is why you wanted me out the house?" I asked directly. "So, you can come up in here, and play Leapfrog."

"It ain't like that, Wisdom," Gigi said.

"Ugh, old dick and balls," Rico went on in disgust, his eyes were screwed shut like he too was trying to rid himself of the memory. It was clear his efforts were unsuccessful. "Old wrinkly dick and balls," he gagged.

"Then what is it like Gigi? Because I'm confused," I stated trying to ignore Rico's gagging. "Chill out, Rico!" If he continued, I was sure to throw up myself.

"Fredrick and I were—" Gigi began.

"Checking each other's heartbeats with your private parts," I finished for her. "I'm all caught up, thanks."

Gigi chuckled a little bit before looking at me with a hint of seriousness. "Now, I get that you're a little upset, but you have about 2.5 seconds to calm your ass down."

"Or what?" I replied.

Gigi blinked, threw one hand on her hip, and tilted her head to the side. "Excuse me? Say that one more gin'," she challenged.

"Or what," I repeated. Rico pulled my arm as if to warn me of the consequences of walking down this particular road with my grandmother. Yet, I didn't care. "You give my daughter's toys away without telling me. Then you have some random old ass man in here."

"Don't you say shit else!" Gigi warned. "I think you forgot who runs this motherfucker, so allow me to remind you… I'm that bitch," Gigi declared. "I don't owe you any explanation for what I do in my own house. You got the game messed up, boy!"

"Oh really," I argued.

"Yes really," Gigi replied. "Coming in here, questioning me about the shit I do," Gigi stated. "Who do you think you are?"

I stood in silence for a second, taking mental notes of all that Gigi said. "You're right, Gigi," I said. "You run this." I threw up my hands, gesturing to the air. "You run all of this…" I paused. "But when it comes to my daughter's belongings you should have asked me."

"For what?" Gigi screamed. "For you to build a shrine of everything she owned. So, we can constantly be reminded of what we lost?"

"Better that than acting like she never existed," I replied.

"Let me tell you something, boy. Grief is going to get your ass whooped," Gigi said.

"By who? You—," I pointed to the ceiling, "—or that old ass nigga upstairs?"

"Watch it, Wisdom," Gigi growled, pointing her finger at me. "Did you think about all we have to get rid of when we have to renew our application for Section 8? And us possibly having to move into a two bedroom because we no longer have a third occupant in this house?" she asked. I stood in silence. "No, you didn't!" she screamed. "But I did. Because I'm the adult, the leader, the HBIC. I ain't got to run shit by you, especially regarding toys *I* purchased for *my* great-grandchild," Gigi declared.

"You ain't buy all of those toys out of your pocket," I argued.

"Wisdom!" It's amazing how a person's name can become a parental threat.

"Nah Gigi, I let you say your piece. Now hear mine," I stated boldly, taking a step closer. "You want to throw away Love's memory. That's fine. You want me out the house, so you can sleep around. That's cool. You want to recreate a whole new family with Mr. Frog. Have at it. But don't drag me along and expect me to put up with your shit."

"Chill, Wiz!" Rico voiced, pulling at my arm one final time.

Gigi charged at me, letting her fist meet my face before I even had the chance to turn around all the way. I hit the floor as my mouth filled with blood. I spat it out on the concrete tiles before standing to my feet. Gigi scowled at me with distaste, begging for me to retaliate with her stance. "Fuck you!" I screamed.

Suddenly, Gigi's hands reached around my neck, choking me. She backed me through the front door and down the sidewalk, still strangling me along the way.

"Let go, Gigi, let go!" Rico screamed, running up to us, trying to loosen Gigi's grip around my neck.

I struggled to breathe, finding my way down to the ground. I didn't have the heart to grab Gigi's hands, so I took the ride down, and my eyes began to look up at the sky.

Right before I could black out, she released my neck from her grip. An influx of air filled my lungs.

Rico leaned down, patting my back as I gasped. "Come on, man!" Rico screamed. "Y'all got to stop this!"

I struggled to catch my breath. Despite being slightly dizzy, I somehow made it to my feet. Gigi's eyes burned with anger and something else. Disappointment.

I gawked at her in utter disbelief. "This where we at now, Gigi?" I asked. She looked away refusing to look me in the eye.

"Get your ass out of here, before I forget you're my grandson," she spit through clenched teeth. She turned around without another glance backwards, walked back to the house, and slammed the door shut behind her.

I spit the rest of the blood that filled my mouth onto the grass. Seeing the red mingle with the green reminded me again of why we were here in the first place. I frowned at the sight in disgust. "Finally, something we both can agree on." I said last, walking down the street as Rico trailed behind.

CHAPTER 10

Cast out like garbage that sat too long in the heat. Forgotten and misplaced behind the other rubble that cascades over the mounds. No one wants you and nobody cares. Phrases that play on the playground of depression, teeter-tottering on both sides of loneliness, patiently awaiting another person to join the team no one wants to be on. Once desired, now abandoned; once respected, now disposed. No one can pinpoint the exact time you expired, but everyone knows the stench. Useless.

I pressed the pavement hard, fuming over my encounter with Gigi. I walked with distaste, still feeling the grip of Gigi's hands around my neck. I pulled on my shirt collar to relieve the pressure. My own thoughts were so loud in my mind, I couldn't even pretend to care what Rico was blabbing about, while pulling my hood over my head to cover myself from the rain that started again. *Am I trippin'? Am I to blame?* I walked aimlessly towards the Tentohamic Bridge, several blocks away from Harrow Park. I could admit, I was way out of pocket for talking to Gigi like that. *But for her to just give my daughter's belongings away and just pretend like she never existed…* It didn't sit well with me. Not to mention, forcing me out of the house so she can have relations with Mr. Frog, her old flame, and more importantly, her boss. *What is going on?* I scratched my head, trying to make sense of it all. Everyone and everything just began to feel so out of place, including me.

"Old dick and balls." Rico's vulgar disgust brought me out of my own thoughts.

"Really, Rico!" I said. "I'm trying to forget it." I pushed him ahead, making him walk in front of me.

"Man, that was crazy," Rico replied. "I told you something like that would happen. Were they wearing Life Alerts? Were there inhalers? Paint the picture for me." Rico's interest was clearly piqued.

"Rico!" I screamed. My mouth was salivating with acid and my stomach turned with the weird feeling you get before you throw up. "Enough, bro!" I begged, holding back a heave.

"My bad, man," Rico apologized.

"For someone so disgusted, you sure want to know a lot about it," I observed.

"Chill on that, Wiz," Rico replied. "I'm just curious to know how old people get down," Rico laughed.

"Trust me, you don't want to know." I said, trying to block out the visuals.

"Copy." With that, Rico made his way to the side of the bridge where construction had begun for a new apartment building. *Gentrification at its best,* I thought to myself, looking at the high starting price of the apartments on the billboard corresponding. We stepped over the rubble where construction workers began framing, continuing our stride near the water.

"Why are we out here?" I asked, following Rico.

"I told you. I have some business to handle," Rico replied. We turned the corner to find Shy and the other Vigilantes huddled near the empty apartment building. I sucked my teeth in annoyance.

"Rico, you're a little late," one of the Vigilantes called out.

"I had some business to take care of," Rico said. Rico dapped his crew member and looked back at me as if to offer me as proof of his excuse.

"Brave Heart," Shy gave me a curt nod. "What's up with you?"

"Nothing much, what's up with you?"

"Nothing much, man. Heard back from the police?" Shy teasingly smirked. The others joined in his amusement with knowing smirks of their own.

"I think you know the answer to that," I replied in embarrassment.

"You are damn right, I do," Shy stated. "They gave your ass the run around."

A regretful "Yeah" was all I had to offer.

Shy smiled, walking up to me. The others stayed behind and let their leader do his thing. He dug into his back pocket and pulled out a gun. I stumbled a bit on a rock as I backed up in quick response.

"Shy, what the fuck, bro!" Rico yelled.

"Calm yo' ass down!" Shy demanded. "It ain't even like that, Rico." Shy turned the handle towards me.

I stared at the piece of steel and at the man holding it out to me. "What's this for?"

"You may have some mean hands, but if you're going against The NK7s, you going to need this," Shy said. "You remember our deal, right?"

"Man, are you really going to hold me to that? You did spring all of this on me at a very inconvenient time."

Shy nodded his head. "Yeah, yeah, I hear all that. But I thought you wanted to know who offed your daughter."

"I do. But—"

"But what?" Shy interrupted. He put the arm that was holding the gun down. "Sounds to me, like you don't want justice."

"Sounds to me, like you are putting words in my mouth," I combatted.

"What if I told you that their hide out is a block from here, and I know that there are only two people there right now," Shy said.

I looked at Rico as he nodded in agreement. "Then I would ask, how do you know this information?"

Shy laughed. "See, y'all smart dudes stay with the questions. Me and a few of my boys found their hide out a while back, and Ice Pick over there—" Shy pointed to one of the Vigilantes. "—been surveilling their house, learning their comings and goings." Shy continued, piquing my interest. "One of their head dogs has recently been released from the pen, and they've been out celebrating and getting him acclimated back to the real world and shit."

"Interesting. So, why do you need me?" I asked, still eyeing the gun he tried to hand me.

"Since there are only two people in the house right now, I thought you could ask them who killed Poodie and your daughter. Then you could off them once you get your answer." Shy stated.

"You mean," I cleared my throat. "Kill them."

"Hell yeah." Shy then tried to force the gun in my hand. "Why not? They had no problem killing your daughter."

I backed up, refusing to accept what Shy seemed to consider a gift. "Chill with all that, Shy!" I warned.

"You scared?" Shy asked, smiling. "That's what it is. You scared."

Of course, I'm scared. What idiot wouldn't be? "Man, they are The NK7s, hood legends," I said aloud. "If y'all so big and bad, why don't you go after them yourselves?"

Shy shrugged. "We thought you would want to take your revenge, being that it was your daughter. But I see we just got to do it ourselves." He put the gun in his back pocket. "Rico, come here for a second," Shy requested.

Rico walked up to him. Shy back hand slapped him to the ground.

"Yo, what the fuck?" I yelped. I moved forward towards Shy and found myself looking down the barrel of the same gun he tried to hand me. I froze in fear.

"I told him he had to get me a recruit after Poodie was killed," Shy said. "He kept saying you were the one, even after I said you were a square ass nigga that won't down."

"I can find somebody else," Rico pleaded from his position on the ground.

"Too late," Shy replied. He kicked Rico in the ribs.

"Stop!" I screamed.

"Vigilantes!" Shy called out. They all crowded around Rico.

"Please. Shy, I can get somebody else," Rico begged. Shy locked eyes with Rico. "Please," Rico begged again.

Shy took a second before fixating his eyes back to me, clenching the gun. "Vigilantes..." He paused with a sinister smirk. "Stomp that nigga!"

"No!" I shouted as The Vigilantes began wildly stomping Rico, who cried out desperate pleas between every kick and strike. "Shy, call them off!" I demanded. Rico tried to fight his way out of the circle to no avail. "Please."

"You know how to make this end," Shy told me.

My gaze flickered between Shy and Rico. Rico continued to beg The Vigilantes while they continued plowing their feet in his body. *I can't let him go down like this.* "I'll do it," I said reluctantly.

"I'm sorry, what was that?" Shy leaned forward, cupping his ear, smiling at me.

"I'll do it!" I shouted. "Now stop this!"

Shy shifted his glare back on Rico. "Vigilantes," he called out. They halted their stomping session. "Enough!"

Rico whined on his back on the rubble and dirt. He coughed, and a bit of blood bubbled from his mouth. "Wiz, you don't have to do this," he wheezed. He held tightly to his ribs as he rolled over to spit out the blood in his mouth.

"Yeah, I do," I said with my head down. "I'll do it," I voiced again, looking at Shy.

Shy walked up to me again and forced the barrel of a gun in my hand while he still held tight to the trigger. "Vigilantes assume the position," he ordered. All the Vigilantes, minus Rico, pointed their own guns at me.

"Wait, I said I'll do it. What is all this?" I asked.

"Nigga, I'm giving you a weapon. This is my insurance policy. You'll be dropped before you even get a chance to do anything."

"That thought didn't even cross my mind," I said, as Shy released the gun fully in my hand. The weight felt strange.

"Whatever man," Shy stated, backing up. "Welcome to The Vigilantes, Brave Heart." He grinned at me while I stared at him with hatred. "Your first assignment is to go to The NK7's house and get some answers on who offed Poodie—Oh, and your daughter, too," he said, like Love was an afterthought.

Rico slowly worked his way off the ground and began shuffling in my direction holding his ribs. "Man, that's suicide."

"Only if you die," Shy carelessly responded. "Besides he owes us. Got us out here paying for wreaths and shit."

"That ain't even cool, bro. Wiz, don't know anything about this life," Rico said.

"You right, he doesn't," Shy agreed. "That's why you are going with him." My best friend dropped his head with The Vigilante leader's order.

"No man, you can't," I told Rico.

He ignored me. "Fine, Shy," Rico agreed.

"Good," Shy voiced. "Black, give Rico your piece."

The Vigilante called Black pointed his gun at Rico with one hand while he dug through the back of his pants for another gun to hand to him.

"I want it back!" Black threatened in a booming deep voice.

"No problem," Rico replied, putting the gun in the back of his waist band. I mimicked Rico, putting the gun I was handed in my own waist band, hoping I didn't shoot my butt-cheek off. I wasn't sure if the safety was on.

"Well, hope you have some news for us soon," Shy stated. "See y'all motherfuckers soon. If not, it was nice knowing you." Shy saluted us with a laugh. Then he walked away. The other Vigilantes walked backwards with their guns pointing at us until they were out of our sight.

"Whew, that shit was crazy," Rico sighed in relief.

"You're telling me. Are you alright?" I asked.

"Yeah, I'm straight." Rico replied.

"Not for long," I said, looking at him. "Look at this shit you got me into. I'm not a gangbanger."

"First off Wiz, no one says 'gangbanger' anymore," Rico teased. "Secondly, as soon as we do this, we'll be good. He's just testing my loyalty," Rico assured gripping his side.

"Well, put it on a piece of paper and make it multiple choice. This is more than your loyalty being tested. Dude, this is your life. And now you got me in this!" I yelled.

All the joking and teasing left Rico's body. Suddenly, he was serious and screaming. "Don't you think I know that!" He paused to let out a shallow breath to calm himself. "Look. Let's just do this, and then you can put it behind you," Rico assured.

"Man whatever. Let's hurry up and get this over with," I replied walking away.

Rico spit another bit of blood into the dirt. "You are going the wrong way," he said.

I turned around. "Fine. Lead the way, and while you at it—" I took the gun from my waist band. "Could you put this on safety? I want to make sure I don't lose a butt-cheek."

Rico chuckled, shaking his head. He made sure that the gun's safety was on before we journeyed our way back over the Tentohamic Bridge. We walked slowly over to Myashere Rd where The NK7's spot was. We tried to look normal as possible. Rico's busted lip and slight matching limp didn't help much. I did my level best not to appear frazzled though my mind was everywhere. I couldn't believe that I was really on this suicide mission to get justice for my daughter. Sweat began dripping from my brow from nervousness. I pushed my hood off to get a little air.

"Wiz, you good?" Rico asked when he saw me wiping the back of my forehead with my hand.

"Just peachy," I sarcastically stated, holding tightly to my bookbag's straps.

"Stop right here," Rico whispered. I halted. "You see that green house with the pealing vinyl?"

I examined the houses on the street until I found one matching his description. I pointed, "Are you talking about that one over there."

Rico slapped my hand down. "Nigga, are you trying to get us killed? Put your God damn hand down," Rico warned.

"My bad," I apologized. "I've never done this before. You're the one that got me in this shit in the first place."

"I know," he agreed. "That's why I want to make sure you live through this, so listen up," Rico instructed. "We are going to bust through the back. You will take the first floor and I'll go upstairs. If you see anyone, call for me. And if you shoot them, try not to kill them until we get some answers," Rico said.

"Shoot. Kill. Upstairs? Man, this is a lot," I voiced nervously.

"Come on, Wiz. We ain't got time for you to punk out. If we do this, you will get justice for Love and Poodie. And on top of that, you'll get out of this sticky mess I got you in. Come on man, I need you." I took a deep breath, looking at the seriousness of Rico's face. My stomach began turning in knots. "Wiz?" he asked in concern.

"Let's hurry this shit up." I replied.

We walked across the street and made our way through the alley that led to the back of the house. I clenched my butt-cheeks tightly together. I felt like I could crap on myself at any point. I was quickly becoming overwhelmed as I followed closely behind Rico, maneuvering our way to the back of The NK7's house. We crouched down behind a bush, while Rico ran over his plan again.

"Alright Wiz, let me see your gun." Rico held out his hand. I handed it to him. Now, I was sure I was going to throw up or pass out. "You good, Wiz?" Rico asked for the second time. I looked at him with my best "Let's get this over with" expression. Rico adjusted the gun and handed it back to me. "Be careful, cause she ready." Rico warned.

"She ready?" I asked, confused.

"Your gun is off safety," Rico explained. My eyes widened in fear. He continued, "So, this is the game plan again: we bust through the back door. I'll go in first, and you come behind me. I'll work my way upstairs as you secure us downstairs. If anything come at you, shoot. But don't kill them. Remember we are here to get answers. After we get our answers then we will finish them."

"'Finish them'? Nigga, this ain't *Mortal Kombat*, this is real life. What do you mean 'finish them'?" I asked, looking at Rico.

"You know what I mean." Rico stated, looking at me. I gulped down my nervousness. "Take off your bookbag," Rico instructed.

"Why?"

"It'll slow you down, we got to move quick with things like this."

"So, you've done this before?" I asked, handing him the gun to do as he told me.

Rico traded the gun for my bookbag, and he hid the bookbag near a bush by the chain linked fence making up The NK7's backyard.

"You ready?" Rico asked, holding his own gun up. It did not miss me that he was actively dodging my last question.

My stomach began to bubble. "Let's go," I declared in defiance of everything in me that told me not to go through with this. I followed Rico over the short chain linked fence. We walked across the patchy grass in the yard, smoothly making it to the back porch unscathed.

"I don't think I can do this man," I whispered behind Rico.

"Come on, bro," Rico whispered back. "It's a little too late now, I need some back up."

I broke out into a nervous sweat again, shaking a little. "Man lets hurry this up," I said for what seemed like the thousandth time.

Rico examined the lock before he put his hand on the doorknob. The door surprisingly swung open when he turned it.

"Bro, this feels like a set up." I whispered, timidly walking behind Rico through the back door and into the kitchen.

"They probably think no one would try anything because of who they are," Rico said. "Stay alert."

I followed Rico through the small empty kitchen. There were pots overflowing in the sink and the kitchen table was covered in some sort of white substance.

"Is that—" I said.

"You better believe it," Rico interjected, inching in front of me. We creeped to the living room at the front of the house where there was an open line of sight to the front and back door.

"Nobody's home, Rico. Let's get out of here," I suggested.

"Let me check upstairs and then we'll go," Rico said.

"Man, hell no!" I voiced.

"Shhh," Rico hushed.

"We need to get out of here." I whispered, lowering my voice. I was scared out of my mind.

"Stay here," Rico instructed. "If anything happens, defend yourself by any means." He inched up the stairs, leaving me to my own literal devices.

I nervously stood in the hall of the living room. *What am I doing?* My hands were shaking, causing the gun to shake too. "Nobody's home Wisdom, calm down," I whispered to myself, attempting to calm my fast-beating heart. I began walking near the kitchen when I heard the front door's knob shake.

My heart sank to my shoes when I saw the dead bolt turn. *Somebody is coming in!* My hands were still shaking as I battled in my mind whether this should be a fight or flight moment. The bottom lock turned, and I dashed into the opened hall closet. I closed the door behind me seconds before a person entered.

I heard footsteps directly after the door was opened. Even though I wasn't accustomed to doing it much, I silently prayed that whoever the person was, they didn't open the hall closet door. The sounds of the person's steps were loud, leading me to believe that whoever this person was had a little weight on them. Luckily, I only heard one set of footsteps. I remained in the closet with my hand clenched firmly on the gun.

"Man, Titan need to hurry his ass up!" A voice growled.

Who is Titan? I wondered until I heard a loud noise echoing through the entire house.

Rico! No! I covered my mouth to keep from shouting what was happening in my brain out into the real world.

"What the fuck was that?" The voice grew from outside the closet. I stood at the door shaking, overhearing steps grow closer and closer to the stairs. *What do I do?* My heart pounded with each step the person took. *I can't let him get to Rico.* With that thought, I swung open the closet door and pointed the gun at whoever was about to climb those stairs.

"Yo, what the fuck?" A large man screamed with his hands up. "What type of shit is this?" The guy yelled.

I held the gun tightly, looking at this large man standing in front of me. He couldn't have been no older than thirty, but the amount of grey in his beard confused me a bit.

"Hey, I don't want to hurt you," I said.

"Lil' nigga, you got a funny way of showing it," the guy stated. "What are you doing in our crib?"

I looked at the stairs in hopes that Rico was on the way. Then I fixed my eyes back on the guy. "I just got a few questions man, and I'll get out your hair."

"Questions? Nigga, who the fuck are you?" The guy asked. "Do you know who I am—better yet– who we are?"

"The NK7s," I said. "Am I supposed to be impressed?"

"You ain't got to be shit!" he countered. "But you being here ain't smart." He slowly brought his hands down. I still gripped the gun with both my hands.

"Don't move!" I demanded, making the guy's hands go back up. "I told you I just got a few questions, and I'll be out of your hair."

"What the fuck you want to know, lil' nigga?" he asked.

"June 10th, Vincent Drive. There was a drive-by out Harrow Park," I said.

"There's always a drive-by out Harrow Park," the guy murmured sarcastically.

"Don't patronize me!" I screamed, holding tightly to the gun's trigger.

"Alright, alright." He stated. "What do you want to know?"

"Who in your group did it?" I asked. The guy began to slide to the left. "Stay still!"

"I'm just trying to adjust myself man," the guy said. "I'm a big dude, you know."

"So, who did it?" I asked again.

"Did what?" he asked.

"Who orchestrated the drive-by!" I screamed.

The top step squeaked making me look up at the stairs. The guy took my moment of distraction to charge at me in full force. "Stop!" I screamed. He continued. "Stop!" I repeated, closing my eyes, and clenching the trigger. Then, I heard the noise of the gun going off and the resounding thud of his body hitting the floor.

"Wiz! Wiz!" Rico screamed, running down the steps as I held the smoking gun in my hands. The guy lied unresponsive and unmoving on the floor. "What happened?" Rico asked. I stood there mute, unable to express myself.

Rico shoved his gun back into the waist band of his jeans, grabbed my shoulders, and gave me a little shake. That seemed to loosen my tongue. "I killed him!" I breathed in absolute disbelief.

Rico took a quick glance at the body and looked back at me. "Come on, Wiz, we got to get out of here."

"I killed him," I repeated.

Rico grabbed me by the arm. I held tightly to the gun. "Wiz, let's go!" Rico screamed gripping my arm and pulling me. I finally ran behind him.

We made it to the backyard, and we both jumped over the fence. We ran back through the alley. I couldn't think straight. I could barely breathe. I just kept running right behind Rico. I shoved the gun in the back of my waist band. My mind was starting to get ahead of itself. I saw flashes of myself in an orange jumpsuit, behind bars. *I can't believe I shot someone,* I recited over and over in my mind. It was like a bad dream I couldn't wake up from.

Making it a few blocks away, Rico and I finally stopped running. We both gasped for air, trying to catch our breath.

"Bro," Rico rasped. "You alright?"

I shook my head, panting heavily, still unable to speak.

"What happened?" Rico asked, huffing, and puffing, while clutching his ribs. A small part of my brain was impressed with his ability to run and move with such a quickness despite being stomped by The Vigilantes over an hour ago.

"He came in when you were upstairs," I answered between my own gasps. "I pulled the gun out on him to ask him some questions. Then he charged at me, and I took the shot."

"Damn, Wiz!" Rico said. "Did he give you any answers?"

"No," I regretfully replied.

"Shit!" Rico voiced. My phone buzzed. "What are we going to do?"

"How am I supposed to know?" I replied, pulling my phone out, scared to read the message.

"Who is that?" Rico inquired.

"Mr. Lee," I said, reading the message. "The former owner of The Oink Shack."

"What the hell does he want?"

"He wanted to know if I could meet him at The Oink Shack, he said he wants to give me something," I said.

"That's perfect," Rico smirked.

"How is that perfect?" I asked in confusion.

"Because it gives you an alibi. Just in case this goes south," Rico said.

"Alibi? What about you?"

"Don't worry about me. The less you know, the—,"

"Oh shit!" I yelped, feeling on my back.

"What?"

"I left my bookbag back at The NK7's house," I said with a panic. There goes my alibi.

"Shit!" Rico shouted. He began to pace the graveled alley. I watched the gears turn in his head, brainstorming what to do next. "Okay, this is what we'll do!" he said. "We'll get the bag later. I want you to take your jacket off and give it to me. You're going to go to The Oink Shack and see Mr. Lee. After that, you're going to go home, and we'll figure out the rest from there."

"Rico, I —"

"Shut up!" Rico interrupted. "You have the book smarts; I have the street smarts. Do what I'm telling you." I could not argue with that, so I took off my jacket and handed it to him. I ran my fingers through my hair to ensure I appeared presentable while Rico draped my jacket over his shoulder. "Give me your piece," Rico instructed with his hand out.

"Piece of what?" I asked.

"The gun!" Rico blurted, shaking his head. I did as I was told with that, too. "Alright, remember what I told you. Go to The Oink Shack, stay there for a bit, then go straight home."

"Man, Gigi don't want to see me," I said.

"Nigga! Do you want to go to jail?" Rico asked.

I shook my head 'no'.

"Then do what I'm telling you to do. Go to The Oink Shack and then straight home, got it?" he voiced authoritatively.

"Got it," I echoed.

Rico gave me a head nod before he began walking down the alley. I turned towards the street.

"Hey," Rico suddenly called out, making me turn around. "I love you, bro."

"I love you too," I replied. He nodded and began running further down the alley.

I turned the corner and began walking down the street. I tried to pretend that I was having a normal day full of normal activities as I began my journey towards The Oink Shack. I tried to blot out all that happened in the past fifteen minutes, making my way to The Tentohamic Bridge, attempting to appear normal in front of the other pedestrians that walked by. *Go to The Oink Shack, then straight home.* I recited Rico's directions over and over in my head like it was a question on a test. My hands were sweating with anxiety. I rubbed at my palms, still feeling the weight of the gun, and recalling the smoke that escaped after I pulled the trigger. *I can't believe I shot someone, better yet killed someone.* For the second time that day, I said a silent prayer. I prayed no one found my bookbag as I kept walking towards The Oink Shack.

I walked up to the Berksdale sign, finally making it to the plaza. The sky was still dark, but luckily the rain was held up. I made it to The Berksdale Plaza and walked down the row of shops, intentionally avoiding Mr. Frog's suit store, just in case he or Gigi made it back to work. I slid down to the end of the plaza, making it to The Oink Shack witnessing Mr. Lee's car, taking up two parking spots right in front of the store. I looked at myself in the windows not even recognizing my reflection. My hair had grown past its normal length and my clothes looked a little baggy on me from not consistently eating. "Who am I becoming?" I asked myself, staring at my reflection in the store's murky glass.

"Wisdom!" I heard a voice calling from behind me. I turned around to see Courtland, my old coworker, crossing the street with a gleeful expression. He walked up to me with a warm embrace, dapping me up in front of the store.

"What's going on, man?" Courtland greeted. "Long time, no see."

"What's going on, Big Court?" I greeted, trying to sound normal.

"Nothing much, trying to get myself together," he said. "What about you, how is your grandmother and your daughter?"

I stood there in silence, trying to center myself as my head spun. I knew he didn't know what happened to Love by the way he asked, but it was still such a hard question to answer. My eyes glazed over, attempting to keep the tears in.

"Gigi is doing well," I managed to get out. "And Love is…"

"My two favorite employees!" Mr. Lee greeted, coming out of the empty store, interrupting me and Courtland's conversation. "Come on in guys, come on in," he gestured as I sped walk towards the restaurant, dodging Courtland's question.

I looked around my former place of employment that was now completely empty. Everything was gone except the cash register.

"Wow, it's really gone." Courtland blurted, as Mr. Lee ensured the front door was closed behind us.

"Yeah, it's really gone." Mr. Lee replied, as we all looked around. "Look guys, I wanted y'all both here because I just wanted to simply apologize." Mr. Lee said, catching my gaze. "Y'all were the main two reasons this place made any money, and instead of taking your input and looking closely at the books; I just put all of my eggs in one basket and ignored your concerns and for that, I sincerely apologize."

"It's all good Mr. Lee," Courtland said, while I shook my head in agreement.

"Thanks gentleman," Mr. Lee replied.

"Hey, Mr. Lee, I got a question for you?" Courtland stated in a weird tone.

"Shoot!" Mr. Lee replied, forcing my mind to recall leaving The NK7's house, making my hands sweat.

"Well, since I'm out of a job and I can't get fired for asking..." Courtland paused. "Were you and Anna knocking boots?"

"What?" Mr. Lee screamed.

"Hey, just asking," Courtland replied with his hands up. "You used to act like Anna could do no wrong, I'm just curious."

"Well, to answer your question. No!" Mr. Lee made it very clear. "My wife, Irene is crazy," he laughed. "To your point, Anna and I served on the same ship in the Navy together and she ran the kitchen there. So, I figured if she could run the ship's kitchen, she could surely run a restaurant," Mr. Lee said. "But as you see I was mistaken."

"You can say that again," I said.

"Right," Courtland added.

"So, I walked all the way from Harrow Park for you to tell us that?" I asked boldly, building my alibi. "You could have sent that in a text."

"Calm down, killer," Mr. Lee stated, making my heart drop. *Does he know?* I asked myself, watching Mr. Lee work his way around the counter. "There is something else," Mr. Lee stated, grabbing two envelopes as my heart continued beating out of my chest. "I know you already received your last checks, but I wanted to give you both a token of my gratitude," Mr. Lee stated, handing us both a thick envelope. "Now I can't pay you what you're worth, but I at least wanted to give you something that could hold you over, until you get another job."

"Thank you," Courtland said.

"Thank you," I added.

"You're welcome," Mr. Lee replied. "Now just in case you guys talk outside of here. I did give Wisdom a little more, because he has that precious baby girl to take care of." Mr. Lee said, feeling my eyes begin to swell.

"I'm cool with that," Courtland replied, as I fought the tears.

"Is that all?" I asked boldly, trying to disguise my pain by appearing annoyed.

"Yeah, that's it," Mr. Lee replied, looking at me with concern. "Are you okay?" he inquired.

"Yeah, I'm fine," I stated clearing my throat, trying not to cry. "Thank you for this," I replied, backing up towards the front door, stuffing the envelope in my back pocket. "I'll catch y'all later," I stated, quickly walking out the restaurant.

"You need a ride?" Mr. Lee yelled out, as I took off down the plaza's strip.

"No, I'm good." I replied, running through the parking lot towards the sidewalk. I stopped and leaned over feeling as if I was going to throw up, as my eyes ran with tears dripping off my face.

I sat up and quickly wiped my face, attempting to look normal, reciting Rico's words in my head. *Go to The Oink Shack and go straight home.* I kept repeating it in my mind as I began trotting toward home trying my best to forget what I've done. Even though I tried to fight it, I just couldn't stop thinking about that guy I shot, realizing that I killed a NK7 gang member. I felt like I had a target on my back, making it to Harrow Park, becoming paranoid trying to pretend like everything was normal.

In the distance, I saw Gigi's Cadillac parked in its usual spot in our court. I didn't know what to do or what to expect as I began walking up to the door knowing how we both left things earlier. The thought gave me pause, and I stood on the porch to take a deep breath before going in. My hesitance gave me time to notice the front door was cracked before I even opened the screen door. Upon further examination, I saw the doorknob was torn off.

"Gigi!" I called out, walking into the dark living room. I didn't make it much further. The hairs on the back of my neck stood up.

"Surprise motherfucker!" A voice stated firmly from behind me. The last thing I felt was a cold piece of metal at the back of my head.

CHAPTER 11

I was fighting for consciousness on the cold floor. The back of my head was throbbing in pain. I opened my eyes and tried to bring my surroundings into focus while trying to muster up enough strength to stand. In the end, I was left unsuccessful. *What the hell was that?* I rubbed the small lump that was quickly developing on the back of my head near my patch. *Did Gigi hit me with her skillet?* I caressed the sore spot in disbelief.

While I lay on the living room floor, trying to get myself together, I heard two voices mumbling in low tones. "Who's there?" I asked. The mumbling turned into distinct, loud laughs, letting me know exactly who these two men were. "Gigi!" I called out again, this time in fear. A firm hand grabbed me by the back of my shirt and forced me to a kneeling position as I looked around in a daze.

"Look, Titan. The little punk is delirious," one of the men teased. *Titan? I thought he was-* I didn't get to finish the thought as whoever was holding me up suddenly let me go. I lurched forward and caught myself with my hands to keep my face from hitting the floor. I blinked a couple times, noticing my vision was clearing, as the concrete tiles were coming into full focus. Someone was slowly walking in front of me; their footsteps came to a halt as they reached my position on the floor. A figure kneeled, forcing my eyes to slowly work their way up to their face.

"Remember me?" he asked.

I looked up in puzzlement, and I was left spooked at the sight. He flashed a wicked smile, making me studder. "H-h-how..." Even my mind stuttered as I tried to get it and my mouth on one accord. "I uh, sh-sh-shot..."

"You shot me," he finished. "That shit hurt like a bitch." He lifted his shirt to reveal a bullet proof vest and slapped it. "Good thing I'm always covered." He leaned forward with a smirk. "I can tell you really ain't about this life. Always check the body." He laughed, as I felt something else pressed on the back of my head.

Is that a gun? I began to shake slightly.

Someone else decided it was their turn to speak, confirming that I did hear a second person's voice. "Next time you attempt to kill a motherfucker. Don't leave your bookbag at their trap with your address in it." The second man threw my bookbag to the ground beside me. Beads of sweat began running down my forehead, and I fought the urge to pee on myself. "Any last words?" he asked.

"Please," I begged, slowly raising my hands. "I just wanted to know what happened to my daughter. She was killed in a drive-by this past June, when y'all were going after Poodie."

The two men were silent until the one holding the gun to the back of my head asked, "Who the fuck is Poodie?"

"That Vigilante nigga?" The guy in front of me said.

I nodded. "Yes. My daughter was killed by a stray bullet. And I just wanted to know who did it," I sobbed desperately. "I didn't mean to shoot anyone."

"You might not have meant it, but I sure will," the voice behind me stated. He pressed the gun harder against the back of my head as I wept. "Dino, since this lil' nigga shot you, did you want to do the honors?"

"Thought you'd never ask, Titan." The guy in front of me pulled his gun out from the back of his waistband and pointed it at the middle of my forehead.

My mind began racing. I looked up at the ceiling, bypassing the gleeful expression on the guy's face, thinking of how I ended things with Gigi. *I can't believe this is it*, I thought to myself closing my eyes.

"Wisdom, is that you?" Gigi called from outside, interrupting my final thoughts. I heard her feet walking on the front porch.

"Run, Gigi, run!" I screamed from the living room.

"Run for what?" Gigi asked. I heard the screech of the screen door as she pulled it. "What the fuck happened to my doorknob?" Gigi inquired. The guy behind me pivoted his weight, and Dino ran up to Gigi, dragging her into the house. "What the hell!" Gigi screamed, as the door slammed shut. I heard the tell-tell gun click, knowing someone had a gun pointing at Gigi. "If y'all trying to rob us, we ain't got shit for you," Gigi aggressively said.

"We don't want your shit, old lady," Dino replied.

"Old?" Gigi questioned, sounding like she was wrestling out of his hold. "Put that gun down, and I'll show you old," she growled.

"Looks like we got a feisty one, Titan," Dino said sounding like he was smiling.

"Gregory?" Gigi said.

"Ms. René?" The one previously called Titan questioned.

She knows one of them. I slowly turned around on the floor, feeling a little more secure to move. If Gigi knew one of the guys who were about to kill me, I had a bit of chance.

"Don't move, motherfucker!" Dino replied, pointing his gun in my direction as I kept my hands raised. "Titan, how does she know your government name?"

"We go way back," Titan replied, still having his gun pointed at Gigi.

"Do we go far back enough for y'all to put those guns down?" Gigi replied sweetly. "And getting the fuck out of my house?" Gigi voiced not so sweetly.

"Not a chance, Ms. René," Titan said. "We have some unfinished business with this motherfucker here." Titan shifted his body back in my direction.

Gigi looked at me with worry. "Whatever it is, we can fix it," Gigi said. "Please don't shoot my grandson."

"Grandson? Lucky got a kid?" Titan looked at Gigi, who was trying her best to keep cool.

"You know my momma?" I asked.

Gigi glared a silent warning at me. Then answered Titan. "Yes, Greg," she said. "Lucky got a kid."

"Greg?" I said, remembering my mother telling Gigi that someone named Greg was out of jail.

Dino rushed me and pressed his gun to my head. "Don't you ever call our leader by no other name than Titan, understood?"

"Understood!" I replied with my hands up again. "Is this the same person mom warned us about, Gigi?" I asked bravely. Gigi shook her head.

"Look! I don't care if it is Lucky's kid or not. This nigga shot my guy, so he got to die," Titan said. Gigi's eyes widened as she looked at me in shock.

"Look at you Titan, rhyming and shit. Jail gave you some bars," he hyped. "Hey, can I still take the shot?" Dino asked eagerly.

His enthusiasm only increased the amount of sweat pouring down my face, intermingling with the tears I'd just cried minutes before. "Please don't," I begged.

"Shut up!" Titan screamed. "As a matter of fact, Dino, I change my mind." Titan pointed his gun at me, and gave a head nod to Dino, instructing him to go by Gigi. "Let me kill him. It's been a little while since the last time I smoked a nigga, I need the practice."

"I don't think you want to do that," Gigi said confidently. Everyone in the room looked at her in confusion. *Gigi, this is not one of your Spades games. Please don't call bluff when my life is at stake.* I stared at her, silently pleading at her to back down.

Dino rolled his eyes in frustration and clear annoyance. "Titan, if I can't smoke the kid, please let me shoot this old bitch."

"Your momma's an old bitch!" Gigi snapped. "I'm THAT bitch, get it right."

"Everybody shut up!" Titan screamed, silencing the whole house. "I'm curious, Ms. René. Give me one good reason I shouldn't smoke this kid," he demanded. I saw Gigi's eyes began to swell with tears.

"Because he's your son!" Gigi said confidently.

"What?" I said in absolute surprise.

"Titan, you got a seed?" Dino asked.

"Man, I ain't got no kids," Titan said. "Besides, how do I know he's mine?"

"He's seventeen years old, do the math," Gigi challenged.

"That don't mean nothing." Titan's words sounded confident, but the tone of his voice didn't completely match.

"Wisdom, when is your birthday?" Gigi asked.

I looked up at Titan, still shocked, and replied, "February 7th."

"February 7th," Gigi repeated. "Go nine months back. That should put you back in May at Lancaster High School's senior prom." Titan looked like he was thinking hard as he processed this new information. "And by looking at that boy over there..." Gigi continued, pointing at me, "It's obvious you did more than just go to IHOP after the prom."

"Old lady!" Titan left me and walked up to Gigi. He pressed the gun to Gigi's temple. "How I know you not lying?"

"Look at him!" Gigi pleaded, as Titan shifted his eyes to me. "You can tell by looking at him, he's yours. Even down to the silver patch of hair on the back of his head."

Titan looked at me for a second before he began walking back towards me. "Dino, keep an eye on her," Titan said over his shoulder.

"With pleasure," Dino replied eagerly.

Titan grasped my head and turned my neck to examine the back of my head, making me cower in his grip.

Could he really be my father? I wondered as he examined me like a pit bull puppy on sale. I looked up at him, hoping what he found would mean he wouldn't kill me. I watched his eyes widen again. He took off his hat to reveal a large patch of silver hair front and center on his head. I instantly thought of Love, and I recognized part of me in his face. *He is my father!* He maintained the same hateful expression as he put his hat back on.

Titan released me, throwing me to the floor. "Let's go, Dino!" he ordered.

"Just like that?" Dino replied in confusion. "So, we ain't gonna shoot him?"

"I said, let's go!" Titan shouted. He grasped the door by the deadbolt lock and walked out.

Dino took one last look at us, shaking his head in actual disappointment. "Y'all some lucky motherfuckers," he said. Then, he followed behind Titan out of the house.

After all of fifteen seconds, Gigi ran up to me. She crashed down on the concrete tiles and threw her arms around me. "Wisdom, I'm so glad you're okay." She squeezed me tightly.

I let out a sigh of relief. "You are? Even after…" I paused, feeling overwhelmed.

"Even after," she assured me, wiping my eyes with her thumbs.

"Gigi…" I started. I was almost too scared to say what else was on my mind.

She pressed my head on her chest. "Yes, Wisdom," Gigi replied with a serious tone.

"Is that man… really my father?"

Gigi grew quiet as she kneeled there on the living room floor with me in her embrace. I listened to her steady heartbeat and patiently waited for an answer. "Yes," she revealed, letting out a huge sigh. "Gregory Boyce, better known as Titan, is your father," Gigi confirmed.

I snatched myself out of Gigi's arms and picked up my bookbag. I began to walk unsteadily upstairs; I was still reeling in dizziness from the hit on the head.

"Where are you going, Wisdom?" Gigi asked. "Are you alright?"

I couldn't muster an answer. I held the banister tightly; the dizziness on top of my fuming anger made it harder to climb the stairs as fast as I wanted to. Gigi's footsteps followed behind me as I busted into my bedroom. "Wisdom," she called out, standing in my doorway. I dropped my bookbag on the bed and held the back of my head, which was throbbing.

"Why didn't you tell me?" I asked, flopping on my bed.

"It wasn't my place," Gigi said. "It was your mother's."

"And she's been MIA for five years," I argued. "You should have told me, Gigi." I reached for my bag, and started going through with one hand to ensure everything was still there. My other hand still held the back of my head. It seemed like holding it helped it throb a little less.

"So, you could have a target on your back?" Gigi walked in and sat beside me on the bed. "So, all the other gang members can hold you hostage, knowing you're the son of a gang leader? Hell no!" Gigi snapped. "I protected you," she said. "Just like your mother."

"My mother?"

"Your father was locked up and, on his way to being sentenced to life in prison when your mother found out she was pregnant with you," Gigi said. "Around that same time a rival gang called The Night Hawks—an old gang that was out way before The Vigilantes were even potty trained— killed his sister and his mother. We couldn't let that happen to you."

"So, it was better to let me think my mom was a ho, who slept around?"

"Better that, than you being killed!" She snatched my hand down from my head so she could get a good look. "We should really take you to a doctor," she murmured.

I shook her off. "I'm good, Gigi." I got up and walked out of my room.

"Now, where are you going?" She followed me to Love's room. I walked in and saw all of Love's belongings in boxes. Some were labeled "keep"; others were labeled "give away".

I turned around to look at Gigi, "So, this is what you were doing?"

"Yes, Wisdom. I have a Section 8 renewal meeting next month, and when they find out there are only two occupants in a three-bedroom home, they're going to have us move out. I'm just trying to get ahead of this."

"So, when were you going to tell me?"

"When is it the right time to tell you anything, Wisdom?" Gigi replied. "You're so up and down. I don't know what information you can handle, so I just handle it myself." Gigi said, as I looked around the room. "We lost Love, Wisdom," Gigi acknowledged. "But somewhere down the line, I lost you too. And your grief is turning you into someone unrecognizable… And what's this I hear about you shooting people? Better yet, where the hell you get a gun from in the first place?"

"The Vigilantes," I said.

"The Vigilantes? Don't tell me you joined them." I stared at Gigi before hesitantly nodding. "Wisdom," Gigi sighed.

"It's not what you think Gigi, they were beating up Rico and the—"

"I don't want to hear shit you got to say!" Gigi replied, cutting me off.

"Fine then," I said passing by Gigi and walking back into my room. I grabbed my bookbag off my bed, before flying down the steps.

"Wisdom, get your ass back here!" Gigi demanded, following me down the stairs.

"I thought you didn't want to hear shit I had to say?" I mocked, walking into the living room.

"Wisdom Nasir Davis, you are trying my patience," Gigi voiced. "If you want to be a part of that street life, you ain't doing it in my house."

"You know, I'm losing count on how many times you put me out this house in one day," I said.

"Oh really? Well, this time can be permanent!" Gigi threatened. "You will not disrespect me in my house. And being a part of some street nonsense is the ultimate disrespect," Gigi continued. "Now in everything there are choices, and yours are my way or the highway. Take your pick..." Gigi paused.

"Gigi," I sighed.

"Bullets have no eyes, Wisdom. They can't see who they're going to hurt!"

"I know that better than anyone!" I exclaimed.

Gigi walked to the end table and lifted a thick envelope from the stacked mail. "Here," she tossed the envelope at me.

"What is this?" I asked.

"It's from Columbia University," Gigi said at the same time my eyes scanned the top portion of the envelope where the sender's address was printed.

I opened my bookbag and stuffed the envelope in. I grabbed the deadbolt lock to pull the front door open. Before I walked out, I looked down at the end table by the door where I saw a framed picture of Love. I grabbed the picture and put it in my bookbag. I zipped it up looking back at Gigi. Her eyes were filling up with tears. "I love you, Gigi," I told her, pulling on the door and leaving Gigi's house.

Once I was out, I came to the immediate realization that I wanted to go back. But I couldn't let myself do it. My father... Love... my life... nothing made sense. I walked down the sidewalk behind the court to Rico's house. I hoped he was home, so I could get my mind off this crazy day.

I walked on to his porch. "Rico!" I screamed, knocking furiously on the door. "Rico!"

After a few seconds, Rico opened the door quickly. He grabbed my arm and pulled me inside. "You trying to get us killed?" Rico asked for the second time that day, slamming the door behind us. He grabbed his ribs. All the running we did in our escape from

The NK7 house seemed to have caught up with the pain from his encounter with The Vigilantes.

"No, why do you ask that?"

"I heard The NK7's leader was out Harrow Park," Rico said. "I think he know we were there."

"Yeah, he knows," I said. "Well, he knows I was there." I stated, taking my bookbag off.

"Wait," Rico eyed the bag. "How did you get your bookbag back?"

"Well, Cliff Notes version, the man I thought I killed had a bullet proof vest on, and him and The NK7's leader found my bookbag in the bushes outside their house. I forgot I had the address tag on my bookbag in case I lost it."

Rico's eyes widened as he blurted out, "Oh shit!"

I continued. "They broke in and held me and Gigi at gun point, but they let us go."

"Wiz, what are you saying?" Rico asked. "You acting weird as shit."

"I'm telling you what happened," I said calmly.

"Wait, what? They paid you a visit?" Rico tried to wrap his mind around what I was saying.

"Yep."

"And you are still alive to tell the story?"

"Yep."

Rico let out a low whistle. "Now see, that's the type of Jesus I need in my life. How in the Genesis through Revelations you pull that off?"

"The leader of The NK7s…" I paused, debating whether or not I really wanted to share that particular fact.

"Yeah," Rico urged me to continue.

"He knows Gigi," I blurted, ultimately deciding it may be better to just leave that piece of information out.

"Dang man, Gigi a whole thug out here!" Rico yelled in excitement. "She knows everybody."

I shrugged. "It looks that way," I said.

"So, we are safe?" Rico asked.

"For now," I said.

"Well, let the good times roll," Rico joked, bringing me in for a bro-hug. "I'm about to go change out of these clothes. Make yourself at home," Rico said. "You gave me the best news of my life."

Rico walked upstairs, and I flopped on the clothes covered couch. I clutched my bookbag, too overwhelmed to move the clothes over. Rico's living room was starting to spin. I grabbed the back of my head and waited for my vision to clear. Once the messy room came to a standstill, I opened my bookbag and grabbed the envelope from Columbia University. I tore open the envelope and went through a slew of papers until I saw what looked like a letter. *Dear Wisdom Davis,*

Congratulations! We are pleased to inform you that you have been accepted into the school of English on a full ride academic scholarship to Columbia University.

The words felt unreal. I wanted to be happy, but it didn't feel right to be happy. I reflected on my mixed emotions as I put the letter back in the envelope and stuffed it in my bag. I grabbed the picture of Love and rubbed my thumb across the frame. I could almost feel that baby soft skin and hear that old woman sassiness. "I miss you, Love," I said, getting up from Rico's couch as he came back down the stairs.

"Headed out, bro?" Rico asked.

"Yep, I'm going to The NK7's house." I said, after only confirming it in my mind just a few seconds prior.

"Stop fucking with me, Wiz," Rico laughed, clenching his side.

My expression remained unenthused. "I'm not," I replied.

Rico's laughter halted. "Wiz, do you have a death wish?"

"Nah bro, I'm just going to get some answers," I said. "They are not going to do anything to me."

"How do you know that? You got lucky once, it might not happen again."

"Well speaking of Lucky. You know how I told you the leader knows Gigi."

"Yeah."

"But I didn't tell you how."

"Oh Lord. Gigi a cougar. Lord, help us," Rico gagged.

"No fool," I said. Rico let out a huge sigh of relief. "He knew my momma before I was born."

"Oh okay. He knew your momma." Rico replied with a stale tone until it clicked. "Wait a minute…You mean to tell me that the leader of The NK7s is…" He paused.

"My father."

"Damn bro, your whole life is a Tyler Perry movie," Rico joked.

I, on the other hand, did not find the matter amusing. "Shut up, man!"

"That's crazy!" Rico replied, grabbing his short locs.

"But that's how I know they won't touch me," I said. "Besides, I need to find out what happened to Love, I can't rest until I do."

"You're serious, aren't you?" Rico asked.

"As a heart attack," I said.

Rico let out a huge sigh again. "Hold on man." He left the room and walked into the kitchen. I could hear him rummaging through cabinets until he returned to the living room. He handed me a pair of gloves. "If we're going to go into The NK7's spot again, you're going to need a piece." He handed me a gun after I slid the gloves on.

"This looks different from the one Shy gave me earlier," I observed.

"It is."

"What happened to the other one?"

"The less you know, the better." He pointed at the gun he put in my hands. "You pull this to take it off of safety," Rico explained.

I nodded. Then it occurred to me when I saw his hands were covered in gloves that matched the ones he'd just given me. "Wait, back up. Did you say 'we'?"

"Yeah, 'we'," Rico said. "You got questions, and so do I. Plus, I ain't letting you walk in there alone, father or not."

"Rico—" I tried.

"I ain't taking 'no' for an answer, Wiz, so let's roll," Rico urged, opening the front door.

I shook my head. "Fine," I replied, walking out of Rico's crib, as he closed the door behind us.

We began walking down the street. The grey clouds remained clustered over our heads. We walked through The Park, noticing that no one was outside.

"I guess your pops scared off our neighbors," Rico concluded, looking at the empty streets as we made it out of Harrow Park.

"Don't call him that!" I warned.

"You got it," Rico replied, as we walked over the Tentohamic Bridge. The sound of the water crashing against the shore brought my mind back to the task at hand.

We made it over the bridge, up the next street, and approached the house. I took in the house's appearance, now being able to look at it in front-facing view. The peeling paint alone was uninviting. A slab of warped wood made up the front door, and almost every window screen was heavily stained with rust. *Maybe this isn't smart,* I began to rethink. Yet, we boldly stepped onto the creaking front porch.

"Should we knock, or ring the doorbell?" I asked.

Rico shrugged. "Man, either one sounds dangerous at this point." We bravely walked up to the unlatched front door. "So, they think since they're The NK7s, they can just leave doors open." Rico pushed the door open right as Dino turned the corner, surprising us at the entrance. Before we knew it, Rico and I were both staring down the barrel of a gun.

"Y'all little punks dumb as hell, aren't ya?" Dino asked, waving his gun in our faces.

I glanced over at Rico, whose hand was slowly inching towards his pocket. "Don't move!" Dino warned.

"It's cool, Rico," I said. "Is Titan here?"

"Lil' nigga, who you think you are?" Dino asked. I stared at his round face, unfazed. "You think just because you might be Titan's seed that you can't get two hot ones in you? And what's up with the winter gloves?" Dino observed. "It's hot as hell outside."

"Dino, who that?" A voice from the back asked.

"Your mistake at the prom and some dusty looking nigga with a busted lip," Dino called out.

"Let them in!" The voice demanded.

"I got your dusty looking nigga, Fat Albert," Rico insulted as Dino lowered his gun and slid to the side, letting us in.

"How original," Dino mocked. He closed the door and walked behind us. Titan met us in the foyer. "Hold the fuck up!" Dino shouted, running up behind us and digging his hands down the back of Rico's and my pants.

"Hold up, Big Worm Jr. This ain't that type of party!" Rico screamed as Dino pulled out our guns.

"Y'all niggas really wanted to try this again?" Dino asked. He tossed our guns behind him, and he continued patting us both down. *So much for protection.* Dino's hand transitioned to the outward parts of my bookbag.

"We just needed them for protection," I insisted. "We didn't plan on using them on you."

"Then who did you plan to use them on?" Titan inquired. Rico and I turned to look at him.

"Anyone that came in our way," Rico stated.

The corners of Titan's mouth turned up into a smile. "I like that answer, young blood." Titan looked in my direction. "I didn't expect to see you so soon."

"Yeah, me either. But I have some questions, and you're the only one who can answer them," I answered.

"Alright," Titan stated, fixating his eyes back toward Rico. "Who's your funny friend?"

"Insurance!" Rico said.

Titan and Dino laughed. "Well, come to the dining room and let's talk." We followed behind Titan to said dining room. I sat down slowly at the table keeping my bookbag straps tight in case this became a fight or flight conversation.

Titan looked at me intensely while Rico and Dino sat at the table alongside each of us.

"Can we get our guns back?" Rico asked.

Titan laughed, "Not a chance."

"In hell!" Dino added aggressively.

"And take those snow gloves off. Y'all look crazy as fuck," Titan demanded. We did as we were told, sliding our gloves off and putting them on the table. I felt the heat of Titan's eyes on me again.

"Why are you staring at me like that?" I asked.

"Man, I didn't know I had a kid until today," Titan said. "It's just taking some time, that's all," Titan confessed. "Where is Lucky, anyway?

"Your guess is as good as mine," I replied. "I saw her about a month ago when she visited, but before that I hadn't seen her in five years."

"Damn little dude," Titan stated. "I'm sorry to hear that. Wisdom, right?" Titan questioned.

"Yep," I confirmed. "Wisdom Nasir Davis."

"Nasir is your middle name?" Titan lit up.

"Yes," I replied, confused at his level of glee.

"Nas is my favorite rapper," Titan said. "I used to get on Lucky's nerves playing his music nonstop."

"Oh wow," I replied. Honestly, I'd never known how I got my middle name, so this was actually interesting.

Titan studied my face carefully. "You kind of look like me," he concluded. "You even got my birthmark."

"Birthmark?"

"Yeah," Titan replied, taking off his hat. "My patch," he pointed to his head.

"Yeah, my daughter had it too," I stated, taking my bookbag off my back.

"Hold up, what are you doing?" Dino asked. He pointed his gun at me, and Rico sat up at full alert.

"Chill, I'm just getting a picture," I said. "You already took our weapons."

"Yeah, but I didn't thoroughly check that bag," Dino speculated.

"Give me the bookbag!" Titan demanded, snatching it out of my hand, opening it up and going through my things. "Columbia University?" Titan pulled out my envelope.

"Yeah, I got accepted on a full ride," I said.

"Damn, you smart like that?" Titan asked rhetorically. "You hear that, Dino?"

"Yeah, yeah, your kid is smart," Dino mocked. "Whoop dee damn doo." Titan glared. Dino straightened up and offered a fast apology. "My bad, Titan."

"Damn, Wiz. I didn't even know that. Congratulations!" Rico said.

"Thank you," I replied, as Titan continued to dig through the bookbag until he found the picture.

He stared at the picture in awe. "She's beautiful." Titan lit up. "Man, you mean to tell me I'm a thirty-five-year-old grandpa?"

"You *were* a thirty-five-year-old grandpa." The past tense made my heart hurt. "She was killed by one of your men who shot up our street in order to kill Poodie." Silence fell upon the table. Dino and Titan exchanged a look.

"Dino, can you check on the other NK7s, and make sure that…" Titan paused looking at us, "That *thing* was handled?"

"They alright," Dino said. "I'll stay here."

"No, you won't. You're going to do what I requested!" Titan demanded. Rico and I looked at them from across the table.

"Yes sir," Dino stated, getting up. "You need anything else, boss?"

"Yeah, pick up a bottle of Henny," Titan ordered. "Looks like I'm gonna need it."

"Anything else?" Dino asked. "I can pick up some Kool-Aid Jammers and some Animal Crackers for your seed and his dusty friend."

Rico cut his eyes at Dino. I felt the heat between the two starting to rise.

"Nigga, do what I said!" Titan shouted.

"Yes sir!" Dino stated. He then addressed us, "I'll be back, lil' juvenile delinquents."

"Spell it," Rico challenged.

"J-u-e-v— nigga, fuck you!" Dino shouted. He picked up our guns by the foyer and slammed the front door behind him.

"Forgive Dino," Titan stated looking at me. "He's a little on edge. After all, you did shoot him."

"Yeah, because he charged at me," I said defensively.

"Yeah, because you broke in our crib and held him at gun point," Titan replied.

"Point taken," I replied. We both laughed almost sounding alike.

"Ha, ha, ha," Rico mocked. "Hate to rain on this family reunion, but can we stick to the matter at hand? Whoever killed Poodie, also killed your granddaughter, and we would like to know who it was."

"I'm sorry to hear about this man, truly I am," Titan sympathized. "But I think you should let this go."

"Let it go!" I shouted.

"Yeah, let it go," Titan replied calmly. "No need to dwell on this," he deflected, shifting his eyes to the wall behind me.

"Tell us what you know!" Rico slammed his fist on the table.

"Let this shit go!" Titan clenched his teeth.

"Did you let it go, when a rival gang killed your mom and sister?" I asked boldly.

The question infuriated Titan. He rose from his chair, grabbed the table, and pushed it out the way in his hurry to get to me. He yoked me up by my collar. My head spun trying to fight the dizziness that occurred from being lifted up so quickly.

"What did you say?" Titan asked.

Rico jumped up, but I gestured to Rico to stay where he was.

"You heard me," I said bravely, staring in his eyes while my dizziness began to subside. "Looks like you haven't let it go." I blurted.

Titan released me and he looked at me as his eyes reddened. "I didn't know," he said.

"You didn't know what?" I asked. He stood there, beginning to sob.

"You didn't know what?" Rico echoed.

Titan looked down at me, revealing his bloodshot eyes. "I was just released from prison a week prior to the shooting," Titan narrated. "I was serving a life sentence for murder until the judge that tried my case was exposed for bribing the jury, for God knows how long. An investigation took place, which led to my case being overturned, and my immediate release from prison."

"What the fuck does that got to do with a grandma in a thong?" Rico questioned.

"Shut the fuck up!" Titan growled.

"Let him finish, Rico," I stated calmly, wondering where this was going. "Go on," I said.

"So, after my release, The NK7s picked me up, and the first thing I wanted to do was hit up the old trap. So, I told them to take me to Scott's store, not knowing it was torn down and some little punks were selling on our turf..." Titan paused. Tears began streaming down his face. "They said some lil' nigga wouldn't move off our turf. So, we went out there, and that was when I saw him."

"Poodie," Rico murmured.

"So, we asked him to leave again, but he ain't want to move," Titan continued. "So, we ended up chasing him through the streets with our truck until he got tired. I thought that he learned his lesson." Titan said. My heart began racing. "Next thing you know he took out a gun and shot one of our headlights out. Now you know we weren't having that shit. So, we chased him through the streets shooting at him. When Dino put the AK-47 in my hands, you know what I had to do." Titan demonstrated with his hands.

"I sprayed the street with bullets trying to angle the gun right, until I hit him," Titan said. "I watched his body fall to the ground as we drove off."

I stood there shocked, trying to wrap my mind around this story. "So, let me get this straight." The tears burned my cheeks falling from my eyes. "*You* killed my daughter."

"Wisdom, I didn't know," Titan cried.

"You killed your own granddaughter!" I yelled.

"I didn't know," Titan repeated. "I didn't know."

"Yo' pops killed Poodie!" Rico shouted.

"I can't believe this!" I screamed in outrage. "How could you do something so careless?!"

Titan straightened up wiping his face. "Because I had to." Titan said, digging through the back of his waistband. He took out a gun.

Is he going to kill me next? I was suddenly paralyzed, too scared to move.

"You going to murk us too?" Rico asked.

"What are you going to do?" I managed to get out, keeping his gun in my line of sight.

"Here," Titan stated, taking the gun off safety, and forcing it in my hands. "If you need to take your revenge, then take it," Titan urged.

"What?" *Why does everyone keep trying to force a gun in my hands?* I wondered, recalling the moment with Shy earlier that day.

"You heard me," Titan said with his hands up. "Gang Rule 101, baby boy: always get your revenge."

"This motherfucker killed Poodie and your daughter, bro!" Rico reiterated. "Do me a favor. Make that shit hurt." Rico begged. My hands began to shake.

"Do it, Wisdom!" Titan stated, walking towards me.

"Stop this!" I warned.

"Wisdom, I killed your daughter!" Titan said.

"Shoot this bastard!" Rico urged again. My mind began to become even more overwhelmed.

"If you're going to do it, then do it," Titan said. "You know you're my seed. It's in your blood, son." Titan said, as his eyes began to swell with tears again.

"Don't call me that!" I warned.

"What are you going to do?" Titan asked.

"Shoot his ass!" Rico shouted, walking up behind me.

"The wind blew as I tossed between the idea of life and death, feeling the power of it in my hands. I thought of the sweet nectar of payback, as the pendulum swung closer. 'Decide now', 'choose one', words that bombarded my mind, pulling me into a frenzy of emotions. Do I take on the role of God, or do I let Him decide? Forgiveness." I recited, pointing the gun down.

Titan let out a deep sigh of relief.

Outraged by my decision, Rico ran up beside me snatching the gun out of my hands.

"Rico, don't!" I screamed.

"Fuck you, nigga!" Rico yelled, clenching the trigger twice.

"Nooooooo!" I screamed. Titan's body hit the floor with two bullets in his head. The blood from his brain began spewing out, saturating the dingy carpet while his eyes remained wide open. "Rico, what did you do?" I cried.

The gun smoked as Rico bowed his head. "I did what needed to be done," Rico answered simply. He dropped the gun. "That was for Love and Poodie."

I frantically looked around in absolute terror. "How are we going to explain this?"

"*We're* not," Rico said. "I am."

"What?"

"I ain't got shit to live for, Wiz," Rico said. "You got everything to live for. A grandma that loves you, a girl that likes you, and even a college opportunity," Rico explained. I stared at him, not believing what he was saying. "And what do I have?"

"Rico," I cried. "You can't just throw your life away like this."

"What life, bro? I'm a third-year ninth grader with a ho for a mother. I have nothing!"

"Rico, I…" I paused, trying to make out the words.

"Give me your gloves," Rico requested.

"What?" I questioned.

"Give me your gloves, Wiz!" Rico shouted. I walked to the table and grabbed the gloves. My hands shook with nervousness. I walked back towards Rico and handed them to him as requested. "Get your stuff and get out of here," Rico instructed.

"But—"

"I said go!" Rico screamed. I ran to the table and put my stuff back in my bookbag before putting it on my back. "Go out the back door," he ordered. I cowardly stepped over Titan's lifeless body to walk towards the back door in the kitchen.

"Rico," I turned around to look at him. "There's got to be another way out of this."

"You were never here." Rico stated, dismissing any idea of an alternate plan. "Go live your life, man." Rico bowed his head again, making his short locs cover his eyes. "I love you, bro."

"I love you, too," I replied. I remained hesitant in my spot, still afraid to leave him there alone.

"Go!" Rico shouted. So, I ran out the back door and through the patchy grass. I cleared the short fence, making it quickly through the backyard. I ran through the alley all the way to the Tentohamic Bridge, doing my best not to stop. The sounds of sirens filled the air as police cars passed me on the bridge, going in the opposite direction towards the NK7's house. I couldn't wrap my mind around the fact that my best friend just killed my father. Those fleeting moments were on replay in my mind as I continued toward my own house. Tears filled my eyes. I made it back to Harrow Park, running up to my front porch where Gigi was standing.

"Gigi, Gigi!" I screamed, running into her arms, crying.

Gigi's warm arms held me tight. "It's okay Wisdom, it's okay."

"No, it's not Gigi. It's not okay," I cried, trying to catch my breath. "Rico…"

"Made a choice, and you made yours," Gigi stated.

I looked up at her in confusion. *Does she know?*

"He went too far, didn't he?" she asked, while I rested my head on her shoulder letting the tears continue to fall. "You can't save everyone, Wisdom." Gigi said. "Sometimes you have to do what is best for you."

Suddenly, the sun broke out of the clouds. Together we realized we hadn't seen the sun in weeks. Gigi draped her arm around me as we admired the sky. "You couldn't survive one day without me, huh?" Gigi teased.

I sniffed and wiped my face. "Gigi, you have no idea," I replied, looking up at the sky. "Hey, Love."

www.ingramcontent.com/pod-product-compliance
Lightning Source LLC
Chambersburg PA
CBHW050341030726
47503CB00008B/2553